SASSY CINDERELLA AND
the Valiant Vigilante

A Ruby Taylor Mystery

SASSY CINDERELLA AND
the Valiant Vigilante

Sharon Dunn

Kregel
Publications

Sassy Cinderella and the Valiant Vigilante: A Ruby Taylor Mystery

© 2004 by Sharon Dunn

Published by Kregel Publications, a division of Kregel, Inc., P.O. Box 2607, Grand Rapids, MI 49501.

Published in association with the literary agency of Janet Kobobel Grant, Books and Such, 4788 Carissa Ave., Santa Rosa, CA 95405.

The persons and events portrayed in this work are the creations of the author, and any resemblance to persons living or dead is purely coincidental.

Scripture quotations are from the *Holy Bible, New International Version*®. © 1973, 1978, 1984 by International Bible Society. Used by permission of Zondervan Publishing House. All rights reserved.

Cover design: John M. Lucas

Library of Congress Cataloging-in-Publication Data
Dunn, Sharon
Sassy Cinderella and the valiant vigilante: a Ruby Taylor mystery / by Sharon Dunn.
     p. cm.
   1. Women detectives—Fiction. I. Title.
PS3604.U57S27   2004
813'.6—dc22   2003022324

ISBN 0-8254-2495-x

Printed in the United States of America

04 05 06 07 08 / 5 4 3 2 1

Because cats seem to keep popping into my plots, this book is dedicated to my feline friends. Especially to Tink and Bill who are gracious enough to let me live in *their* house and wait on them hand and foot.

Acknowledgments

Special thanks to Mountain Locksmithing for giving me just the right details to make the locks work, and to Detective Fillinger and Tom Weightman of the Bozeman Police Department for answering all my silly questions and giving me a tour of the place. As always, I am grateful to my number one cheerleader and provider of gun detail; thanks, Michael. And to Jonah, Ariel and Shannon— you keep me inspired. I am delighted with and grateful to Steve, Janyre, Dave, and everyone at Kregel Publications for taking a second chance on the redhead with an attitude. Bruce and Becky, thank you for your expert help and for knowing that *karate* was a Japanese word.

SASSY CINDERELLA AND
the Valiant Vigilante

Chapter One

Jesus, chocolate, and a mocha with the steam rising from it. Jesus, chocolate, and a mocha with the steam rising from it.

Thinking about my three favorite things as I fall asleep is my new coping strategy for short-circuiting The Dream, which starts in a room where I am surrounded by mirrors.

A voice that sounds like a cross between Elvis and James Earl Jones asks me, "Where are your feet pointed?"

An invisible weight squeezes my skull and chest—pressuring the answer out of me.

I always wake up with cold, tingling skin. My insides feel like they've been stirred with a hot crowbar. Typically, a good twenty minutes pass before I can go back to sleep. My number-one goal has become not to finish this dream.

I have been working late at my new job on purpose, just to avoid what used to be my favorite place—between my comforter and cool cotton sheets.

This Thursday night was no different. I put together lesson plans up at the university until ten and trudged home long after Mom was in bed. Yes, I'm thirty-one and I live with my mother. She went to prison for embezzlement when I was sixteen, so I figure she owes me a few years of mothering. That's the short version of a long story.

As I slip into unconsciousness, thinking about my three favorite things helps me create my own mental happy place. I pull the comforter up around me, close my eyes, and picture me and Jesus sipping mochas at an outdoor café with a big plate of dark chocolate between us.

Jesus, chocolate, and a mocha with the steam rising from it.

My eyelids felt heavy and my muscles relaxed. *Two chocolates and a Savior. Can I get that in a to-go cup?* I rolled onto my side—drifting and swaying, swaying and drifting. *Chocolate in liquid and solid form . . .*

"Ruby, someone's tapping at the window." A voice came from far away. "There's someone outside."

The pressure of a hand on my shoulder sucked me through a chocolate-drenched tunnel of unconsciousness. My eyes popped open. I rolled over.

It took me a moment to process what was in front of me. Mom in her white cotton nightgown, long salt-and-pepper hair draping down her back, the room heavy with her rose-scented perfume.

"What?" I waited for the fairy dust of sleep to drift off my brain.

"Outside—there is someone outside in the yard."

She hovered over me.

I sat up. The red light of my alarm clock said 2:13 A.M.

Mom leaned over and turned on the nightstand lamp. I squinted, blocking the light with my hand.

"There is someone in the yard," she whispered. "He was tapping at the window." She patted her chest with an open palm. "My window."

Oh, okay. Intruder alert. Intruder alert. I tossed off the covers, grabbed my bathrobe at the end of the bed, swung my legs around, and planted my feet on the cold wood floor. I only wobbled a little bit when I stood up.

My first suspicions ran to a weird kid in one of the beginning composition classes I was teaching. Maybe he had moved up from lurking outside my office to following me home.

I reached over and turned off the nightstand lamp. "He doesn't need to know we know he's out there."

Maybe this guy wasn't even real. Hopefully my mother was having bad dreams too and had not been able to separate them from reality. I kind of doubted it, though. Mom was the levelheaded one in this house. "Go down the hallway and phone the police. Don't go by any windows."

"Ruby, I'm scared." Her hand found my mine in the dark. Clammy fingers trembled beneath my touch.

I squeezed her hand. "It's all right. Just get the police."

I scampered in the opposite direction down the hallway to her bedroom. When I crossed the threshold, I dropped to my hands and knees so I wouldn't be seen from the window. Mom's touch light by her bed glowed in the darkness. Cool air from the open window filled the room. Don't ask me why, but until the dead of winter, Mom insists on sleeping with the window open—something about the fresh breezes being invigorating. With sweat dripping from all my major body parts, I crawled up on her bed and peered over the rim of the window.

A streetlight some distance away provided a little illumination. I could make out the silhouette of the weeping willow and the smaller trees in the yard.

Then I heard it. Flesh crashing into metal, followed by a curse word. Whoever was stumbling out there in the dark hadn't seen the lawn mower. I slumped back down on the bed. My throat constricted. I couldn't get a deep breath.

"Ruby?" That one word from Mom held a ton of explosives.

After slipping off the bed, I crawled quickly toward her. Fear pulsed through my burning muscles. I felt every fiber of carpet rubbing against my knees.

Her lips were very close to my ear. "He's at the patio door in the kitchen."

The phone was at the end of the hallway, right before the kitchen where the patio door was. "Did he see you?"

"I don't think so."

"Are the cops coming?"

"I called them."

"That door's locked, isn't it?"

"Yes, they all are."

"Then we just wait." I crawled into the hallway. "The police will get here."

Pressing my back against the wall, I stared at the ceiling and willed my heart to quit thudding in my chest. A single incandescent bulb with a frosted cover on it partially illuminated the hallway. Most of the light fell on the photographs Mom had hung up.

To try to calm myself, I took an inventory of the pictures. Mom and me at a friend's wedding. *Deep breath.* Mom working her booth at a farmer's market. *Deep breath.* Me and my brother, Jimmy, when we were maybe eight and six. *Deep breath.* It was the oldest photo on the wall. Why had Mom put it up there? Jimmy's opened-mouth smile took up half his face and revealed a big gap where his front teeth should be. We both had our father's red hair and could have easily taken first prize at a freckle festival.

Mom scooted up beside me. She tucked her long, salt-and-pepper hair behind one ear and pulled her knees up to her chest, resting her hands on them.

I draped my hand over her trembling fingers, rubbing her soft skin. She shook her head and released a noise that was half cry, half sigh. Mom is the Rock of Gibraltar. I'd never seen her this shook up.

The creep must have noticed Mom's open window and peered in. *No wonder she was shaking.* How terrifying would it be to have only a screen between you and some demented weirdo? I sandwiched her hand between mine.

She closed her eyes and pressed her head against the wall. "Oh, Jesus, keep us safe."

I took in a shallow breath that was filled with silent prayer.

Where was the intruder now? Was he still standing at the patio door, or—

I exhaled through clenched teeth. Why hadn't I closed that stupid window in Mom's room? It would be a reach to get the screen off from outside. Maybe that's when Mom had heard the tapping. He'd been trying to work the screen off, not realizing a bed was right below it.

I held Mom's hand in my own until the trembling stopped. In the silent hallway, her steady, rhythmic breathing was amplified.

Then I heard the tap, tap, tap on glass.

Blood froze in my veins.

"He wants in," Mom whispered.

Pressure squeezed my heart. "I can't wait for the cops." My arm and leg muscles tensed. "It's time to play defense." I don't like it when people back me into a corner and play on my fear. How dare someone do this to my mom, the nicest person I know.

She tugged at my bathrobe as I stood to go down the hall. "Ruby . . . please . . . no. . . ."

I pulled my robe out of her grasp and strode to where the hallway ended and the kitchen began. Once I stepped out from behind the wall, he'd see me through the glass door. But there was no other way to get to the kitchen knives, the only available weapons.

For an egghead like me, whose idea of an action-packed time is reading a book on the couch, this was a little too much stimulation for one night. I gulped a deep breath, as if preparing to dunk under water. Bending over to minimize my profile, I ran toward the kitchen.

When I glanced at the patio door, I saw blackness. I opened a drawer. Nothing but spoons and spatulas. We weren't big meat eaters, but you would think we'd at least own one sharp steak knife. I slammed the drawer shut and shuffled through all our cutlery in a second drawer. Did we need all these soup spoons? I pictured the headline in tomorrow's paper, "Man Stabbed to Death with Fork" or "University Instructor Bludgeons Intruder with Soup Ladle."

Finally, in the third drawer, I found an assortment of knives. I chose one with a seven-inch straight blade and a sharp point. It looked reasonably scary.

Across the chasm of the kitchen, my mother stood at the edge of the hallway, her hand gripping the corner of the wall. Even in the dark, I could read fear in her expression. I didn't need to turn on the light to know that the two worry furrows between her eyebrows had become canyons.

If the intruder wasn't at the glass door, where had he gone? Why had he tapped on the window and then stepped away? Had he been checking to see if anyone was home? Or maybe he had been using some kind of tool to jimmy the lock.

Please, God, don't let him go back to Mom's window and find a way to crawl through. Crouching, I peered out the bottom of the kitchen window.

I had the strange sensation of an anaconda-like pressure twisting around my chest. *What I'd give for two fully inflated lungs . . .*

I squinted and leaned closer to the window. He was there under the weeping willow. Just standing there. The branches of the willow waved in the wind like the tentacles of a sea monster. Only a few dried leaves clung to the trees. The breeze kicked up, and a whirlwind of leaves sprayed through the yard.

I swallowed hard. What now? I didn't want this guy running away before the cops came. He'd ticked me off, and I needed to make sure justice was done. If he backed down the alley and got away when he saw the cop car, he'd only come back some other night. Or worse, he'd never come back, never be caught, and we would be endlessly tormented by the fear that he would come back.

His head tilted up slightly and turned in my direction. I ducked. He must have seen me when I ran past the glass door. My fingers curled around the knife handle.

Maybe this guy wasn't interested in getting into the house. Maybe he just got his jollies from intimidating women: waking them up, scratching at their windows, lurking in their yard.

I peered over the windowsill. He turned his whole body so more of him was illuminated by the streetlight. I could see the top part of his head distinctly. My eyes fixed on the coppery shade of his dark red hair, and I was drawn back down a corridor of memories.

I was sixteen when my parents were sent to prison for embezzlement. My little brother and I were thrown into the foster-care system. The last time I'd seen Jimmy, he was fourteen. I hadn't lived with any of my family since then, until a couple years ago when Mom and I reunited.

I peered out the window again, hoping to discern more facial features. Jimmy's hair was a unique shade of dark auburn with orange highlights that I'd never seen on another person. The man shifted slightly beneath the willow tree, placing his hair and half of his face in the light.

I leaned closer to the window. Were my eyes playing tricks on me? The word escaped my mouth before I could swallow: *"Jimmy?"*

"Jimmy?" Mom stepped out from the protection of the hallway and gazed out the patio door. Shadows shrouded her. A band of gray covered her eyes, and light from the hallway reflected off her hair. Her arms hung at her side. She stepped forward, zombie-like.

I must have said Jimmy's name louder than I realized. "We don't know, Mom. We don't know."

She was already halfway across the kitchen. Her long, white nightgown, made gray by the dim light, seemed to float across the floor.

"Jimmy—it's Jimmy." Her fingers wrapped around the handle of the patio door.

"He might have a gun. I can't tell for sure. I don't know if it's him."

I watched her push up the lever that unlocked the door.

"Jimmy. Jimmy." Her voice filled with irrational joy. I knew that what she wanted more than anything in the world was to undo the past, to have never lost her children. Now that desire drove her to do something unsafe—impulsive.

A burst of cold air filled the room as she slid the door open.

The man took a step toward her. She ran across the lawn in bare feet. Arms held out.

The man uttered a single word, "Mom," and fell into her arms.

"You found us. You found us." Mom's voice fluttered—half crying, half laughing. The last we'd heard of Jimmy, he'd run away from a foster home. I hadn't seen my little brother in fifteen years.

I turned on the kitchen light and walked to the patio door. This guy's face was pudgier and squarer than the Jimmy I remembered.

Mom separated one arm from the hug, and she and Jimmy walked toward the concrete slab by the sliding door. Waving her hand, she ushered me to join them. I stepped the few feet into a three-way embrace.

Jimmy smelled like breath mints. His forearm pressed into my middle back.

Suspicions rose up in me that I could not dismiss. Since her conversion, Mom had been praying for her children to come back. God answers prayer, but nobody's life works out *this* nice. And if this was Jimmy, why didn't he just knock on the door at a decent hour? Why was he lurking around the house, scratching on windows?

"We have so much to talk about." Mom stepped back and wiped her eyes. "Come inside. How did you find us?"

"This is Grandma's old house. We came here every summer, remember?"

"Of course I remember, Jimmy." She put an arm around his shoulders and escorted him through the patio door. "When your grandma died, she left me the house."

I straggled behind. *Lord, forgive me for my pessimism. Something feels wrong here.*

As we crossed the threshold into the kitchen, Jimmy slipped

from Mom's arm, giving me a backward glance, then lowering his eyes. The exchange lasted only a moment. I stared at him without blinking, hoping to see some nervous twitch, some unveiling of the eyes that would give him away. His expression was a virtual poker face.

Mom bustled around the kitchen, filled a kettle with water, and pulled tea bags from a cupboard. She glanced in our direction, smiling and raising her eyebrows at Jimmy. She was effervescent, almost glowing. "Have a seat. Have a seat, both of you."

Jimmy pulled a chair out, and I sat down kitty-corner from him. I wanted an explanation as to why he had been scratching at Mom's window—but somehow this didn't seem like the right time.

"I'm sorry I came so late at night." Jimmy combed his fingers through his hair. "I got off the bus at one o'clock, and I couldn't wait."

Mom opened the cookie jar. "Oh it's all right. It's all right, Jimmy." She stopped bustling for a moment, gazed at him, and brought a hand up to her heart. Her eyes glistened with new tears.

"We're just glad you are here," I said, hoping my words didn't have a hollow ring to them. I could see him better in this light. The Jimmy I remembered had been skinny, gaunt, with real distinctive cheekbones; a lot like a male version of me. Jimmy had been one of those kids who could eat anything and not gain weight. This guy was almost chubby. I could even see a little bit of a paunch under his black T-shirt. Then again, people could change. Fifteen years is a long time. His hair and eyes were the right color.

Headlights flashed across the living-room wall and a car pulled up outside.

Jimmy sat up straight in his chair, turned his head toward the living room, and then narrowed his eyes, questioning and suspicious.

"It's the cops. We thought you were an intruder," I almost whispered, addressing my comments to the floor. Then my back stiffened. Why should I feel any shame for calling the cops? He was the one who had acted like he was trying to break in. "You and Mom talk. I'll go outside and let the police know everything is okay."

I walked through the living room, opened the door, took the four steps across the porch, and descended the stairs to our front yard and walkway. I shivered and wished I had grabbed a coat to ward off the October chill.

A uniformed officer with a crew cut got out of the driver's side of the police car. He was dressed like every other cop in Eagleton, but I would recognize that distinctive confident stride—almost a swagger—anywhere.

It had been a year since Wesley Burgess and I had decided against any romantic involvement despite the strong attraction we felt for each other. A year ago, I was a new Christian. Because I'd had a really ugly history with men, I decided that a brand-new romance wouldn't be a good idea. I didn't want to repeat the patterns of the past. Wesley and I had parted, and he had attended a different church so we wouldn't be tempted to fall into a relationship until we had worked the kinks out of our faith.

"Thought I recognized the address when the call came in." His voice still had the marvelous, silky quality that made my rib cage tighten and my feet melt in my footwear.

"I'd heard you'd been training to be a cop." Honestly, I hadn't tried to ferret out the details of his life from friends we had in common, but my mind had drifted back to him more than once in the last year.

"Finished up at the academy about four months ago. Did my training with a senior officer before that." He stood with his legs shoulder-width apart, as lean and handsome as I remembered him. "I sold the roofing business—needed a steady paycheck."

"I suppose all that marine army-guy stuff you did years ago helped you get this job?"

"It was a selling point to the police department. I'm pushing thirty. I couldn't roof forever; my body was getting pretty beat up—I ached every night when I got home."

And what a body it was. He hadn't changed much in that respect. He was probably running laps while the other cops were at the doughnut shop. Other things about him were different. He wasn't wearing the glasses that made his green eyes seem even bigger and rounder. Maybe he had gotten contacts.

While I did my mental inventory of the six feet of gorgeous standing in front of me, Wesley surveyed the street from east to west. Yes, the way he looked made my little heart beat faster.

"What's going on here? Is this a false alarm?" He glanced toward the house.

Duh, Sherlock. At the rate he was going, he'd make detective in no time. All sorts of sarcastic responses ran through my brain. *No, dinglefritz, the intruder let me out to talk to you.* I actually grimaced at the thoughts galloping through my head.

I knew where this sarcasm came from. All these emotions ricocheting around my psyche scared me. My attraction for Wesley hadn't dimmed even after we put time and physical distance between us. But I wanted a relationship I'd be proud to show God, and I wasn't sure I could do that once I stepped into the whirl-wind of feelings that attraction created. "It's a long story. But I guess there's not an intruder."

"You guess?" He stepped toward me. "Don't play games with the police, Ruby."

"I wasn't playing games. There really was. . . ."

It was past two in the morning; I didn't have the energy to ex-plain the whole "Jimmy" saga to Wesley. I didn't like the way he implied that I had resorted to crank calls. Why is it that anytime he showed up, my emotions could do a one-eighty in a nanosec-ond? I groaned and rested my forehead in my hand.

"Don't get upset." He held a hand up, palm toward me. He spoke slowly, annunciating each word. "For the record, why did your mom phone the police?"

Now he was talking to me like I was five years old. "It involves having to tell you my entire life story."

"Ruby, I'm trying to do my job here. I can't leave until I am sure you are in no danger. Did you hear something and think it was an intruder? Do I need to have a look around the place?"

"Don't get mad at me. I'm sorry my life doesn't fit into a one-paragraph summary."

"I'm not getting mad. I'm just trying to follow procedure. Are you and your mother in any danger?"

"No." I glanced back at the house. What was the "Jimmy" sit-ting in our kitchen capable of? He had scratched at Mom's win-dow—probably tried to open the door. "I mean, we thought it was an intruder, but it was just . . . just my brother Jimmy."

Wesley rolled his eyes. "Make up your mind."

He was trying hard to sound neutral, but I could hear the

frustration in his voice. I could read the subtext under his words. His emotion wasn't about police procedure. I'd stirred up old feelings in him as much as he had in me. Now we were even. So there.

I stood for a long time, getting a headache because my teeth were clenched so tight. I hadn't meant to jerk him around emotionally. It just happened. "Honest, Officer. We're okay. Thank you for doing your job."

I cleared my throat. My voice had actually sounded husky. "I think that Jimmy is going to be staying with us."

"Okay, good. I can call this in as a false alarm." He stood about three feet from me, not budging, bathed in the soft glow of the streetlight.

"Your hair looks different." Without thinking, I reached up and touched the wavy soft hair at his temple. The gesture was almost involuntary. His gaze locked on me. I felt that familiar electric charge travel over my skin. I swallowed hard and stepped away before I had a Wicked Witch of the West moment. You know: Help me, I'm melting, I'm melting.

"I had to get it cut for the job." He brought his fingers up to where I had touched his hair. "So things are good with you?"

His voice had entered the sultry zone.

"I got a new job too, part-time at the U. Some guy died, and I took his place. I'm hoping it will turn into more—better money and using all that education I got. I'm still helping out at the feed store."

He nodded and stared just long enough for me to tremble all over and wonder if I had food stuck in my teeth. His uniform looked so pressed and smoothed over and gorgeous. I balled my hands into fists to keep from touching him again. "Glad you came by. Thanks, Mr. Policeman."

He grinned with only one side of his mouth turning up. "Still as funny as ever, aren't ya?" A forest of thick lashes surrounded his green eyes.

Yeah, and you, dear Wesley, still make me feel like I'm about to spontaneously combust. But let's not go there. I took a step back and managed a very businesslike tone. "Stay safe out there." I was impressed with my ability to sound neutral despite the raging river underneath.

"Be seein' ya." He sauntered back to the patrol car. Once behind the steering wheel, he gave a half wave before craning his neck and backing up.

When was that man going to learn to use his rearview mirror? Light from the streetlamps shone on the car in such a way that I could see Wesley's tanned skin and the strands of muscles in his neck. What he needed was a good woman to teach him how to use the rearview mirror.

He pulled forward and drove past the house.

Stop it, Ruby. Put the brakes on that fantasy, girlfriend.

If God wanted me to stay single and take care of Mom, I could learn to be content with that. And now we had Jimmy to deal with. It would take a while, but I could learn. Still, a guest appearance from Wesley was enough to stir up those old feelings. I glanced up at the dark sky. The North Star twinkled back at me. *What am I supposed to do, God, hmm? You tell me.*

The screen door creaked. "Ruby, is everything all right?" My mother's voice drifted out from the doorway.

A heaviness settled into my arm muscles. It must be three o'clock by now. "Yeah, I took care of it."

"Come on back inside." She was almost singing when she spoke.

"I got the photo album out. We have so much to learn about Jimmy. So much lost time . . ."

Her voice trailed off. Was there something underneath her joy—a question mark? Or was I reading things into her words because I was such a doubting Thomas?

Other than incredible cruelty, I couldn't think of what motivation someone would have for impersonating my little brother.

I caught myself yawning as I trudged up the stairs into the living room, but I didn't want to go back to sleep. I wasn't that jacked about walking down memory lane with Jimmy, either. *Jesus, chocolate, and a mocha with the steam rising off of it. Find a happy place, Ruby.*

Mom put her arm around me and ushered me into the kitchen where my alleged brother sat flipping through a photo album.

Chapter Two

What's up with that kid hanging out by the rare books collection?" Professor Donita Hall leaned against the doorway of my office. "He was there last night too, wasn't he?" Her fuchsia blazer with large shoulder pads made her look even thinner than she was, which put her in the toothpick category for body type. She clutched a well worn copy of *The Brothers Karamazov.*

I pushed my wheeled office chair back from the colossal desk and gazed at the ceiling. "Is he wearing a long coat that looks like it came from army surplus, medium height, medium build?"

She craned her neck so she could stare down the hall, then stepped toward my desk. "Yep."

"His name is Dale Cutler; Monday-Wednesday-Friday class. He hangs out around my office late at night like he wants to talk to me, but he never does. Never comes by during the day when I have regular office hours."

"Nifty, your own personal stalker." After setting her book on my desk, Donita scooped up a handful of M&M's out of my goodies bowl.

"I thought stalkers were issued by the university—part of the benefits package." I walked my chair back to the desk and grabbed a handful of chocolate. "Really, it's the only benefit I'm getting."

"Our beloved department head didn't give you bennies?" Donita sat down on the corner of my desk and swung one of her long, skinny legs back and forth. "You're a short-timer. I didn't realize."

"I'm hoping for more."

I had been a Christian for a year. The depression episodes were fewer and farther between. I was so much stronger and felt ready to handle more than my minimum-wage job at Benson's Pet and Feed—ready to put the *M* and the *A* that were behind my name to good use.

"The guy you replaced, Theodore Aldridge, was a Ph.D." Donita locked her elbows and stared at her hot pink fingernails, fingers splayed.

"Yeah, they told me he killed himself three weeks into the semester. I know I was a last-minute replacement, but still—"

"Cameron might be looking to hire someone who can handle the upper-division classes too." She must have seen my shoulders slump and picked up on my disappointment, because she reached over, patted my back, and winked at me. "Get good evaluations. Something might open up."

So far, Donita was the only professor who had talked to me. We seemed to be making a habit of chatting and eating chocolate at night. Just the three of us—me, Donita, and my stalker—hanging out in Truman Hall. Now I had two reasons for not wanting to go home—the dream and Jimmy. I didn't know why Donita stayed so late at night.

She had this sort of latent Cyndi Lauper quality. On my first day of work, I'd seen her wearing lime-green tights with a very businesslike navy suit. Her hair stuck out at odd, sharp angles. I pictured her styling it every morning with a large can of mousse and a weed whacker.

"Theodore was fun. I miss him." Donita gathered more chocolate from my bowl and spoke between bites. "He could be a little moody."

I patted her hand as she reached toward the bowl for the third time. "Don't eat all my chocolate. I keep it around for medicinal purposes."

Donita laughed. "Better than Prozac, huh?"

I picked a few chocolates from the bowl. "Cheaper, too." The tension eased out of my shoulders as the chocolate melted in my mouth.

Donita sighed and blew a strand of hair off her face. "I better get home and write that great American novel I'm supposed to produce—or at least some tripe for a journal. You know what our beloved leader says . . ."

We spoke the words together. "Publish, publish. Published means prestige, and prestige means students, and students mean money."

Every prof in the English department knew that little ditty by heart. Cameron Bancroft, head of the department and all-around budget balancer, raged up and down the halls with his version of a pep talk.

I rose to my feet and shoved the seventy-odd papers scattered across my desk into my briefcase. My vision was blurry from reading. I could record the grades this weekend and hand them back at the next class.

Donita turned her attention to the books on my shelf on the wall opposite the desk.

I picked up my Bible and shoved it in my briefcase with a craned-neck glance at her. Mentally, I kicked myself. Why had I done that? So what if she saw that I carried a Bible around? No one here even knew I was a Christian.

I kept thinking about the Christian groups I saw around campus, throwing tracts at people and running away. One of my students had left a tract on my lectern. He hadn't bothered to get to know me, to look me in the eye, to have a conversation with me. He had automatically assumed I was an atheist. Hit-and-run evangelism seemed like a bad idea.

Donita turned back around.

I pulled my Bible back out of my briefcase and very deliberately laid it on the desk. I did a Vanna White sweep over the Bible as if to say, Look, I have Christian stuff. Ask me why.

Donita was utterly oblivious to my game-show performance. I tapped my fingers by my Bible. Here was this person whom I liked, a potential friend, and I had no idea how to share the most important part of my life with her. *Can I get a segue please?*

"Did you find the key to that drawer?" She adjusted the shoulder pad in her blazer and walked toward the desk.

I brushed my palm across the smooth top of the wooden desk. "No, it would be nice to have the space to put my stapler and dictionary."

"I don't think it's been moved in fifty years. The last time they renovated, they just built around it. That desk is gimungous and heavy."

Gimungous, I liked that word. Donita's little history lesson explained why the desk took up most of my microscopic office. I had room for my chair and a bookshelf on the opposite wall. A family of five, however, could live quite comfortably on top of the desk. It was made of a rich dark wood, maybe walnut. A rectangle of copper covered most of the top.

Donita strutted back to the doorway and leaned out. "It's ten o'clock on a Friday night. He's a kid. You would think he had better things to do."

I plunged back down in my chair and spun around. "You would

think *we* would have better things to do." Yet another benefit of this job was the spinning chairs. There were no spinning chairs at Benson's Pet and Feed.

Donita stared at the floor. "Not much to do on a Friday night since I quit drinking," she whispered. Her words were far away, not meant for me.

I shrank back from the sudden coldness she exuded. "Don't you get together with other professors?" Dummy me, I had assumed there was some huge social circle of academics that I had been excluded from 'cause I was the new girl in town. I slipped my Bible back in the briefcase. Maybe I would get another chance tomorrow night.

"They all drink. The ones that don't drink are busy doing things with their kids." She hit her forehead with the heel of her hand. "Darn, I forgot to have kids." She shrugged and stared down the long hallway. "Life's kind of a bummer when you have to go through it sober. But it's too dangerous to go through it drunk." Her voice was full of lightness and air, but the joking seemed forced.

"I'm glad you come by and talk to me. Otherwise, I'd have to actually get my work done."

The tightness in Donita's expression softened. "Tell you what." She made a come-closer motion with her finger. "You call that kid down here and find out what he wants. I'll kind of lurk outside to make sure he's not a perv."

I leaned out the door. "Hey, Dale. Do you need to see me about something?"

Donita wrapped a supportive hand around my upper arm.

He stuck his head out from behind the rare books display case. "Professor Taylor, I was just waiting until you were done talking."

Donita giggled. "Professor Taylor."

Dale didn't understand the pecking order of the U. I was not a professor with three letters behind my name. I was just a lowly adjunct.

"Professor Taylor. Nice ring to it," Donita teased.

I pressed on her foot with my own. Out of Dale's earshot, Donita let out an exaggerated squeak. "My visitor was just leaving, Dale."

He stepped from behind the bookshelf and ambled down the hall.

Donita slipped past me. "I'll be lurking. Just in case," she whispered. She did a slicing thing in the air with her hands. "I know karate—and twenty other Japanese words."

"Get out of here."

I listened to Donita's heels tap, tap, tap down the hall, but the tapping stopped when Dale stepped into my office.

Dark brown hair stuck out from beneath a black cowboy hat. His eyes were close together and slit-like. He had pudgy cheeks and bunched-up lips.

"You wanted to see me, Dale?"

"Yeah, um," He tugged on the collar of his coat. "Um . . . I was just wondering . . . um . . ."

He shoved his hands in the pocket of his jeans and wandered over to my desk, where he poked at the rivets that held the copper sheeting to the wood. "I was just wondering if you had those papers graded yet."

"You've been hanging out all this time just to find out your grade?"

Dale slipped his hat off. "I need to get an A in this class." A row of red, round scars and pinholes arched over the top of one of his eyebrows where silver studs must have been at one time. Judging from the few days I'd seen him in class, he seemed to be trying on identities. On alternate days, he'd come dressed in the cowboy attire he wore now, and the other times he'd had on a pastel polo with slacks—very frat boyish. "I took this class because Dr. Aldridge was teaching it." Dale twirled the cowboy hat, then placed it on the desk by Donita's book. "What did I get?"

I set the briefcase on the desk and pulled it open. "This is really why you have been hanging out for the last couple of nights?" I shuffled through the papers until I found his and handed it to him.

Dale did that thing where he didn't quite make eye contact. Instead, he stared at my neck. "I'm pretty busy during the day." He flipped through the pages, totally ignoring all my witty written comments. I put the grade on a back page so the student doesn't have to be embarrassed by other students seeing his grade.

He flipped to the last page. His jaw dropped, and his shoulders slumped.

"You didn't do any research. All your examples are personal experience. You need a little more support for your argument." I spoke as gently as I could.

Dale's reaction to the C was remarkably civilized. When I'd handed papers back in class, the student responses had ranged from shooting daggers with their eyes to confronting me after class. Some students had a gift for twisting things around in their head so that they believed their bad grade was all my fault. Dale hadn't done that.

"Yeah, Dr. Aldridge said I had good ideas, but I needed to learn how to do research."

"You liked Dr. Aldridge?" I pulled the paper from his tight grip.

"I am a sophomore. I put off taking this freshman class so I could take it from him." He raised his gaze from the floor. Again he did not look me in the eye. "I was in his scriptwriting class last year—spring semester." Dale ran his hand over the top of the desk. "He was nice. He was helping me . . . with some things." He fixated on the desk, tracing the grain pattern with his fingers.

Was there something more he wanted to say to me? "Dale, what are you doing wandering around campus on a Friday night?"

Dale shrugged and shoved his hands into the deep pockets of his trench coat. His jawline stiffened as his defense shields went up. His expression was smooth, masklike. "I got lots of places to go."

"Good." I shoved the paper back in my briefcase. I smiled, hoping pleasantry would help me find the kid behind the defenses. "I've got an action-packed weekend of recording grades and writing lesson plans myself." I snapped the briefcase shut. "Sounds like you miss Dr. Aldridge."

Dale ran a hand along the side of the desk and stopped at the drawer. "I do. I do miss him."

"I'll see you in class on Monday."

He nodded for about five seconds. "Yeah, on Monday. I'll try harder on the next paper."

He grabbed his cowboy hat and left. I listened to his tennis shoes pad down the hallway while I gathered up the rest of my stuff.

When I glanced down the dark hallway, Donita was nowhere in sight. "Hey, what happened to my protection, woman?"

Donita popped out of her office three doors down. She had put on a bright purple wool poncho. "I would have heard you scream."

"Yeah, right. But could you get here fast enough?" After picking up Donita's book, I closed the door to my office and fumbled through my briefcase for my keys.

"I listened outside your office for a while," Donita said as she closed the door to her office and shoved the key in the lock. "The kid is a little weird, but not violent. Poor guy sounds like he really misses Theodore."

All this talk about my predecessor had piqued my curiosity. "So why did Theodore kill himself?"

Donita walked down the hall toward me. "Same reason I thought about suicide when I was drinking—'cause booze messes with your head." She readjusted the large tote she had draped over her shoulder after she dropped her keys in it. "But no more stinkin' thinkin' for me."

What a strong lady, I thought. Any English professor who made up words like *gimungous* was okay in my book. I handed her the worn-out copy of *The Brothers Karamazov*.

"Thank you." She held the book to her chest. "My most treasured possession."

"If I'd known that, I would have held it for ransom. You know, bring two stuffed weasels and a bag of chocolate to the corner of Wilshire and Main if you ever want to see your book alive."

"Two stuffed weasels would be a small price to pay to be reunited with Ivan." She slipped the book into her tote.

"Ivan?"

"Ivan Karamazov. The brother who falls into despair because he thinks too much about stuff. He's my favorite character in the book."

"Oh, right." I nodded as if I knew what I was talking about. I must confess; I could never get past page forty of any Russian novel without either falling asleep or becoming really sad. "Come on. I'll walk out with you."

We made our way through the dark maze that was Truman Hall, two women with nothing better to do on a Friday night than hang out at their place of employment. *A date would be nice with, oh, say, Wesley.* But I was not going to force that to happen. If Wesley was still interested, he would have to do the pursuing. Besides, I couldn't come up with a reasonable excuse to get in touch with him.

Donita and I walked slowly down the dark stairs. Our footsteps were the only noise in the empty building. None of the staircases adjoined each other, so we had to descend a flight, walk the length of a hallway with a few turns, and then go down another flight.

My cowboy boots echoed on the linoleum of the first floor. I was convinced the architect for this building was either forgetful or a former prison inmate who wanted to feel at home. Hardly any windows graced the halls. The decorator had chosen a theme of concrete and dim lighting. All the department offices and grad carrels looked exactly alike, so it was easy to get lost. You thought you were headed toward the biology department and you ended up in religion and philosophy.

The outside door creaked open, and we stepped into the crisp fall evening. I could just make out the silhouette of the mountains that surround Eagleton. The town itself rests in a valley and was originally a fort, a stopping place for settlers on the way to the better, greener land on the West Coast. At fifty thousand and growing, Eagleton is one of the larger cities in Montana. Within a 150-

mile radius, you'll find only little agricultural towns of one thousand to five thousand people. So most of the good shopping is in Eagleton, and the U is here.

Donita said good-bye and headed up the hill.

"Thanks for being the protection, Guido."

"Any time," she shouted as she walked away. "I know lots of Japanese words."

"You and Ivan have a good time tonight," I shouted back.

Entranced by the easy-listening sounds of my boots pounding on the concrete of the parking lot, I let my thoughts drift to Theodore Aldridge. For me, curiosity doesn't just kill the cat, it takes it to the taxidermist and stuffs it.

My nemesis, a sort of geriatric Nancy Drew who lives inside my head, asked the burning question, *Why did Theodore kill himself?*

I dreaded the thought of going home. Not only was I haunted by strange dreams, but Jimmy had a dreadful snoring problem that I could hear through the whole house. The world conspired against me getting a good night's sleep.

Maybe finding out some interesting tidbit about Theodore's death would give me an excuse to go see Mr. Policeman.

Who am I kidding? The campus library is open tomorrow. Home hasn't felt like home since Jimmy showed up. Reading the newspaper reports about Theodore Aldridge will be a good excuse for getting out of the house.

Get your walker and perfect hairdo, Nanc. We're going asleuthin' tomorrow.

Chapter Three

Honestly, Ruby, it's been fifteen years." Mom readjusted her tote bag as we stood outside the university library. The bag is a little quilted job she made out of fabric scraps. Mom has a gift for taking the things that other people throw away and turning them into something beautiful.

I've christened the tote "the purse with everything and everything in the purse." Flashlight, umbrella, lip balm, Bible—Mom has her whole life in there. If I dug deep enough, I could probably find the kitchen sink.

We ascended the steps of the library. Jimmy had been home for a little over a day. So far, he seemed more interested in sleeping than in repairing the family. He came out to eat a late lunch with us before we left for the library, but he complained about fatigue and was reluctant to talk. He wasn't giving me any opportunity to press him about details of our childhood, which made me even more suspicious of him.

Finding out more about the dead man I had replaced provided distraction from my messed-up family.

With Mom trailing behind me, I pushed open the glass door. "I'm just saying he doesn't look like the Jimmy I remember. And don't you think it's kind of weird the way he scratched at your window?" We entered the library lobby.

Mom put her hand on her hip. "People change. I think he looks better with a little meat on his bones. I used to worry about that boy—scrawny little thing ate like a horse but never gained a pound."

I had worked an early morning shift at the feed store, unloading some things that had been delivered. My boss, Georgia, is letting me come in on an "as needed" basis when she can't get relatives to cover or she has extra work like unloading. She told me she could put off posting a "help wanted" sign in the window. Straddling the fence between two jobs leaves very little free time, but I don't want to give up the feed store until I'm sure I have something permanent at the U. There's nothing glamorous about shelving bags of alfalfa cubes, and it sure doesn't require the level of education I have, but I really like Georgia and the people who come into her store.

"I still think the way he stood in the yard was weird." I traipsed across the library's mosaic floor to a table displaying books that were new in the library. "Why didn't he just ring the doorbell?" I picked up a history text about mining in Montana and flipped through it.

Mom had spent the morning teaching a painting class at the senior citizens center. I'd thought maybe after we'd had some sleep and time to think she might have been willing to address the part of the Jimmy picture that looked questionable.

Mom did that thing with her face where she draws her lips into a straight line and her cheeks bunch up. "Maybe I didn't hear those noises at the window. Maybe I just imagined them."

I tilted my head and glared at the high ceiling of the library lobby. "You were scared out of your wits."

"I've prayed for this for years." She narrowed her eyes at me. "I've got my son back. You've got your brother back. Don't go spoiling it with your pessimism. Don't you think I would recognize my own son?"

We walked past the long, marble checkout counter, where a young woman stood staring at her fingernails. As we skirted around the copy machine and went down the stairs to the newspaper room, the only words I could manage were, "I'm sorry." *I do need to quit being such a naysayer.*

"I am just so glad he is back in our lives," Mom said as we entered a room that was labeled "Newspapers and Microfiche."

I didn't want to think about Jimmy anymore. "The stuff on Theodore Aldridge is recent enough. We should be able to find some of it in hard copy."

A counter with a computer on it stood just inside the door. No one was behind the counter. The decor for the basement consisted of early modern concrete accented with sleeping students. The place smelled like damp leather. Apparently the concept of windows was foreign to the designers of this university building, as well. I walked over to the row of computers positioned against the far wall.

Mom tagged behind, taking short mincing steps. She actually dressed up for this morning. She has a way of dressing that is somewhere between standard senior citizen and sixties radical. Today it was a white peasant blouse and a velvet patchwork skirt. Her shoes are those "comfortable shoes" that look like little chunky blocks on her feet. All the ladies she teaches crafts to at the senior center wear the exact same kind of shoes, only in different colors. Mom coming to help me with my research was her idea. Jimmy was sleeping in the guest bed in the room where Mom kept her sewing stuff. Her excuse was that she wanted the house quiet so he could rest.

I entered the keyword "Theodore Aldridge" and found plenty

about him in the campus newspaper. The *Eagleton Gazette,* the town newspaper, had second-page news about his death. He'd died three weeks into the semester on Friday, September 20. I had stopped reading the newspaper months ago because it was so depressing. At the time, I was probably the only one in town who hadn't heard about Aldridge's death.

I skimmed stories about him being named professor of the month and professor of the year; his article had been featured in this journal and that magazine; a book on Edgar Allen Poe was set for publication. He had already written several other well-received books over the course of his career. Much of his writing focused on Poe. Apparently, Aldridge had taken Cameron Bancroft's words to heart and published, published. He'd founded a film festival, helped the department set up a rare books collection as an investment, and was chairman of this and head of that. His face stared back at me in black-and-white photographs. A lean, tall man with gray hair, round, wire-rimmed glasses, and a welcoming smile.

He had also made an appearance in the police report for drunk driving this past summer. Maybe Donita was right and his drinking had led to the ultimate despair.

Sitting in a hard plastic chair in the basement of the university library where musty, thick air settled on my skin, I watched a life full of achievements and accolades pass before me—*and end with suicide?* Even though I knew from personal experience that high achievement didn't bring happiness, I couldn't picture the smiling man I saw in the photographs killing himself.

Then again, maybe I was trying to create a crime where there was none so I would have an excuse to go talk to Mr. Policeman,

Wesley Burgess. I sucked air through my gritted teeth. No matter what I did, my thoughts seemed to circle back around to Wesley.

I turned my attention to the reports of Aldridge's death. Feet padded up behind me. I assumed it was my mother until a very male voice cleared his throat.

I levitated three inches off the chair but managed not to scream.

When I turned around, Dale Cutler grinned at me. He wore jeans with a belt buckle the size of a saucer and a western-cut shirt loud enough to break eardrums. It had vertical stripes of different widths in hot pink, lime green, gray, and black. I resisted the urge to ask him if he had crashed into a kaleidoscope. God and I have been working hard on me learning to hold my sarcastic tongue. I know what the psychology rule books say about sarcasm—that it is a defense mechanism, a way of keeping people at a distance, blah, blah, blah.

"I don't have your paper, Dale." I resettled myself into the uncomfortable chair.

Dale drew his eyebrows together. "I work here, Dr. Taylor."

I loved him calling me "Doctor" even though I am not. "Oh . . . yes . . . of course you do." He seemed fairly normal, but I still wasn't over him lurking outside my office. Maybe he was just shy. I could feel my cheeks getting hot as I turned around and focused on a newspaper ad for doggie daycare.

"Let me know if I can help you find anything." A moment passed before I heard his tennis shoes pad across the concrete.

I flipped through a few more articles and then glanced around the basement. Last time I'd seen Mom, she had been reading on the dilapidated brown couch in the corner. A large man wearing burgundy slacks and a baseball cap sat there now. I had a horrific image of Mom being squashed, cartoon style, beneath the large man. She was petite, but not that small. She must have wandered off. The care and feeding of moms is complex, but at the very least you shouldn't let them wander too much.

I needed to stretch my legs anyway. I found her upstairs, swapping cake recipes with the reference librarian. Mom can make friends with anyone.

"Mom, you said you were going to help me with my research." I approached the library counter.

Mom nodded at me. After she finished writing her list of ingredients on a sticky note, she handed it to the librarian. I knew what she was writing, because she announced each item as she wrote it down. "One-half cup flour, teaspoon baking soda, just a pinch of salt . . ." She readjusted her tote bag on her shoulder. Like always, she had braided her long hair and swirled it around her head. Her hand moved quickly across the tiny piece of paper.

Mom is pushing sixty, and although her skin has that leathery quality that comes with age, the crow's-feet and lines around the mouth have just started to emerge. Maybe it's because I'm her daughter, but I've always thought my mom had an unpretentious elegance about her.

Why did she come with me today? Obviously, it wasn't to actually help me. Did being alone with Jimmy scare her? Maybe she would get to talking with him and realize he wasn't her Jimmy.

She followed me back downstairs to the table where I had my research laid out. I glanced at the pile of newspapers and grabbed the one on top. The article didn't look familiar.

Mom leaned close. "What is it?"

"I don't remember pulling this article up." I skimmed it.

"What's it about?"

"Well," I continued to read, "looks like Dr. Aldridge co-taught a scriptwriting class with some film professor."

"Is that important?"

I looked back at the color photograph: Aldridge sitting at that huge desk—my desk—with a woman standing beside him. She was fortyish with auburn hair and dressed in a blazer with a jewel-neck blouse, the standard uniform for all female professors. "This article is from last year."

I glanced around the basement: stacks of newspapers on metal shelves, microfiche machines, and several droopy-eyed patrons reading or clicking keys on computers. I honestly couldn't remember pulling this article. Then again, I'd found more than thirty articles either in hard copy or from the computer archives. I was probably just exhibiting signs of early onset senility. The walker and big-people diapers couldn't be far behind.

Mom put a hand on her hip and patted the back of her head. "This place could use a coat of paint."

Before Mom had a chance to remodel, I dragged her upstairs, not allowing her to give a recipe to anybody on the way.

I shaded my eyes from the afternoon sun as we stepped outside. The sky was clear marble blue, streaked with brush-stroked clouds. Compared to weekdays, the campus was virtually abandoned. A smattering of people, most of them walking alone, trickled across the lawn and stone walkways. Most wore backpacks; some pushed bikes.

A young man wearing jeans and a T-shirt that made a reference to Jesus walked by us.

I pointed at the student. "I need to get me one of those."

"Ruby, he's way too young for you," Mom scolded.

"Not him, the T-shirt. You know, something that says 'I Love Jesus.'" I ran my fingers across my chest and stomach to show her where the words should go.

Mom sat down on a nearby bench and crossed her legs at the ankles. "And why do you think you need something like that, Ruby?"

"Maybe I should get one of those three-foot crosses to hang around my neck. The kind that glisten so much people have to shade their eyes as you come down the hallway." I mimed someone trying to haul a cross that size around her neck by leaning back and sticking my stomach out.

Mom's mouth curved up into a smile. "Sounds like a lot of extra work to me. Could throw your back out."

"I'm a Christian now. I should have the official uniform." I plopped down beside her. The metal bench was solid against my back. "At least that way, when I showed up some place, everybody would say, 'Here comes that Christian lady.'"

Mom laughed, shook her head, and patted my hand. "Oh, Ruby."

I hate it when she does that. I was hoping for a little advice—a little wisdom from the senior member of the God Squad. Instead, she's going to make me figure it out on my own. I don't like feeling like two people, yakking it up about Jesus at Bible study and then growing silent when I get around people who don't share my beliefs.

"It bubbles up from inside," Mom said absently after a moment of silence. She stared off into space.

"What?" I scooted away from her. *It bubbles up from inside?* Was she just having a senior moment where pieces of recipe instructions fell out of her mouth?

We sat for twenty minutes. The mid-October sun warmed my arms—Indian Summer, they call it. Montana's last-ditch effort at a little warmth before six months of cold set in. A few people passed by and entered the library. Patches of brown had invaded the lawn, and most of the trees sported a gold-and-red hairstyle or had gone bald.

Mom didn't seem to be in any hurry to go home. She took out a book and read. I don't think either of us knew what to do with the stranger sleeping at our house. We could only look through so many photo albums of happy memories before the past barreled down on us at a hundred miles an hour.

Except for the embezzling thing, we had been the picture of an All-American family. Dad moved us from one city to the next every two or three years. We settled into suburbia, had barbecues, rode bikes with the neighborhood kids, and painted our fences white. My whole childhood had been a lie.

I didn't even know my parents were criminals until the cops came and hauled them away when I was fifteen. By the time I was sixteen and Jimmy was fourteen, we had worn out our welcome with relatives and were in foster care. I suppose there had always been an undercurrent of suspicion. Normal families didn't move around like we did. Normal families didn't change their appearance every time they moved.

I'm sure Jimmy had wounds and scars, just like I did. I patted Mom's leg. "We gotta go home." The mom who had gone to prison was very different from the mom I had now.

Mom closed her book and put it back in her tote. "I know." She didn't make eye contact. Instead, she looked far off in the distance, across campus to a parking lot, and beyond that to a vast open field. "I know, Ruby."

When we got home, Mom set her stuff down on the kitchen table. "I'll go wake Jimmy."

I trudged to my room with the articles I had copied. The stories in the *Gazette* said that Theodore Aldridge had hanged himself. Wesley, (aka Mr. Policeman), would have access to the details about the death. I banged my forehead with the heel of my hand. *Come on, Ruby, be honest with yourself. You know you are just looking for an excuse to see him again so you can marinate in those mushy feelings.* I need to stop letting my mind wander down that path. I am not going to chase men. That was the old me. If anything was going to happen between us, Wesley would need to make the first move.

I placed the articles in a desk drawer. *Okay, so I am looking for an excuse. It has been a year. I'm a lot stronger spiritually, and I feel like maybe sexual temptation isn't as big an issue anymore. I could start dating again. Maybe Wesley has worked through his treating-women-with-dignity issues. Wouldn't that just be cozy?*

Mom stepped into the doorway. Except for two bright red patches on her cheeks, her light skin was even paler than usual, like she'd been sick. Her lips moved up and down several times before any words came out. "I can't find Jimmy."

My stomach clenched. "Did you check outside?"

"He's not there." Her voice cracked and slipped into falsetto.

"It doesn't make sense to panic right away. Maybe he went for a walk. Did you look for a note?"

Her hands balled into fists and her chin jutted out. "He's not here."

"Don't snap at me."

She collapsed into a chair by the door. "I'm sorry. I . . . I just . . ." She buried her face in her hands.

I had that awful sensation of needing to run really fast and not being able to move at all. If he was gone, there was nothing I could do. The four feet to where Mom sat felt like a marathon. I touched her shaking shoulder. Her hands still covered her face. They were fragile-looking hands, skin so thin and milky it was almost transparent. The placement of muscle and bone underneath was easy to discern.

"How about I make you a cup of tea?" This was actually a technique I had learned from Mom. Hot beverages made with love have healing properties. "Men are not real good at leaving notes. He probably just stepped out. We'll wait."

We waited through the late afternoon, through a plate of cookies and a pot of tea. Mom sat with her hands folded in her lap—back straight and chin parallel to the floor, like she was balancing an invisible book on her head.

I went to my room and worked on lesson plans for several hours. When I came out, she was still sitting at the kitchen table. Her neck was bent, and she stared at the grain pattern in the wood.

When I touched her, she was rigid, like granite beneath my fingers. I knew what tape she was playing in her head. It was the same one I had to keep myself from listening to. The one about the past and all the mistakes you made and how you wish you could undo it.

My tape was a little different from hers. I wished I hadn't slept with all those men, hoping for a commitment. I wished I hadn't wasted so many years consumed by bitterness and blaming everyone else.

I knelt beside her and put my arms around her narrow shoulders. "Don't do this to yourself. God forgave you for prison and everything."

"Forgiveness doesn't make the consequences from the past go away, Ruby. Every day, I wake up and wish I hadn't let your father talk me into stealing. Wish he hadn't died in prison. Wish I hadn't lost my children."

I squeezed her shoulder.

She closed her eyes. "I pray through it. I remind myself of the good things God has given me." She patted my hand. "So many wonderful things. But some days . . ." A tear formed at the corner of her eye and drifted down her finely wrinkled cheek. "Some days," she whispered, "I just don't feel strong enough."

I had never seen my mom this fragile, never heard her express doubt that Christ's love was enough to get her through another day.

I didn't say anything, because everything I could think of sounded trite. Still hugging her, I slipped into the chair beside her. Our breathing and the ticking of the kitchen clock created a repetitive song—don't give up, don't give up, don't give up.

I held her a while longer until she reassured me she was okay. Then I trudged back to my room, finished recording grades, and started some reading.

Two hours later, when I came out, Mom was cooking—and I do mean cooking. The mixer, the bread machine, and every kitchen device buzzed. Steam drifted up from two casserole dishes resting on the counter. One had melted cheese on top of it, and the other looked like some kind of potato-broccoli thing. Salt and cinnamon aromas swirled through the moist air. The table was covered with chocolate chip cookies. She punched bread dough together and pounded it with her fists, then she moved to a mixing bowl and stirred for a while. Then she quit that and took up chopping vegetables. On the countertops, the kitchen table—everywhere, unfinished cooking projects sat scattered around.

Mom looked up at me and smiled brightly. "Thought I'd do a little baking."

"Okay." The mood change was strange. I had the sense that she was smiling for my sake. When I can't cope, I go fetal and sleep. I guess Mom cooks.

She handed me a plate and pointed. "Try the chicken Parmesan. I think it will be quite good."

The steely look in her eyes and tight lips told me I was not allowed to argue. It was past dinnertime. The sugar buzz from the plate of cookies had long since worn off.

I shoveled a bite of chicken into my mouth and looked around at the mess on the counters. If she kept this up, I would weigh three hundred pounds. How much baking would she have to do before she was over Jimmy? There was still a chance he would come back— but somehow, in my heart, I knew that chance was slim.

I was angry with my brother, if he even *was* my brother. I could guess at what had driven him away. The same things I wrestled with a year ago—that push-me/pull-you feeling of wanting to love Mom, to be connected to her, but being consumed by bitterness for how her choices had hurt me. Still, I hated him for his cruelty to Mom. It would've been better if he had never come back at all. And I hated myself for allowing that thought into my head.

At about nine o'clock, the kitchen stopped buzzing. Mom ate a plate of something-or-other casserole and stood by the living-room window, staring out into the street. She looked small against the high window and ornate curtains that swept to the floor. Curtains she had sewn.

Jimmy wasn't coming back—no matter how long she stood there.

I wanted to believe he had just stepped out, but something told me that wasn't true. If he was my brother, memories had driven him away.

When I went to bed, Mom was still standing at the window.

The next morning was church. I had dressed and finished breakfast, and Mom still wasn't up. When I went to her room, she was lying beneath the covers.

"Ma, church?"

"Go without me, Ruby. I'm too tired."

Mom hardly ever misses church.

Her bent form beneath the blankets looked tiny enough for me to gather into my arms. I stood in the doorway. Was it my turn to be the spiritually strong one?

'Scuse me, God. I'm not quite ready for this lesson. Can we go back to "You are forgiven and valued by God"? I liked that one.

"Are you sure?" I gripped the trim around the doorway so fiercely, my fingers hurt.

"Yes, go."

I got to church and sat at the back like I always do. Took me a while to work up to that. When I was first saved, I prayed in a garbage dump. I pray all the time, and God and I are working on me feeling like I belong with other Christians. The whole thing is very foreign to me, like being tossed into a strange country and having to learn the language and customs. People in my Bible study fascinate me. The leader will say, "Okay turn to Denominations 12:13," and whammo! They know right where it's at in the Bible.

From the pulpit, Pastor Carpenter announced, "Please greet and say hello to the people around you." I always plan a potty run during this time, because I hate this part of the service. I hardly know anyone. The one thing you don't want is to be standing there looking totally pathetic and lonely.

The two people I saw from Bible study were already hugging and engrossed in conversation. I took in two deep breaths. *Take a risk, Ruby. That's what growth is about.* The chatter around me increased in volume and quantity.

If Mom were here, I'd hug her like we hadn't seen each other in ages. I hoped I'd done the right thing, leaving her alone to sleep off her sadness.

People continued to mill around the church, greeting each other. My throat grew dry. *Come on, Ruby, take a chance.*

I took another deep breath and started shaking hands like I was running for office. I introduced myself. People told me their names. Five minutes from now, I wouldn't remember a single name. What was the point of this part of the service—this howdy-doody time?

"Good to see you, Ruby."

A firm male hand slipped into mine; green eyes looked down at me. I got an eyeful of six feet of gorgeous. Wesley, minus his uniform, smiled at me like it was the most normal thing in the world for him to be there.

"Wes . . . I . . . what are . . . ?" I gripped his hand.

He wore jeans and a royal-blue button-down shirt. His short hair was hard to get used to. When it was long, it had a kinky, curly quality to it. Now there was just the hint of waviness at the ends. It still had those wonderful, glittery gold highlights against light brown.

The chattering died away, and people started to sit down. Pastor Carpenter cleared his throat.

"Good to see you too, Wesley." I delivered my line with the monotone of a stewardess explaining what to do in the event of a water landing. Water landing indeed. This could be an all-out crash with tons of flying debris.

Why had he come here today? A year ago, we had agreed to go to different churches. Was this his way of saying, "I'm ready to start a godly relationship with you"? Was this his version of a first move? Of course, he just couldn't come right out and say that. Heavens, no. That would be way too easy. It all had to be delivered in signals and codes. Time to get the decoder ring out. Why was Wesley showing up here, now, after a year? It had to be that the 2 A.M. false alarm on Friday reminded him that I was still around—still available.

We returned to our respective seats as Pastor Carpenter started on his sermon.

I sat there, placid smile on my face, old-fashioned washing machine of emotions chugging away underneath. I sat there and decided I was ready to start a relationship with Wesley.

I don't remember what the sermon was about. I spent the whole time studying every hair on the back of Wesley's head five rows in front of me. If I talked to God through every step, maybe Wesley and I could make this work.

Marriage, and then—later—kids. I might actually be able to salvage some normalcy out of my life.

After service, I would find him and tell him exactly how I felt. No more coded messages. I'd tell him straight out. *Wesley, I want a relationship with you.* No more fuzzy, ambiguous, subtext-heavy language.

The choir finished the final hymn. People filed toward the back door. My heart reverberated in my chest as I rose from the pew.

Chapter Four

I saw him from across the church parking lot as he ambled toward his Jeep. With each step, I rehearsed what I would say. *Wesley, I think I am ready to pursue a relationship with you.* No, too clinical. *Wesley, hey, how about it, you and me?* No, too buddy-buddy. I was within thirty yards of his car. My heart pounded. I ran my fingers through my hair, an utterly pointless activity, but it took care of some of my nervous energy. Twenty yards and closing in on my target. Wesley stood beside his car, arms crossed, surveying the parking lot. He hadn't seen me yet. I knew what I would say. *Hey, Wesley, how about you and I try a date—you know, one we wouldn't mind showing to God.* Yeah, that sounded good.

About ten yards from the Jeep, I stopped. At the same time Wesley spotted me, a tall blond woman came up beside him. Wesley put his arm around the woman's shoulder and kissed her. No matter how hard I tried, I could not interpret the gesture as merely friendly or brotherly.

"Hey, Ruby." He waved me over.

The woman's hair was a rich, golden shade of blond. It fell in organized waves and curls to her shoulders. I knew her first name was Vanessa, because she had sung solos in church from time to time. So that's why he'd come here today. It had nothing to do with me.

"Ruby, good to see you again." He was all smiles. His hand pressed into Vanessa's shoulder. "You probably know Vanessa Prentice."

I smiled. "I've seen you around church." I felt like Saran Wrap thrown on a fire, shrinking in on myself. Soon I would melt away and be nothing—not even ashes on the concrete. I wanted to get this over as quickly as possible. In one of the finest performances of my life, I pulled pleasantries up from my gut. "Good to meet you."

Vanessa nodded and held her hand out. I barely touched her cool fingers. She had a finely pointed chin that made her face heart-shaped, set off by big, wide-set eyes. The only fault I could find was that her eyebrows arched so symmetrically that they had to be penciled in.

Once, years ago, I had tried plucking my eyebrows. After much wincing and tugging, I managed to yank a single hair out. The pain was so excruciating, I doubled over and hit my head on the sink. When I looked in the mirror, I had a bruise on my forehead and a bleeding chasm where the hair used to be. Somehow, perfectly arched eyebrows didn't seem worth a trip to the emergency room.

Vanessa kissed Wesley on the cheek. I cringed.

"I'll see you Wednesday night," she told him, then looked at me. "Good meeting you, Ruby." She slipped from Wesley' embrace.

I coated my words in sugar. "Yes, you too." Emily Post would have been proud of me. The constriction in my throat that always precedes an all-out crying jag made it hard for me to talk at all. But I held it together.

We both watched as Vanessa made her way toward her car. I willed her to fall down some unseen mineshaft in the parking lot. "I didn't know you were dating her."

"We met at a singles retreat."

"Oh." *Forgive me, Lord. If Wesley has met someone, I need to be happy for him. We didn't have any agreement that we would eventually get together. What did I think would happen in a year?*

"So." Wesley's tenor voice made my rib cage vibrate.

Accepting that Vanessa was not going to meet with an accident, I looked back at Wesley. Mentally, I reshuffled my cards. I couldn't use the actual reason I'd come over to talk to him. "Do you know anything about Theodore Aldridge's death?" Yes, that was it. I was here on official business.

Wesley gave me what I can only call a "cop look." One of those expressions where the intensity of the gaze and the slowness of the response tells you that he knows way more than he is saying. "You read the papers. It was a suicide."

"Yeah, but was it? I know he had a drinking problem, but he kept it under control enough to be quite successful."

"Ruby, come on. I got a job to do. It's my first year on the force; I'm still a probationary officer." He sliced the air with his hand. "Don't push." He punctuated his comments by drawing his eyes close together.

Ashamed, I took a step back. "I'm sorry." My pressing for details had little to do with Theodore Aldridge. Hurt is an emotion that likes to wear disguises. My pain wore a lovely costume of pushiness. "I haven't gotten much sleep lately. Jimmy came in on the 1 A.M. bus the night you came over, and I've been having this strange dream."

"There is no 1 A.M. bus. That side of town is part of my patrol; the last bus comes in at eleven."

Anger ricocheted around my brain. I bit my lower lip. Why had Jimmy lied? Why wasn't he here for me to confront him? I directed my anger with Jimmy toward Wesley because he was the one standing there. "Why don't you just tell me what you know about Theodore Aldridge?"

His shoulders bunched up. "Cops talk—to each other. Just to each other."

I wondered if he shared details of his work with Vanessa. *No, Ruby, don't go there. Be nice.* "I'm working at the university. I might be able to help. If I got you some inside knowledge, it would look good to your boss." *Why am I doing this? Am I trying to win him back by helping him with his work?* I did want to know more about Aldridge. My motives were so tangled.

Wesley wet his lips, glanced across the parking lot, and looked back at me. "All I can tell you is that there are some inconsistencies. They are keeping the investigation open—unofficially." He raised an eyebrow at me. "Don't go playing detective on me."

"I won't. It's just that sometimes you can pick up details from people talking that you won't get in a police interview."

He looked at me way longer than he had to. I could read affection in his expression. Or was it just wishful thinking on my part?

"Thanks." He gave me a brotherly punch on the shoulder. "It would help me look good to the chief."

Walking backward, I made my way toward my car. "Glad to help." And I was. I wanted good things for Wesley. Maybe Vanessa was a good thing. I believed that—in my head anyway. It would just take a while before my emotions downloaded the message.

He waved at me and stepped up into his Jeep.

I sat behind the wheel of my Valiant and spent a good ten minutes gripping the steering wheel, squeezing my eyes shut, and praying the hard prayer. The hard prayer usually involves me saying

"Thy will be done" about a hundred times, because that is all I can manage through clenched teeth. As my jaw relaxed, I was able to say, "If you want Wesley to be with Vanessa, help me to be happy for them. If I am to spend the rest of my life alone, help me to find joy in that."

Finally I was able to unclench my hands and take in a deep breath. I rolled down my window. The parking lot was empty. The sun beat down from a clear sky, and warm fall air drifted in. This late in the year, the temperate weather was deceptive. I'd lived in Montana long enough to know that chill and heavy snowfall lurked around the corner.

When I got home, Mom was baking again. Two neighborhood kids, boys about eight years old, sat at the table, eating her brownies. The boys had their heads together, looking at a handheld game.

Mom hadn't spoken of Jimmy since she entered into cooking therapy.

"Hi, Ruby." She smiled at me over a dish of steaming casserole. Sweat beaded her forehead, and her whole face was red.

"Hi, Mom." I wasn't about to bring Jimmy up. If she wasn't talking about it, neither was I.

All that pop psychology about getting things out in the open just doesn't apply to our family. We don't ignore the elephant in the living room, we just dress it up and decorate it.

The jerk was gone. It was a moot point that he had lied about coming on the bus. I sure hoped Mom started feeling better soon. At this rate, we'd still be eating thawed-out casserole next spring, and all the neighborhood kids would pimple and pudge up.

She sat the steaming dish beside two other steaming dishes on the counter. "How was church?"

What a loaded question. "Fine. Just fine."

I spent the afternoon finishing the readings I had assigned to my students for discussion. I'd already read them once, but I was hiding. Hiding from the pain of knowing Wesley had met someone else. Hiding from not being able to ease my mother's anguish and loss.

I found myself wishing Georgia would call and ask me to work at the feed store. There was something therapeutic about stocking shelves or sorting receipts. But she wasn't open on Sunday.

My mother bakes. I actually have three very sophisticated coping strategies: hide, sleep, or run. I know, I should write a self-help book and make a million.

Let me see. I had tried to hide, and I wasn't tired, so that left . . .

I decided to go for a drive. Somewhere between driving around town and getting out on the highway, I checked a phone book for Theodore Aldridge's address. I did need a key to that desk drawer. As it was, I had to get out of my chair every time and pull the stapler off my bookshelf. I was wasting valuable time and costing the university money. Maybe his wife or kids would be home.

Thinking about Aldridge's death was easier than thinking about my life. Besides, Wesley's reaction seemed to indicate there was something more to Theodore's death.

The good professor had lived in an older part of town not far from the university. The houses in his neighborhood were built prior to 1950, not the usual cookie-cutter, pastel boxes that were going up in the new subdivisions.

Eagleton is an odd mixture of old and new. Old, mostly poverty-stricken farmers and downtown business owners who have been here for generations are interspersed with a new thin layer of pretentious telecommuters and trust-fund East and West Coast escapees who would like Eagleton to be the Little Aspen of Montana.

I drove along the wide street, checking the numbers on mailboxes. I passed a few Victorians. Many of the houses had brick exteriors with large front windows and good-sized yards. Judging from my own paycheck, Aldridge couldn't have made that much as a professor. He must have bought his house before the telecommuters decided that these neighborhoods were quaint and the price of real estate went through the roof. The only reason Mom and I can afford to stay in Eagleton is because we inherited the house after Grandma died.

Aldridge's house had cream siding and a chain-link fence. I clicked open the door of my Valiant and crossed the street. After opening the gate and slipping through, I headed up the sidewalk. The sky was overcast. A thin patina of gray covered any potential for sunshine. Earlier it had been warm and clear. If you don't like the weather in Montana, wait ten minutes.

Two flower beds, now full of brown weeds, stood on either side of the stairs leading up to the front door, which was ajar. I could hear things being slid across the floor. I knocked gingerly.

The sliding stopped and footsteps pounded toward the door. It swung all the way open revealing a fortyish woman with a single blond streak running through her dark brown hair. A fringe of bangs about an inch long offset a slender face and pretty eyes.

"Yes?"

I hadn't thought of what I was going to say. "I'm Ruby Taylor. I work up at the university. I have Dr. Aldridge's office. Are you his wife?"

"Ex-wife." She said the "ex" like she was grinding something into the ground.

Behind her, I could see boxes piled on the couch and floor. The paneled walls of the living room were bare. "I know this must be a hard time for you."

"Not really. There was no love lost between Theodore and me." She stepped back, indicating that I could come in. "I realize he was everybody's golden boy up at the university, but he never had time for me and the kids." Kneeling on the floor, she tossed a pile of books into a box. "After twenty years of marriage, I decided I was wasting my time hoping he would change."

The former Mrs. Aldridge was giving me way more personal information than I needed. I could see more boxes piled on the dining room table. Her coldness about her husband's death was surprising. Going through his stuff probably stirred up memories for her, some of them apparently unpleasant.

Without my prompting, she continued. "He left the house to me and the kids." She sighed and threw a thick textbook into the box. "Just one final slap in the face, as far as I am concerned. I have to clean the place up and try and sell it. Meanwhile, I have to pay taxes and upkeep."

I wondered how many days she had been in this house, packing and stirring up old bitterness. I kneeled down on the floor beside her and handed her a book.

"Thanks." She clutched the book in her hand. "You're the first person from the university to come by." She slammed the book onto the pile in the box. "Of course, they all came to the funeral. That way they had an excuse for a big drinking jag afterward." She stood up and brushed dust off her thighs and knees. Her eyes traveled the circumference of the room. "A lot of people become college professors so they can keep acting like college students, drinking and being irresponsible. Theodore was just a little boy. A very intelligent little boy." I detected a slight tremble in her voice. "I'm sorry. Why did you come here?"

I rose to my feet. "I inherited Dr. Aldridge's desk. It's got a locked drawer."

"So you got the dinosaur desk, huh?" She shook her head and put her hands up toward me, palms out. "The key is probably somewhere in this house, but don't ask me where."

Twenty years ago, the former Mrs. Aldridge had probably been an attractive woman. She was still slender with close-set, almond-shaped eyes and distinctive cheekbones. But the bitterness of the years was etched on her face. Her tight mouth and the worry lines on her forehead overshadowed her pretty features.

I suppose, as a Christian, it was my duty to offer a speech on forgiveness, but everything I could think to say to her sounded stupid and judgmental compared to the hugeness of her unresolved pain. *Lord, what could I say?* "Are you taking these boxes somewhere? I'll help you load them." The words fell out of my mouth.

The rigidity in her shoulders softened. "Thanks." The tightness of her expression smoothed over. "I didn't mean to vent. You probably didn't even know Theodore."

In the dusky light of evening, we loaded the boxes in the back of her pickup. I could feel God smiling on me as I strained to pick up a heavy box of books. This weird impulse I felt to speak little biblical truisms to everybody was a false obligation. People didn't need verses thrown at them. Jesus just hung out with people and met their needs. Right now, Mrs. Aldridge needed to get these memories donated and out of her life. I carried the box down the stairs and toward the truck. Its bed brimmed with boxes.

Mrs. Aldridge locked the front door and walked down the stairs toward the truck. She glanced back at the house. "I'll be glad when I get this place cleaned out. Every once in a while, I see some weirdo in a long coat lurking around here." She shrugged. "Probably one of Theodore's heartbroken students."

Dale Cutler wears a long, olive drab coat, and he's pretty weird.

She squeezed my shoulder. "Thanks again for your help."

"Do you think Dr. Aldridge killed himself?"

She shrugged. "He did like to play the suffering artist from time to time, and he drank like a fish." She climbed into the driver's side of the truck.

"But he was successful and pretty happy at the end of his life?"

She turned the key in the ignition and shouted over the chugging of the engine. "I don't know anything about that." She didn't quite make eye contact. "We really didn't talk that much."

She did know something about that. For some reason, Mrs. Aldridge was content with her ex-husband's death being a suicide, even if the police department wasn't. Maybe that was justice for her and maybe . . .

I wondered just how deep her hatred ran.

I stepped back from the truck as she shifted into first and revved the engine. My Valiant was parked across the street. I had just opened the door to my car when she pulled up beside me.

She leaned out the window and shouted, "I haven't gotten to the back rooms yet. He kept a bunch of keys in a file cabinet. The front door is locked, but I think the back one is open. I'll be back in a few minutes."

"Thanks."

I watched as she drove off, then recrossed the quiet street. Cars occupied the curb in front of almost every house, but only a few people were outside. An older woman at the house next door raked leaves into a pile. She had a slight hunch to her back and wore a floral scarf. A couple houses down, some children played in the front yard. This late in the year, it got dark around six, which was about half an hour away.

The backyard consisted of a concrete slab with a barbecue in one corner, a little stretch of browning grass, and an old tree with wavy branches. When I jiggled the knob on the back door, it was locked. But the window next to it was wide open with no screen. The polite thing to do would be to wait until Mrs. Aldridge got back. Then again, she had given me permission to go into the house.

Theodore Aldridge had been two people: the successful, friendly professor and the negligent, drunken husband and father. I felt an affinity with him. I was one person when I was around other Christians and a different person when my support system fell away.

When I glanced around the yard, I noticed some logs piled by the side of the house. One of the logs might as well have had a "use me to get in" sign on it. Curiosity and impatience trumps politeness every time. I only had to stretch my legs a little to crawl in through the window.

As I straddled the windowsill, my foot found something solid. I angled my upper body through the window and prepared to pull my other leg in. The something solid I found wasn't that stable. While one of my legs was still in the air, my foot slipped, and I sailed backward. The time in the air offered a surpassingly long moment to think.

I'm thirty-one years old. What am I doing crawling through windows? I should take up knitting and buy a rocking chair.

I landed with resounding heaviness on my behind. The pain vibrated up my backbone.

In front of me the "solid footing" lay spread all over. More books. The room I was in was dim, lit only by a thin slit of light between the drawn curtains. This must have been Aldridge's office. I rose to my feet and rubbed my lower back. At least nobody had seen me fall on my behind.

I clicked on the overhead lamp, which was bolted onto a metal desk. The file cabinet Mrs. Aldridge had spoken of was in a dark corner by the window. Two of the four walls were lined with books and videos. A VCR and television had been built into one of the walls. In a corner by the door was a plush easy chair with papers piled in it and books stacked around it.

Little hairs on the back of my neck stood up. There is something creepy about being in a room that belonged to a dead person. Almost a month had passed since Aldridge's death, and the dust had already begun to settle. A book lay open on the desk. *Does someone planning on killing himself leave a book open?*

I checked the title on the book. Maybe he had been reading Russian literature and had been driven to despair by its contents. I could have finished a cup of coffee in the time it took to read the title. It contained a colon and two commas and—near as I could tell—was a lengthy diatribe on imagery in T. S. Eliot's poetry and how it related to modern man, blah, blah, blah. The kind of stuff only other professors cared about.

Books like this had contributed to my burnout with academia. Actually, my personal life had had a lot to do with my leaving academia. Before I became a Christian, I was a quasi-feminist, believing that the way to achieve equality was to behave as bad sexually as men did. Only, in feminist circles, you didn't call it promiscuous behavior; you just claimed that your inability to hold a relationship together made you "independent." I bought into the lie of no-boundaries behavior. Everything was okay as long as you had a big, important job. All I'd gotten out of that deal was a shredded heart.

My stomach tightened as I laid the book back down on the desk. I had been in God's fix-it shop for a year, getting the tears in my heart mended. I had taken this job thinking I would return to my old career track a stronger person because of my faith. So far, the choice felt awkward at best.

My feet hardly made any noise at all on the lush carpet as I walked toward the file cabinet. I thought about opening the curtains for more light. My hand even touched the edge of the drapes. Curse my wild imagination. I kept thinking of the lurker in the long coat Mrs. Aldridge said she had seen. I envisioned him standing at the window now. If I didn't open the curtain, I would never know.

The light was so dim, I opted for letting my fingers do the walking through the file cabinet. Behind the papers stacked vertically in folders, I felt more papers and then something hard and metallic. Even without much light, I knew the gun was a Hi-Standard .22 automatic.

The one skill—if you want to call it that—that my father taught me was a thorough knowledge of guns, or "firearms" as he used to call them. I clicked out the magazine, catching it in my hand. By running my thumb down the open slot in the middle, I could tell the magazine was fully loaded. A loaded magazine in a firearm violated all kinds of safety rules about guns.

There are two reasons why a man would have a gun loaded and ready to go in his house. The first is that he is feeling deficient in the manly macho department and bragging to his friends about his fancy loaded gun kicked up his testosterone levels. Somehow, I couldn't picture Dr. Aldridge smashing beer cans on his forehead and shooting guns to feel manly. The second reason was because a man feared for his life and thought being able to get to a loaded gun quickly would save him.

I wrapped my hand around the pistol grip. *Why would someone with a gun kill himself by hanging?*

I put the .22 back where I found it and felt around until I touched cool, narrow metal. I pulled out a metal ring with about fifty keys on it and held them up to the narrow slit of light. *Of course they're not labeled. That would be too easy.*

The keys jingled as I walked over to the shelves of books and read through titles. The usual scholarly stuff. Aldridge had books on Poe and Eliot, one on the values of first editions, several on film and film structure—even a couple versions of the Bible. He had titles on feminism, neocolonialism, and an assortment of books about how white guys of European descent had ruined the world. I had just pulled down a collection of Poe short stories when I heard a noise in the living room.

Gripping the book in both hands, I listened. Footsteps. Mrs. Aldridge coming back? These footsteps weren't distinctive. They were soft and far apart like someone inching along a wall, trying to be quiet.

I thought to call out Mrs. Aldridge's name and decided against it. Certainly, she would have called out for me. My heart rate increased. A shiver slithered down my spine.

Who else could it be? Didn't she say the front door was locked?

My gaze darted from one corner of the room to the other. There was one doorway, which probably led to a hallway and then out to the back door, or I could go back out through the window. The footsteps grew closer. *Step, slide, step.* They were as subtle and indistinguishable as fish popping to the surface of a lake to feed. If it hadn't been a quiet evening in a quiet house, I wouldn't have heard them.

I could hide behind the desk. But that would take some explaining if it was Mrs. Aldridge coming toward the office. I needed to keep her trust. Having her think I had paranoid delusions was not a good strategy. I turned and headed toward the file cabinet where the gun was kept. If it was Mrs. Aldridge, I could just casually point out the gun. If it wasn't her, I would be ready for whatever Mr. Inch-Along-the-Wall had in mind.

Chapter Five

My thumb pressed against the metal tab on the file cabinet. Willing it to be quiet, I eased the drawer open. I slipped my hand into the drawer and felt for the gun and the magazine.

I swallowed hard. My heart raced. Sweat made the crooks of my elbows sticky.

The footsteps stopped. Without hearing it, I had the sense of someone inhaling and exhaling. The quiet contained an undetonated heaviness.

I jammed the magazine into the base of the gun until I heard the click that told me it was locked in. I wrapped my hand around the grip and held my finger straight above the trigger. Carefully, I lifted the pistol so it pointed at the ceiling.

Footsteps.

My back was still to the door. I heard quick footsteps and a thud like someone had leaped the last three steps.

"I got backup coming. Put the gun down and turn around slowly."

Still holding the gun, I raised my arms even higher. Tension and fear dissipated like rain on a hot day. In the deepest, darkest echo chamber, I'd recognize that silky voice anywhere. *Wesley.* Of all the police officers in this town, why did it have to be him?

"Backup is here," came a voice from outside the window I had so recently crawled through. The evening light allowed me to see only a silhouette of an officer in uniform.

"Drop the gun and turn around slowly." Wesley was using his

police officer voice, low and commanding. I wondered if he had to take actual classes in sounding tough, Cop Voice 101.

I let go of the gun. It fell on the carpet with a muffled thud. As commanded, I turned around slowly. "Hi, Wesley."

Fancy meeting you here. Do you come here often? So did you just bring this one cop, or did the whole SWAT team come with you? What's a nice cop like you doing in a dark room like this? Hands still in the air, I bit my lower lip and bowed my head. My face felt really hot. Not a good thing on a fair-skinned redhead.

He gripped the gun with both hands, elbows locked. "Ruby?" His arms relaxed slightly, but he kept the gun on me.

I didn't like having a weapon pointed at me, especially by him. Didn't he trust me?

The cop from outside the window shouted, "Burgess, what's going on?" His words pelted my back along with an evening breeze from the open window.

"I think I got it under control, Cree. I know the perp."

Perp? What was he doing calling me a perp? Arms held high, I turned my head sideways. I actually knew Officer Cree, as well. "Hey, Officer Cree, do you remember me?"

I turned toward the window and waved. "Remember me? You found me sleeping in my car the night God turned me into a new critter in Christ."

Recognition spread across Cree's dark features. "Oh yeah, Garbage-Dump Woman—you pray there." His dark brown hair, craggy nose, and high forehead suggested he might be part Native American.

Wesley cleared his throat. "Excuse me, I hate to break up this coffee klatch."

I turned back around to face him.

Cree came and leaned into the window. "You got this under control, Burgess?"

Wesley nodded. "I don't think she's dangerous." He glared at me. "I just need her to give me some answers."

Fun. Fun. Wesley's going to interrogate me. I clenched my teeth.

"Next time, you need to make sure backup is in place before you draw your weapon." Cree stepped away from the window.

"I know. I got excited. This was only my second intruder call." Again, he looked at me. "I keep thinking they are going to be real."

"Catch you at the station later."

Wesley and I stared at each other while Cree's footsteps faded.

He put his Glock back in the holster but left it unsnapped. "What are you doing breaking into people's houses?"

"Breaking in—?" A gurgle came out of my mouth. I hated being accused of breaking the law, especially by Wesley. Even if there would never be anything between us, it mattered what he thought of me. My hands dropped to my sides, and I shook my head.

"Your actions are very suspicious, Ruby." He crossed his arms.

"Come on, it's me. I'm not here to rob this place."

"The neighbor lady saw you crawl through a window. Is that true?"

"Well, yes—" *Okay, so it did look like I was breaking in.* "But I have permission to be here."

"Most people with permission go through the door, Ruby."

Oh, he made me mad. "Hey, the front door was locked. How did you get in anyway?"

Wesley's cheek twitched. "That's not important."

"I would have heard the door breaking down. Don't tell me you picked the lock." I watched his face, waiting for him to give something up in his expression.

His Adam's apple moved up and down as he swallowed hard. "I didn't pick the lock." He shifted his weight and glanced at the floor. "I pushed the front window open."

"So it's okay for *you* to crawl in through a window." I put my hands on my hips.

"Stop." His voice was tainted with anguish. I'd pushed too far. "Just stop it, Ruby. You broke in. You were holding a gun when I found you."

"I know what it looks like, but I—" I hated the way he kept saying my name like I was some dumb kid. "Mrs. Aldridge will be back in a few minutes." I pushed the file drawer shut. "She can tell you. I'm not a criminal."

"Fine. We'll wait." His eyes bored into me, like he was trying to figure me out. *Good luck, Officer.* He checked his watch.

The disapproval I saw in his expression and posture bothered me. He didn't trust me. For crying out loud. We had almost been an item a year ago. I had spent two days tromping through the woods with him, trying to find his missing friend. "Wesley, you know me. Come on."

"Do I? The other night you put in a false intruder call. Do you have something against the police? Do you have a problem with authority?"

"Don't be so paranoid. Of course I don't have anything against the police. What, do you think that in the year since you have seen me I have entered into a life of crime?" *Yeah, that's right, Wesley. I'm so distraught about you taking up with Vanessa that I've turned to robbery.* My toes curled in my shoes. Tension rose up at the back of my neck. "You know I wouldn't—"

"You sneak into a stranger's house. I find you with a gun in your hand. What am I supposed to think?"

"What does 'procedure' tell you to think?" My words dripped with unexpected anger. What does the Bible say? Out of the fullness of the mouth the heart speaks. My heart was speaking; in fact, it was doing a full operatic production. Ain't love funny? If I couldn't have Wesley, I'd hurt him. What was my problem? I wanted to be nice to him, but everything I said came out mean.

I was not about to play any "steal my boyfriend" games with Vanessa. She was a Christian; they were dating. I was not in the picture, and I needed to trust that God knew what he was doing. Yet none of that logic stopped the pitter-patter of my heart every time Wesley entered a room. And now he thought I was some kind of criminal.

I took a step toward him.

"Come on, Ruby. This is hard enough as it is. I just need some straight answers." He shifted his weight from foot to foot. "Everything says you were breaking in here. Do you think it's easy to draw a gun on someone I care about?"

"Care about?" Warmth flooded through me.

"Cared about."

Ice froze me.

He tilted his head and resumed an official stance, shoulders squared, feet shoulder-width apart.

"How is Vanessa?"

He turned toward me, head held up. Even in this the dim light, I could see him shake his head and squint. He found me perplexing. "She's fine. Wonderful in fact."

"She's pretty, and she seems nice." I'd pulled those words up from the underside of my feet. Each syllable took considerable effort. I stepped away from the file cabinet.

"Yes, she is, real sweet and soft spoken, supportive."

Great, everything I wasn't. To me, all opinions were worth expressing and every day was a bad hair day. "I'm not a law breaker, Wesley." That was the one thing I wanted clarified before we left.

"Then what are you doing here?"

I nodded toward the floor. "That gun is Theodore Aldridge's."

His gaze did not waver. "Ruby, leave the detecting to the police." Again, the scolding tone. He did everything but waggle his finger at me.

"If you wanted to commit suicide and had a gun, would you hang yourself?" I hated not being able to see his face, not being able to read his reactions. I took a step toward him. His body tensed. "Permission to come a little closer to you, sir."

His lips curled in a half smile. "Sorry."

"I know they teach you how to do that poker face nonreaction at cop school, but you don't have to do it with me."

"I'm just trying to do my job."

"Your job has made you paranoid and tense."

His jawline stiffened. Obviously, I'd just poured lemon juice on an open wound. Seems to be a gift with me. "Don't you think I know that? What I've seen in my months on the force would curl your stomach." He balled his hands into fists. "I have to arrest people for DUI that I sit across from at church, I—"

Now I understood why he didn't trust me. If he was arresting churchgoers for drunkenness, he was probably thinking no one was who he or she seemed to be. "I didn't know you had to deal with that." Now I was sorry for everything I had just put him through. Poor guy. "I'm glad you're a policeman. You're good and decent."

"Thank you." His tone softened.

"Can you at least turn on another light, so I can see your face better? It really bothers me when I can't read people's expressions."

"For you." He switched on a light standing by a large plush chair in the corner by the door. His face glistened with sweat. That was my fault too. Now I could see his eyes, the big green things that they were.

"Theodore Aldridge didn't kill himself, did he?" I took a few steps toward the metal desk.

"We don't know. The marks on his neck were consistent with suicide by hanging, so they wrote it up that way. But there was no suicide note."

"Of all people, an English professor would leave a note," I said.

"Exactly. The coroner declared it a suicide. But we called in a pathologist and sent some samples to the state lab. There should have been more investigation. This house should have been declared a crime scene. It's not a high-priority case. We haven't gotten the tox screen back yet."

"Now Mrs. Aldridge is hauling potential evidence away." After scooting some books aside, I sat down on the professor's metal desk.

"I know." I heard frustration in his voice. "Greta Aldridge really pushed for suicide and wanted the body back." Wesley moved the paper pile aside and sat down in the chair by the door. "That gun is just one more thing that doesn't fit. You're right; statistically speaking, a guy is more likely to kill himself with a firearm."

"What else doesn't fit?" I picked up a book and flipped through it idly.

"The neighbor called about a strange smell coming from the house. The officer sent to the scene said the place smelled like rotten lemons and someone had built a fire in the fireplace. It was a warm September day. There was no reason to have a fire."

"I'll let you know if I find anything up at the school." The heels of my boots banged softly on the metal desk.

Wesley rose to his feet, took a step toward me, hands on his hips. "Don't go putting yourself in any danger."

I liked the concern I heard in his voice. "I can take care of myself."

"I know that."

I liked the admiration I heard in his voice. "What makes you think I might be in danger?" A year ago, Wesley and I had dodged gunfire to find his missing friend.

"The coroner said that Aldridge had an inverted V-shaped bruise on his neck." He pointed to the side of his own neck where the shape would have been.

"Meaning he was hung rather than simply being strangled."

"Right, if he had been strangled with a scarf or rope, the bruise would have been a straight line. Hands would have left finger and thumb marks. That means whoever did it got him unconscious, strung him up, and let him choke to death."

I shifted on the desk, crossed and uncrossed my legs. "So you're saying whoever did this has a pretty cold heart." My fingers fluttered up to my own neck as my throat constricted.

"Beyond cold hearted—vicious. The motive had to be pretty strong."

"Do you think a woman could do that?" An icy chill traveled up my back. "His ex-wife hated his guts, and she inherited his stuff."

"It would have been hard for Greta Aldridge to do that by herself. But she has a nineteen-year-old son. The kid is very bitter about his dad having all the time in the world for his students and never being able to come to his baseball games." Wesley slumped back into the plush chair in the corner with a heavy sigh. "It's nice to talk to somebody on the outside about this."

"I won't tell anyone. I don't want to get you in trouble." Didn't he talk to Vanessa about these things?

"Thanks. I meant what I said about you playing detective."

"I'll be careful."

A screen door slammed against the frame, and Mrs. Aldridge called "hello" from the front of the house.

"Back here," I shouted.

Wesley rose to his feet. Mrs. Greta Aldridge's footsteps echoed through the empty house. She had gone from being the nice lady who let me root through her husband's stuff to being a murder suspect. I needed to prepare my reaction accordingly.

She filled the doorway. "What's with the—" She pointed toward the front of the house, then stared at Wesley. "I saw the police car out front." Her gaze traveled from Wesley's feet to the top of his head.

I shuffled through the possibilities of how to make a long story short. "Greta, this is Officer Burgess—"

She snapped her head around at me, raising an eyebrow. I shrunk back from my own stupidity, slouching and wishing I could melt into the desk. I had blown it. She had never told me her first name. Now, she knew Wesley and I had been talking about her. *Tactic number one, pretend like I didn't say that.* "Mrs. Aldridge, would you explain to the officer that you gave me permission to be here?"

Wesley scolded me with his furled eyebrows. *Okay, so I blew it. I messed up.* I eyebrowed him back.

Greta crossed her arms and continued to give me the hairy eyeball. "Did you find the keys?" She couldn't have made her words colder if I'd she'd stuck them in a Frigidaire overnight.

I reached across the desk and picked the keys up. "Found them." I jingled the keyring and used my cheerful airline hostess voice.

She didn't fall for it. "Good, so you can go." She glanced back at Wesley.

I could guess what she was thinking. And take the meddling little policeman with you.

Wesley cleared his throat and adopted his official tone. "Mrs. Aldridge, if you could just confirm that Miss Taylor had your permission to be in the house."

"Didn't I already imply that?" She pivoted and glared at me with her hands on her hips. "I thought you said you worked at the university."

"I do." I could feel myself getting smaller by the moment. Pretty soon, I'd only be visible under a microscope. Her suspicion and anger could either be because she was hiding something or simply because this whole situation defied explanation.

Her shoulders drooped. She massaged her forehead with her fingers. "It's been a long, hard day." Her gaze went to the bookshelf, the file cabinet, the desk. This room had "Theodore Aldridge" written all over it.

"We'll go. Thanks for the keys." We left the former Mrs. Aldridge to sort through the memories and bitterness.

Outside, Wesley punched me in the shoulder. "Smooth."

I held my hands up defensively. "I admit it. I messed up."

"You might as well have said, 'Here, Greta, we have a "murder suspect" sign for you to wear.'"

Despite his berating, I felt a kinship between us. "You don't know that was what she was thinking." I glanced back at the house. I longed to have a more thorough look at Aldridge's room before his ex hauled away the secrets it held.

"Ruby, I'm trained to read people's body language." His voice held a warm quality, a tone of affection. We were working on this thing together—like Batman and Robin. I could play the role of faithful sidekick.

He followed me as I walked toward my car. I could be his friend. I could keep these emotions under control, quit wishing Vanessa would be abducted by a UFO. That way, I could still be in his life. I crawled into my car and shut the door.

He peered through the open window. "Now leave the investigating to the professionals."

"I promise." I held my hand up to my forehead. "Scout's honor."

"All right then." He ambled back to his police car.

The ring of keys jingled as I set it down on the passenger seat. My Valiant roared to life with its characteristic chugging sputter.

I clicked on the push-button shift and pulled out onto the street.

I glanced at the key ring. Good thing I'd never been a Girl Scout.

Chapter Six

The aroma of the hot mocha I held in my hand made my mouth water as I stood outside my office. Even through the thick paper cup, the liquid warmed my fingers. I turned the knob and pushed open the door. The scent of steaming coffee mingled with an unfamiliar perfume. I sniffed the air. Or was it cologne?

A tingling electricity at the back of my neck, similar to the physical reaction a body has to an approaching storm, caused my danger antennae to perk up. I surveyed my office: the bookshelves, the computer, the papers piled on the desk and floor.

Someone had been in here.

He or she had been careful. The place hadn't been ransacked. The perfume and some primitive instinct had clued me in. The chair was separated from the desk. I was in the habit of pushing it in when I left. The stack of papers on the desk was at a slightly different angle. After I set my coffee down, I ran my fingers along the bookshelf. Some of the books were pulled out from the wall.

I had been gone maybe twenty minutes to get the coffee—and I hadn't locked the door. At two in the afternoon, traffic through the building was heavy. Anyone could have popped in here, shuffled my papers, and pawed my books without being noticed.

I slumped down into the chair and tried to shake off that awful feeling of violation, the sense that private territory had been treaded on. I wrapped my hands around the warm coffee cup and prayed with my eyes open, watching my door. I prayed until I felt peace return and the urge to lock the door left me.

It was just an office. But someone had shuffled through my personal stuff—my stuff. Why? I opened my eyes and stared at the desk. My fingers went to the keyhole on the desk drawer. Had those scratches always been there?

I took a big swig of coffee and stuffed a handful of M&M's in my mouth. The chocolate would kick in at any moment, and my heart would quit racing. I stared at the desk. It was already Friday, and I still hadn't tried the keys I'd gotten from Greta Aldridge.

I reached into my briefcase, which was propped against the desk. I felt something sticky but no keys. I searched several other pockets and crevices. My fingers touched something mushy, and I got a paper cut but no keys. This thing was a black hole. I dropped to the floor and shook it out. A shower of pens, papers, receipts, candy wrappers, paper clips, and a very black banana fell out, but no keys.

"You made a mess," a voice cooed above me.

I looked up in the pixie face of Celeste the Cleaning Woman. That's what everyone called her. No one had ever used her last name. Like Catherine the Great or Peter the Lionhearted. I wondered if her checks said "Celeste the Cleaning Woman" on them.

"I know; I'm looking for something." I tried not to lash out at her. It wasn't her fault I'd misplaced the keys. Maybe I had left them at home or in my car. I glanced back at the desk. Or— . . . somebody had taken them.

"I'll help you clean up." Celeste had the cherub features, apple cheeks, and the small nose of a Down's person. Soft brown curls framed a her round face.

I could see her cleaning cart behind her in the hallway. She'd decorated it with rainbows and glittery star stickers.

"I can get it, Celeste."

She looked at me with small, round eyes. "It's okay. It's my job." She was already on her knees gathering paper into her hands. "This was Theodore's office."

Had it been anybody but Celeste pointing out that fact to me I would have screamed, "Don't you think I know that?" Instead, I gave a very diplomatic answer. "Yes, it was. Now it's my office."

"Theodore was nice." One point of the white collar on Celeste's button-down shirt stuck up. The shirt was a soft pink with pearlized buttons and eyelet around the collar.

It depends on who you talk to, I thought. "That's what I heard."

"He was my friend." Celeste sorted the paper clips into a pile on the floor. She scooted them toward me. "I miss him. But he's in heaven with Jesus."

I gathered up the paper clips. I didn't think I needed to shatter her simplistic theology if it gave her comfort. "That's nice, Celeste."

"He always said 'hi' to me. He was my friend."

Her comment caught me off guard. Nobody in this building even knew Celeste's last name. In the two weeks I had been here, I must have walked by her a hundred times and not noticed her. Yet all a person had to do was say "hello," and she would consider them a friend. I patted her hand. "Thanks for helping me clean up, Celeste. I'm glad you are here."

Celeste glowed. "Thank you." She tilted her head sideways and pushed her tongue to the inside of her lower lip so her mouth hung open. "You're my friend, just like Theodore."

"Just like Theodore," I patted her leg. My cheerfulness faded as I noticed the disturbed pile of papers on the floor. "Celeste, have you been working in this hallway for a while?"

Celeste nodded, eyes blinking rapidly.

"Did you see anyone come into my office?"

She shook her head. "I had to clean the bathroom." She pointed through the wall in the direction of the restrooms.

"If you do see anyone come into my office—ever—let me know." My hand curled into a fist. A surge of tension traveled up my arm, pinching the back of my neck. "Okay?"

"Okay," she said vaguely.

The intensity of my voice must have frightened her. She rose to her feet and stepped into the hallway with a nervous backward glance.

"I'm still your friend, Celeste," I spoke gently.

"Okay." She gave me a half wave and a straight-lip smile before pushing her cart out of view.

As the rolling of the cart's wheels dimmed, Cameron Bancroft's voice crescendoed up the hallway. "Publish. Publish. Published means prestige. Prestige means students, and students mean money."

Cameron popped his bald head in my office. "Dedication at the museum tonight." His gaze fell to floor where I sat cross-legged, surrounded by empty candy wrappers and decaying food bits. "Hope to see you there."

Nothing in his expression suggested that he thought finding an instructor sitting on the floor in a nest of trash was weird. He didn't even draw his thick eyebrows together or purse up his plump lips.

"Dedication at the museum? What dedication?"

"I sent out a memo." He narrowed his wide-set eyes at me like a lizard about to snap up a fly.

Cameron sent out twenty memos a day. Anything that was on his mind, he turned into a memo. I'd stopped reading them after the one that suggested the department invest in a literary-themed coffee cart. The idea of the department making money on *Pride and Prejudice* prune Danish and T. S. Eliot espresso seemed demeaning.

I looked up at Cameron. A fringe of sand-colored hair surrounded his bald spot, which glistened beneath the fluorescent lights. "I'm sorry. I must have missed that memo."

Cameron drew his thick lips into a pout. His bushy eyebrows got so close together I could have sworn there was a prehistoric caterpillar crawling across his forehead. He shot daggers with his eyes.

I slouched, shrinking farther into the floor. Okay, the one thing you did not do around here is actually admit you hadn't read the memos. "It's probably on my desk," I offered hopefully.

He glanced at the stacks of papers and books on and around my desk.

"You know what they say. Messy office, organized mind," I said. A gurgle of a laugh escaped from my throat.

"Who says that?" he snapped.

"Nobody, I guess. I just made it up." Whatever remote possibility I had of getting a permanent teaching contract was quickly slipping away. He had probably put me in the moron category by now. "I'll find the memo and read it." I hung my head like a repentant child.

"Good." He nodded at me for several seconds before turning his vertically challenged body and leaving. His voice slowly faded as he made his rounds through the maze of the English department. "Publish. Publish. . . ."

I tossed a pile of candy wrappers in the trash.

Donita stuck her head into my office. "Don't tell me you actually admitted you didn't read his memo?" A thick line of blue eyeliner made her tiny eyes look even smaller. Her effort at conservative dress with a gray pantsuit was destroyed by the scarf around her neck, a combination animal and floral print done in psychedelic colors.

"Okay, I learned my lesson." I rose to my feet. "Don't you have better things to do than listen outside my door?" I sat down so hard in my chair that it rolled backward. Every time I glanced at the desk drawer, a shiver rippled over my back.

"You are going, aren't you? To the dedication." Donita stepped into my office. She walked lightly on the balls of her feet—almost dancing.

"I don't want to go—not even for two stuffed weasels and a bag of chocolate."

She smiled at our inside joke. "Major brownie points. Not to belabor the obvious, but after that memo faux pas, you could use some brownie points."

I had more important things to think about than a dedication. I thumbed through the pile of papers. They didn't look out of order. Someone had just lifted them up and set them back down. I shook the drawer. Still locked . . . or relocked.

Donita placed her cold hand on my shoulder. I jumped. She giggled. "Coming back to this planet anytime soon?"

The iciness of her touch faded. "I don't want to go to a boring dedication." I sounded whiny. Brownie points were becoming less important to me. The money from teaching was nice but not worth this feeling of being out of place. No matter how hard I tried, I couldn't make the new me fit in the place the old me used to feel so at home. Why had I taken this job? What was I trying to prove?

"Your social calendar all booked up?" Donita grabbed a handful of M&M's.

I swatted her fingers. "Not really." I did have plans to go home and watch my mom cook enough food to feed a small country.

"They are supposed to be doing some sort of salute to Theodore and his work." Donita scooped up another handful of M&M's. "And another retired prof who died over a year ago."

I drew the bowl of M&M's toward me. "I am going to have to start charging you for these." The thought of learning more about the life and death of Theodore Aldridge pricked my curiosity.

"Run a tab." She poured some back into the bowl. "I don't think I'll need that many anymore." Her hot pink lips curled up into a smile. "I'm seeing someone new. Come to the dedication tonight and meet him."

The glowing Donita with her bright lipstick and giggly demeanor was a contrast to the guarded Donita I'd come to know. Donita was fun and friendly, but I always got the feeling she would only let me so far into her life before the defenses went up. Was that all it took to cheer her up—a new relationship?

She traced a pattern in the wood on my desk with her finger. "You might meet somebody."

I sorted through a stack of papers. "Guess I'd rather let God choose my relationships." The words fell out of my mouth without me even thinking about it. I couldn't grab them out of the air and stuff them back down my throat before they got away.

Donita spoke between bites of chocolate. "God? What does he have to do with it?"

I stared at her bright, blank face. There it was—a wide open door for me to walk through and share my faith, and it happened without prescripting or planning. I held a piece of paper in mid-air, and my heart pounded in my chest. *Oh, Lord, don't let me blow this.* "I don't know. I just spent so many years making poor choices and being hurt by men or hurting them. Maybe God can do a better job than I did at finding me someone." I let go of the paper, and it drifted down to the desktop.

Donita didn't respond until the paper landed on the desk. She shrugged. "Whatever." She stepped toward the doorway. "See you tonight. It's a very hoity-toity affair, so dress up." She strutted out of my office.

Well, there it was. Donita knew I was a Christian, and her reaction had been complete indifference, which I suppose was one step above hostility or ridicule.

Shortly after I had started teaching, I'd heard a conversation outside my door between two professors. One of them was talking about how a Christian student had written a paper offering arguments from books the prof called "religious drivel." The other professor laughed and said he had received a paper that was "peppered" with Bible verses. The tone of their voices dripped with disdain and condescension. I had sat in my office, listening to their laughter fade down the hall, feeling my chest grow tighter and tighter. Christians were few and far between around here, and most people assumed Christianity was for the feeble, the simpleminded. To liberal academics, Christianity and stupidity were a boxed set.

I rested my forehead on the desk. The day had already been too much, and I still had a class to teach.

~

After class, Dale Cutler stood at the back of the room. His face glistened with sweat. Circles of perspiration darkened the armpit areas of his polo shirt. As the rest of the class shuffled out, his eyes locked on me. He pressed his back against the wall, holding a single piece of paper in his hand. Everything about him communicated nervous agitation.

"But why can't I use this as a source for my report?" Nicole Adams waved a fitness magazine in my face. Her brown, shoulder-length hair had intense contrasting blond streaks. She had used styling products so it cascaded around her head in chunks making her look unkempt on purpose. She was a pretty girl with big eyes and a tiny, upturned nose.

Three other students stood behind her, waiting to ask me a question. One of them, a man holding a book by Plato, rolled his eyes and glared at the ceiling.

"Nicole, the assignment is to summarize a journal article."

"Like the *Ladies' Home Journal*?" Nicole offered brightly.

At the back of the room, Dale pushed himself off the wall and shifted his weight from foot to foot.

"No, an academic journal like *the Journal of the American Medical Association* or the *Journal of Agricultural Economics*," I explained.

I could feel Dale staring at me.

Nicole gazed down at her magazine, which featured a muscular woman who looked as if she had fallen in a vat of olive oil right before the photo was taken. The poor dear apparently could not afford clothing and was forced to cover her personal parts with fabric remnants. My prayer was that she had been paid well for the photo and could at least purchase a pair of pants and a shirt. "This has lots of good information in it."

"Nicole, it won't work for the assignment. The reference librarians will help you find what you need."

With a heavy sigh, she turned and left the room. I felt a little twinge of delight as she stepped out the door. She was about to enter a whole new world. The world of books without pictures. Don't ask me why, but there is some sick thrill in dragging a student kicking and screaming to knowledge and then watching them drink. I liked this part of my job.

While I dealt with the other students' questions, Dale paced.

When the last student stepped out into the hallway, Dale remained at the back of the room.

I packed up my books and overheads. "Did you have something you wanted to talk to me about, Dale?"

He took a few steps toward me. "I . . . ah . . . I . . . um . . . I need to drop the class."

"Is it about that C? You could still bring your grade up."

"No, it's not that." He glanced out the door again. "I just have too many classes."

"Come over here. I'll sign your drop form." I spoke to him without looking up as I shoved books and papers into my briefcase. I set the briefcase on the floor. "Dale, I can't sign your drop form from across the room."

He licked his lips. The drop/add form in his hands was held so tightly that the edges curled up. He took a few more steps toward me.

I held my pen up. "I'm ready. If you're not sure about dropping the class, I think there's another week before the last drop day."

"No, no, I'm sure about it." He handed me the paper. "I can't take classes—not in this building."

What a strange thing to say. I stared at the paper, then at Dale, then at the long trench coat he had hung over the back of the chair. Greta Aldridge had said the lurker around the house wore a long coat. And now someone had been snooping around my office.

"How well did you know Dr. Aldridge?" I re-sorted my overheads, trying to sound casual.

Dale let out a tiny grunt. His slit-like eyes grew rounder. He took a step back, pivoted, and then answered without making eye contact. "I . . . I was taking this class from him before. . . ." He paused to lick his lips again. "He and Dr. Philips co-taught the scriptwriting class I took last year." A stream of sweat trickled past his temple. His Adam's apple moved up and down several times. "I just know him from class, that's all."

Dale was not a good liar. Obviously, there was more going on between them than simply a student–teacher relationship.

"You never saw him other than in class? I thought you said he was helping you with some things."

Dale shook his head.

I leaned closer to see if I could smell his cologne. My olfactory memory isn't the greatest, but it was worth a try. Mixed with the acrid tang of sweat, it was hard to tell if his woody cologne was the same I had smelled earlier in my office—but it was close.

He took a step back. "Just sign my form, okay?" He pushed the paper toward me, but I didn't take it.

I edged toward him. "Were you rooting through my office earlier today?"

Dale shook his head. I could actually see his pulse throbbing in his neck. "You don't understand."

"I understand that you went through my personal stuff."

"No, no, you don't get it." He stalked across the room and picked up his coat.

"Dale, wait."

He ran toward the door.

I yelled down the hall at his back. "Did you take my keys?"

I trudged back to the room and slumped down into a desk. A thought popped into my head. It sure would be nice to go home and talk to somebody about how hard my day had been. It would be nice if that somebody was Wesley. *No, Ruby, don't go there.* If Wesley was going to make guest appearances in my head just like that, I had been telling myself a lie. I couldn't be "just friends" with him. Using that as an excuse to be close to him meant I was still hoping for more. I didn't want to be responsible for Vanessa being hurt. We weren't Batman and Robin. We were Batman and Cat Woman.

A heavy net of depression loomed over me. I couldn't burden Mom with my problems either. She was dealing with enough. I guess that left God. I closed my eyes and said, *I will trust you, Lord,* about fifty times. The prayer came slowly, the tension melted off, and I felt like I could move out of my chair and make it home to get ready for the dedication.

What does one wear to such a hoity-toity affair anyway?

Chapter Seven

I opened the living-room door, and a mishmash of spices assaulted my nose: cinnamon, lemon, basil, and some kind of pepper, topped off with just a hint of my mother's rose-scented perfume. I could detect three different kinds of chocolate. She was still at it—still cooking.

In the kitchen, the two children who had been there before had multiplied and turned into a flock: little blond heads, medium-sized heads with brown hair, curly and straight, long and short. Some of the critters around the table were in diapers, some wore in-line skates, some still had their ski jackets on. Males and females of every shape and size ran or skated around the table and darted in and out through the patio door. Three shoved handfuls of cookies and fudge into their mouths. Sugar glistened around their lips. Others had brown smudges on their faces. Some actually sat at the table, eating with forks and spoons, scooping up the casserole in front of them.

I couldn't get an accurate count because they kept moving, but I estimated twelve in all. Because they were all eating, the noise level was low—lots of crunching, chewing sounds and the occasional, "Hey, I was going to take that one."

Mom stood whisking something in a metal bowl. Behind her, the electric mixer whirred away. The air in the kitchen was heavy, hot, sweet, and spicy.

"Hi, Ruby. Are you hungry?" She gave me a Miss America smile. Her eyes had a glazed look to them.

I empathized with my mother's pain, but honestly, this was starting to feel like an episode of *June Cleaver Goes to Bellevue*. I had to do something to get her over this cooking addiction . . . but what?

I felt a tug on my pant leg. I looked down into a pudgy little face topped off with a tuft of blond, troll-doll hair. Fat little fingers gripped an empty bowl. "Got any more?"

Only a yellow residue remained in the bowl. I had no idea what had been there. I took the bowl. "What were you eating, hon?"

Mom pointed to the yellow, three-tiered cake on the edge of the counter. "Lemon cake with pudding filling. Freddy loves it." She stopped stirring and addressed the little troll directly. "Don't you, honey?" Mom poked the air with her finger and made one of those silly noises you are only allowed to make when children are around.

The little boy giggled, revealing an even row of pearl-like teeth. "You funny, Mizzuz Taylor. You funny." Freddy patted his big round belly as I cut a small piece of cake for him. "Tank you." The little critter waddled back to the table on Pillsbury Doughboy legs.

The moms in the neighborhood were probably delighted that the Taylor house had become an unofficial snack shack. Freddy opened his mouth wide for a big bite of cake. If Mom kept this up, the whole block would be poster children for the Diabetes Association. I was the only one who knew my mother's behavior was manic. The rest of the neighborhood would just think she was the grandmotherly type who baked for everyone. This was not the peaceful woman I knew—this was not my mother. She might as well have locked herself in a room with a bottle of scotch.

"Ruby, get that worried look off your face." She wiped her hands briskly on a towel that hung on the refrigerator door.

I must have been staring while I strategized the intervention possibilities.

She yanked open the refrigerator door. "How about some strawberry shortcake?" Cradling a heaping bowl of fruit, she scurried to the counter.

I filed through a catalog of possibilities. Words and speeches weren't going to work. Anything I could think of to say sounded trite or judgmental or cruel. On top of everything, I was sure we didn't have the money to buy all this extra food.

Mom hummed away as she sliced the little green heads off the fruit.

Jumping up and down and screaming, "Stop it! Stop it! Stop it!" probably wouldn't help either.

The only option was to join in the madness. I grabbed an apron from the hook by the stove. I touched the rim of a metal bowl. "Whatcha got started here?"

Mom held her knife in midair. "Scrambled eggs." She turned the knife in such a way that it caught a glint of light.

Scrambled eggs and strawberry shortcake, a combination served in all the finer restaurants. "Why don't I finish it for you?" I have a sarcastic streak in me a mile wide, but I swallowed hard and resisted the impulse to comment on the weird combination of stuff she was brewing. The kids didn't seem to mind. Fudge as an entrée with tater tot casserole for dessert was the most natural thing in the world to them.

Every time Mom sliced a head off a strawberry, the counter vibrated. I whisked the eggs and smiled at her. I didn't see a single cookbook around. She must be working from memory. The mixer chugged away. Bowls with half-mixed concoctions cluttered the counter.

"Ouch." Mom held up her index finger. A crimson strand of blood flowed across her palm.

"I'll get it." I grabbed a clean white towel out of a drawer and wrapped it around her hand, covering the cut finger. "It's just a nick."

A growing red circle stained the white material. I cupped her hand in mine. Her skin was soft and cool. I pressed the cloth a little tighter against her finger. Our heads were close together.

She touched my cheek with the gentleness of butterfly wings.

"When your children are babies, you have such dreams for them." Her voice faltered. She glanced at the children bustling through the kitchen. "You and Jimmy were so bright and perfect and beautiful. You could have done anything, gone anywhere, if I hadn't—"

"Ma, don't."

"I know why Jimmy left. He hates me. He hates what I did to his life. When he saw me, he realized he couldn't get past it."

I let go of her hand and pulled open several cupboard doors. "Don't we have a Band-Aid here somewhere?" I couldn't argue with her, because what she said was partially true. When Mom had first found me, I'd felt the same push and pull—anger and a longing to reconcile.

"Where are those bandages?" I slammed one of the cupboard doors so loudly several of the children looked up from their bowls, mouths open, spoons suspended in midair. "Eat your food." I placed my hand on my hip and waggled my finger. "Don't waste."

Now I sounded like my mother. The children dutifully returned to their meals. Several of them filed out the door with side glances at me.

Sometimes the anger toward my mother surfaced, but I wanted a relationship with her. God and I could work through the bitterness. Mom was a different person from the woman who had helped her husband embezzle all those years ago. Jimmy hadn't stuck around long enough to see that.

"On the night your father told me he was stealing from those companies and he wanted my help, I should have taken you kids and left him." Mom clicked off the mixer with her good hand. "I thought about it." She crossed her arms and leaned against the counter. "Believe me, I thought about it." A deep red circle a little bigger than a quarter stained the cloth still wrapped around her wound. "That night, I checked on you and Jimmy as you slept. Jimmy had that fuzzy red hair. He always slept with his hand on his cheek." The white cloth slipped from her finger and fell to the floor. She placed a hand on her cheek. "I thought about it, but I—"

"Can't go back in time." I took her place at the strawberries. "Sooner or later, you've got to play the cards you've been dealt. You get to trade some, but your basic hand is the same." One. Two. Three. I sliced the little green heads off the strawberries. "You can't ask for a different hand, and you can't demand to play Scrabble instead."

Mom's lower lip quivered, but she managed a smile. "But I like Scrabble."

"Nope, that's not how it works. Just the cards in your hand. Not Parcheesi or Monopoly."

"Not even checkers." She moved over to where I was working.

I shook my head. "Becoming a Christian didn't wipe out the consequences of our past."

"I know that." She picked up a strawberry and rolled it in her fingers, studying it. "I just don't want the past to own me."

All the children but Freddy slowly trickled out of the house via the patio door. Freddy stuck his head in his bowl and licked it. When he pulled his face out of the bowl, he had yellow frosting eyebrows, and cake crumbs littered his nose.

I needed to divert my mother's attention, and I needed to get her to quit cooking. "I've got to go to this stupid dedication at the museum—very hoity-toity. Why don't you come with me?"

"I don't know, Ruby. I've got so many things started here."

"I'm ordering you."

She wiped her eyes with her apron and sniffled. "I'm very good at hoity-toity." Mom walked over to the table and touched Freddy's fuzzy head. Freddy tilted his head and leaned against her hip. She glanced around the chaotic kitchen.

"It can wait, Mom."

She gathered Freddy into her arms. "I suppose you are right." Freddy nuzzled against her neck.

As I watched Mom holding that little boy, guilt pangs snaked around my rib cage. Somewhere out there in the world was a little girl I had given up for adoption. She would never know her grandma. Mom knew just about everything about my past, about the years we were apart, except for that one secret.

Mom kissed Freddy on the cheek. "Okay, I'll go."

"You're the queen of hoity-toity. I need your help and your moral support. Can I borrow one of those designer rip-off dresses you scwcd up?" My idea of dressed up was to put a blazer over my T-shirt and to wear flats instead of my cowboy boots.

We gave Freddy one more piece of cake before sending him home with a substantial sugar buzz. An hour later, we were primped and rouged and perfumed. Mom found a fake silk number in purple that was only a little big in the waist and a little too high up on the leg for me. I'm nearly six feet tall, and Mom is five-foot nothing, so we were lucky to find something that fit. The dress had one of those flirty, flyaway skirts that made me feel like I might be able to dance and actually look good. The fabric swished when I walked.

I topped the whole thing off with light brown mascara on my white lashes. I liked what I saw in the mirror. This was the face God gave me, freckles and all. I hadn't dressed up to please anyone but myself, and that felt good.

"Come on, Ruby, I've got the Caddy started," Mom yelled from the living room. Mom's Caddy is an older seventies model that runs a little better than my 1968 Valiant. If my car were spiffed up, painted, and had the dents pounded out of it, I could pass it off as a classic. On its better days, it's a clunker.

The Museum of Northwest Exploration and Discovery (NED) was about two blocks away from campus, though it was considered part of the school. History and archeology professors guest-lectured, consulted for the museum, and helped with exhibits. The photography and art departments had an upstairs gallery to display work from students and professors. Now the English department would have some sort of affiliation with NED. If I had read Cameron's memo, I would know what that affiliation was.

Oh well, life is more fun when it's full of surprises.

A dark dome of sky arced over us when we pulled up. Light from the interior of the museum and the lampposts revealed about ten cars in the parking lot. We were past regular museum hours, so all these people were here for the shindig.

My legs instantly goose-pimpled when I stuck them out of the car. This was probably not the best getup for a late fall evening. We'd been lucky to get this far into October without snow. Still, the air held a threatening chill. But I didn't care. I looked good and felt good. So what if my legs turned to blue icicles before the evening was over. I gathered my iridescent wrap around my shoulders, opting to leave my warmer but bulky jacket in the car.

Once inside, we walked past the vacant greeter's counter toward the sound of voices. A life-size bronze of Sacajawea with a dog, a baby, and a canoe stood at the entrance to the first exhibit. Her face looked heavenward, serene and hopeful. How unrealistic. If I had to tromp around the woods with a bunch of smelly men and carry a baby on my back for months on end, I'd be demanding some bubble bath and disposable diapers. Bare minimum, a pound of chocolate. And I sure wouldn't have that look on my face.

To the side, opposite the statue, was a door that said Lewis and Clark Theater.

Mom walked a few paces in front of me. She wore an Audrey Hepburnish black dress with white pearls. The dress had a full, gathered skirt that cascaded down to her ankles. She seemed almost cheerful. Getting her out of the house had been a good idea.

The chatter got louder as we walked through a display on westward expansion that featured covered wagons, actual pieces of railroad track, and the ever popular "history of barbed wire" display, complete with samples of each kind of barbed wire. A jail cell, stuffed buffalo, and Native American artifacts were also part of the extensive exhibit.

We turned a corner. Twenty, maybe twenty-five, people mingled, holding glasses of wine and little paper plates. Waiters dressed in black pants and white shirts refilled the trays and poured glasses of punch.

Greta Aldridge stood at the goodies table, loading up her plate and glancing around nervously. She'd pulled her short hair back and up with some sort of hair dealy. She wore black pants and a black shirt with a multi-colored jacket. A tall teenager stood beside her, holding a paper cup. He looked like Theodore Aldridge, only thirty years younger. He had the same slender build and narrow features, except the round, wire-rimmed glasses were absent and his hair was a light brown instead of gray. A shorter, skinny boy with hair the same shade as the teenager's stood with his hands in his pockets, staring at the floor and swaying.

Greta's mouth tightened into a straight line when she saw me. Nope, I wasn't going to be getting any information out of her tonight. Mom busied herself complimenting the serving staff on the wonderful food and thanking them for their hard work.

Donita perched next to a table with a small banner that said, "In honor of Dr. Theodore Aldridge and Xavier Konrad." She was dressed in a very elegant short navy dress and red canvas high-top sneakers. Her hair had its usual chaotic bigness to it. The ever-so-fashionable I-stood-too-close-to-the-nuclear-blast look. What caught my attention was what Donita had hanging on her arm. Six feet of handsome, with wavy brown hair, perfect skin, and a charming smile made a nice accessory for her—much better than a sequined evening purse.

Just 'cause I'm a good Christian woman doesn't mean I stopped being human. He was magnetically good looking. *Thank you, God, for making handsome men.* Enough of that. I was happy Donita had met someone. I hoped everything worked out. It had cheered her up quite a bit.

Cameron Bancroft stepped up behind the podium; he tapped the microphone and cleared his throat. "When Professor Emeritus Xavier Konrad left a substantial amount of money to the English department, he specified that all the money should go to a rare books collection. . . ."

Donita scooted up beside me while Cameron droned on. She whispered in my ear, "Cameron was none too happy about that. He thought he was going to get the money for the department to spend as he pleased."

Cameron droned on. "My good friend and colleague Dr. Theodore Aldridge was instrumental in setting up that collection at the university last year. . . ."

I loaded my plate up with mints and pretzels and grabbed some punch. I recognized some of the other people as English profs. I was pretty sure the woman in the beige pantsuit was the scriptwriting professor whom Aldridge had co-taught a class with. I had seen her photo in the pile of articles I pulled up at the library. She was a slender, fortyish woman with auburn hair.

Donita grabbed a cup of punch and took a gulp. "So what do you think?" She tilted her head in the direction of the tall guy by the banner.

"He's very good looking."

Cameron raised his voice. "I feel a special affinity for NED. As an undergrad, I did my internship here, often studying and taking my lunch in the loft where I could view the whole museum." He glanced up toward a panel of windows with nothing but darkness behind them. "I am honored now that. . . ."

"Could Cameron possibly be more long winded?" Donita leaned closer to me so I could hear her. "We met at AA, so that avoids my pattern of attracting men who drink like fish. I think my problem was that I was always going for the suffering artist type—both my husbands were." Mr. *GQ* smiled in our direction. "He's a very successful contractor."

Cameron continued. "This collection of frontier diaries for the museum will be a memorial for two men who loved the written word, Dr. Theodore Aldridge and Professor Xavier Konrad. The legacy of both men will live on. . . ."

"We're thinking about moving in together," Donita whispered.

I stopped munching my mints and looked right at her. Of course they were sleeping together. Why had I hoped otherwise? I tried hard not to sound like her mother. "How long have you known each other?"

She glowed with the radiance of romantic attraction. But I had used that drug myself and knew it didn't last. Been there, done that, they don't make a T-shirt for it.

Donita smoothed the skirt of her dress. "We've known each other a year, but we've only been dating a week." She craned her neck to get a gander at Mr. Gorgeous.

"That's awful quick, don't you think?" I crumbled a pretzel in my hand.

Donita's expression hardened. She squared her shoulders and thrust her chin in the air. "We've known each other a year. We just seem to mesh. I'm sober now; I'm not going to make the same bad choices I made before."

I ground the pretzel into dust with my fingers. Everything I could think of to say to her was wrapped in Christian jargon and judgmental phrases. How could I make her understand that I was trying to pull her from the same burning building that had incinerated me? "I hope things work out okay for you. I really do. But if they don't, I'm always around to talk, and I have lots of chocolate."

"I'm happy." She crossed her arms and shook her head. "Can't you be happy for me?"

"You deserve good things in your life, Donita. I just . . ." What could I say?

Momentarily, almost indiscernibly, she bit her lower lip. I saw a flash of something in her eyes, an emotion that faded with her masklike smile. "I'm just so happy. Be happy for me. That's all you have to do." She gave her guy a little wave before strutting across the floor to join him by the banner.

Mom came up beside me. "These have too much paprika in them." She pointed to a cracker on her plate with goopy stuff on it. "I saw a catering van outside. I might call them tomorrow and give them my recipe."

I wrapped my arm around her. "Okay."

"Why are you smiling at me like that, Ruby?"

"Because you are you." I gave her shoulder a squeeze.

Cameron introduced Aldridge's widow, failing to mention that Greta was Aldridge's ex-wife. She stepped behind the podium and bent the microphone up and down for several seconds. She gripped the sides of the podium. Her hands slid back and forth as she spoke.

"Theodore was a good professor and a scholar. He was much loved by his students." Her chest moved up and down as she took a deep breath. "He was a father to his two boys. . . ."

She was being very diplomatic in her word choices. While she spoke, her younger son wandered away from the reception area. He turned a corner and disappeared into another part of the museum.

Sometimes kids talk more than parents do. *Maybe I could find out something more about Aldridge from his youngest son.* I slipped past the reception table. The boy had wandered into the dinosaur exhibit. Huge pterodactyls hung from the ceiling, suspended by wires. Several replicas of dinosaur skeletons towered twenty feet into the air.

The kid trailed his hand across a display of dinosaur eggs. He hesitated at the exhibit about different kinds of rock before turning the corner.

I raced after him. He had stepped inside an alcove with a television and bench in it. Tiny, quarter-sized lights shone from the ceiling. I came up behind him just as he was about to push the button that would run the video about dinosaur digs in Eastern Montana. "Hi, you're Dr. Aldridge's son, aren't you?"

He was maybe ten or eleven, a tall, skinny creature with narrow, unmuscular arms. His short-sleeved dress shirt and slacks had a rumpled appearance, and the shirt was buttoned crooked.

Applause filtered in from the next room. *Greta must be done with her totally honest speech.* The chatter grew louder.

When the kid didn't respond, I approached him and touched his shoulder. "What's your name?"

He didn't make eye contact with me. "Benjamin. My name is Benjamin." He touched the television screen, then stared at his shoes.

I angled my head to try and make eye contact. He looked at

me, then sat down on the bench by the TV screen, angling his head away from me. Jagged bangs hung over his eyes.

"I bet you miss your dad, huh?"

"Yes. He used to bring me books about magnets and locksmithing. Did you know locks were invented in Egypt?"

"No, I didn't know that."

"They were the pin-and-tumbler type with lock and key." He half stood up, rubbed his thighs, glanced nervously at me, and sat back down. "Dad gave me a book." He spoke without much inflection or emotion.

"That was nice of your dad."

"Benny, you need to come back into the other room." The older son had come around the corner. He leaned into the TV room.

Benjamin stood up and touched the television. "Those locks were made of wood."

"He's really into learning about locks right now." The older brother must have noticed me dancing, trying to make eye contact with Benjamin. "He has a learning disability, a form of autism. He's very smart, but social situations—eye contact—are hard for him. It's called Asperger's Syndrome."

"I haven't heard of that one."

Benjamin scratched the back of his head, stepped out of the alcove, and wandered over to a coloring station with pictures of dinosaurs. "Most locks have tumblers inside of cylinders but not all, not all."

The older Aldridge kid put his arm around Benjamin. "It's also called the Little Professor Syndrome. He has incredible rote memory. He can tell you everything you need to know about magnets or anything technical that fascinates him. He fixes all the appliances at home."

Benjamin made eye contact momentarily, then addressed his comments to the coloring table. "I'm not stupid. My brain is just wired differently."

"You seem really smart." His social ineptness had a certain charm and vulnerability to it.

Benjamin grinned.

"Sorry, guess I overexplained." The older kid rearranged the crayons on the coloring table. "I just want people to know what a neat guy Benny is." He touched his brother's upper arm.

"He is a neat guy. I'm Ruby Taylor, by the way." I held out my hand. "I took over your father's lower-division classes."

"Eliot Aldridge." The elder son gripped my hand firmly.

"I didn't know your father, but he was well liked at the university."

Eliot mimed throwing a baseball. "I guess. Everybody loved Dad."

"I don't think he killed himself."

Benjamin sat down at the coloring table and picked up a red crayon.

Eliot perked up. "Really?"

"Did you know he owned a gun?"

"No, but I never thought he killed himself." Eliot leaned over the short table and pushed the other crayons toward his brother. "Dad changed right before he died."

"Changed how?"

"I don't think you boys need to be talking to her." Greta Aldridge's voice cut the air like a hatchet.

Benjamin jumped. Several crayons rolled off the table.

"Eliot, get your brother and come on." She stalked across the carpet and put a protective arm around her younger son. "We have nothing to say to this woman." She'd penciled in her eyebrows and drawn a thick layer of liner on her upper lid. The intense makeup drew attention to the wrinkles in her forehead. The rest of her skin was pale, including her light pink lips.

"She says Dad didn't kill himself."

"Your father was an alcoholic. He was up and down with his emotions all the time. He lived alone and was estranged from his family. He was a prime candidate for suicide."

"He changed, Mom. You just want to keep on hating him even though he's six feet under."

"I can take locks apart," Benjamin offered brightly.

"People do change, you know." Eliot narrowed his eyes at his mother. "I'm just so tired of you bad-mouthing him."

"He never had any time for you boys. Maybe if he'd spent more time with Benjamin—"

"Stop it, Mother. You even find a way to blame *that* on Dad."

"You don't know what it was like being married to that—that jerk." She tugged on Benjamin's sleeve. "Come on, we need to go home."

"He was trying to make things right. You were just so full of hate, you couldn't see. Can't you just drop it? You've been divorced for eight years, and now the guy is dead."

"I'm taking Benjamin to the car." Greta grabbed her younger son at the elbow and yanked him across the floor.

Benjamin addressed his comments to the floor. "I know lots about rocks and minerals, too."

"Are you coming, Eliot?"

The older boy shoved his hands in his pockets and set his jaw.

"Fine then." She disappeared around the corner, dragging her younger son with her.

"Sorry you had to see that." He hung his head.

"It was entertaining." I shifted my purse from one shoulder to the other. "You guys aren't boring."

"Being angry at Dad has become some kind of hobby for her." Eliot unbuttoned his cuffs and rolled his sleeves up. "They used to fight all the time when I was kid. Screaming, throwing things. I cut my feet on broken glass more than once." He glanced over at me, smiling faintly. "They both got Ph.D.'s. You would think people with all that education would be more civilized to each other."

I shook my head and shrugged.

"Let me know if you find out more about Dad." He stalked off but yelled back at me, "Her degree is in counseling. Isn't that funny?"

I stood among the dinosaurs. All the book smarts in the world didn't keep you from hurting people who cared about you.

The model of a triceratops stared at me with beady little eyes. "Isn't that right, my prehistoric friend?" The dinosaur offered no opinion. If Greta Aldridge had killed her ex-husband, I didn't think she'd gotten any help from either son.

My cell phone rang, and I pulled it out of my purse. I didn't recognize the number.

I clicked on. "Hello?"

"Ruby, Wesley here."

An electric charge zapped my heart, but I managed to rework my mushy feelings for Wesley into indignation. "What are you doing, calling me?" I wasn't about to give up the ship and let him know how I actually felt. My true feelings would only be ammunition for him to hurt me more, since he was with Vanessa.

I regretted giving him the impression we could be friends the last time I'd seen him at Greta's house. Everybody knew Batman and Cat Woman were mortal enemies.

He hesitated. "I got some rather intriguing information about Aldridge."

"What?" Again, my tone made it sound like it was a dreadful inconvenience for me to exchange words with him. I had decided I needed to keep physical distance between us, and he calls me. How irritating.

"I got his bank records. His income was going up by five hundred to a thousand a month. Even during the summer when he wasn't working."

"Maybe he was consulting or editing. Or whatever English profs do to make extra money."

"The deposits were in cash. Very fishy looking."

My thoughts went to Dale and his strange behavior earlier today. Had he and Aldridge been selling drugs to students? What was the connection between the two of them? "You think he was involved in something illegal?"

"Maybe. We need more information before we draw any conclusions."

"Listen, I think a student named Dale Cutler might have something to do with this. I'm going over to talk to him tonight."

"Ruby, let the police take care of this."

"Make up your mind. First, you give me what is probably confidential police info and then you tell me to let the police take care of it."

"I . . . Ruby . . . I . . . just . . . I . . ."

While Wesley struggled to relearn the English language, I could hear a woman's voice in the background: Vanessa's voice.

A hot, tight strand of anger twisted around my spine, traveling all the way up to my neck. "Look, I'm just a concerned instructor going to talk to a student. I can handle myself."

"At least go at a time when I can go with you."

Vanessa's voice got louder. I could hear other voices in the background, laughter and chatter—a party. Of course he couldn't come now; he was hanging out with Vanessa. With each syllable Vanessa spoke, my chest got tighter. This was mean on Wesley's part.

"What do you care about my safety? You haven't earned the right to be concerned about my safety. I'm a big girl. I can take care of myself." I clicked the off button. *What a flake. What a tease.* I'd show him. I could talk to Dale by myself. I checked my watch. Nine o'clock. Dale was probably still up, and I was sure the museum had a student guide with his address in it.

Chapter Eight

I found a copy of the campus directory at the greeter's counter of the museum. Dale's address was listed as 421 1/2 South Preston, about five blocks from campus. I was still steaming about the call from Wesley. Here I was being a good girl, keeping my distance, and not playing games, and he calls me—with Vanessa talking in the background. What was he up to? I didn't want to believe that Wesley was that cruel or that insensitive.

Honestly, he wasn't making any sense at all. *He tells me to keep my nose out of police business and then he shares police business with me.* Mom came up beside me, waving a piece of paper. "I picked up an application to be a volunteer here. It'll keep my mind off of . . . well . . . other things. I'm going to get through this." She touched my arm above the elbow. "Is everything okay?"

She must have noticed my shoulders touching my ears. Trying to figure out Wesley made me so tense, I had developed a serious case of no-neck syndrome. "I have a student I'm kind of concerned about. What say we swing by his place on our way home?" My motives were all mixed up. I wanted to find out what was going on with Dale, but I also was struggling with an I'll-show-you-I-can-take-care-of-myself attitude where Wesley was concerned.

Mom folded the application and placed it in her monster purse—the quilted job, the "purse-with-everything-and-everything-in-the-purse." Once, I'd actually witnessed her pull a first-aid kit out of there when she saw one of the neighborhood kids fall down on the sidewalk. "If that's what you want to do, Ruby. I sure don't have anywhere to go."

$$\backsim$$

I drove slowly when I hit Preston Street. It was a residential neighborhood with older, box-like houses. The homes were fairly close together, each with a small front yard, some fenced, some not. The addresses were hard to read in the dark. Mom had taken cross-stitch out of her purse along with a little light on a headband.

"Got a man in that purse for me, Mom?" I slowed to a crawl as we passed the six hundred block of Preston Street. "You seem to have everything else."

Mom opened her purse and stuck her head in it. "Let's see here. Makeup kit. Bible. Nope, no man in here. Were you in need of one?"

We were on the five hundred block. We passed a house with all the lights on. Music and college-age people spilled out the front door onto the lawn. "Some days." *If I could just meet someone else, I could forget Wesley.* "I am trying to accept God's timing in this."

"But you get a little anxious?" She adjusted her lighted headband. "Concerned that God lost your prayer request in a pile of paperwork?"

"Something like that." Seeing Wesley again served as a reminder that I was human. I could still feel attraction for a man. Even though I was loved by the Savior of the universe, I could still get lonely for human arms. "I'm starting to think that God's timing is that I never meet anyone."

"And you spend the rest of your life taking care of your wacky mother." Mom turned toward me, lightbulb head and all.

We were in the four hundred block. My crawl slowed to a creep. It was past ten o'clock. Most of the houses were dark except for a kitchen light or the glow from a television. "You're not wacky, Mom. You take care of me more than I take care of you."

"Maybe you're right, Ruby. Maybe it's time you moved out."

I gave Mom a double take. "That's not what I said." Where did she get this stuff?

"You could almost afford it with your job at the university." She jabbed a needle through her cross-stitch.

"Right now, it's a semester-long contract." I turned the wheel and pulled into an open spot by 421.

"I thought you said they might give you more work."

"I'm not sure that's what I want," I said. I had thought I wanted a job at the U. Now I wasn't so sure.

"When I found you, you were like a wounded bird. You are so much stronger now, Ruby. I love having you in that house, but it's not healthy for you."

"You want me to move out." Her words hurt. Why was she pushing me away like this?

"I want you to think about it." She folded and refolded her hands over the top of the cross-stitch. I witnessed a nanosecond in which her blue eyes glanced at me, and then she closed them and turned away. She clicked the light on her head off. Shadow covered her face, as if a gray veil had fallen over it.

Realization hit me like a blow to the stomach. Now I knew why she was saying these things. She was feeling unworthy as a mother because of Jimmy. She thought she would be doing me a favor if she wasn't a big part of my life. What a lie.

I reached over and touched her shoulder. "What if I do meet

somebody?" I wanted her to know how much she meant to me. Of course, I couldn't come right out and say that. My compassion was all in code. "What if God answers that prayer? I want to do things right this time—no sex until I'm married. If I stay with you, I'll have someone to be accountable to."

"But you haven't met anyone."

"Don't rub it in." My teasing was winning her back. The softest of smiles crossed her lips. "I know. The reason you want me to move out is so you can party and have all those old widowers from the church over."

Mom waved the idea away with her hand. "Oh, Ruby!"

"How about that one guy in your Bible study, the guy who owns the carpet cleaning business?"

"Frank Wychoski? He falls asleep during Sunday school and drools."

"Okay, so you will at least need someone who can stay awake and doesn't have saliva issues."

She tilted her head toward her chest. "Ruby, don't match-make."

"Sorry, it's just that nothing is going on in my dating life, so I've got to interfere with other people's." I squeezed the steering wheel. "Seriously, do you ever think about getting married again?"

"I'm not very good at picking husbands. Look at the father I gave you and Jimmy. I'm happy being single." Head still bent, she rubbed the pearls around her neck.

Now I'd blown it. I'd brought her back full circle to the cause of her pain. "Come on, let's go find out what's going on with Dale." I winked at her and pushed open my door.

A motorcycle and a newer model truck were parked out front. Because the address had a fraction attached to it, I assumed Dale's apartment was in the basement down the dark stairs. No lights glimmered in the upstairs rooms, but a yippy little dog barked in falsetto behind the door.

The neighborhood for the most part was quiet. Someone started a car down the block. Streetlamps illuminated the empty sidewalk.

Mom shone a flashlight down the dark stairs. Yes, she pulled that out of her purse too. I was so glad I brought her and her purse. We descended the stairs. The landing was surrounded by a five-foot concrete wall on two sides. Upstairs, the dog continued to bark, and it sounded like it was spastically flinging itself against the screen door.

I rapped on the door. No answer. I knocked harder. "Dale?"

"Does this boy have a substance-abuse problem?" Mom held the flashlight on the door.

"I'm not sure. He was just acting very strange in class today. I don't know what he's involved in."

Upstairs, a porch light went on.

I knocked until my knuckles hurt. "Dale? Dale? Are you in there?"

"It is awful late at night, Ruby." Mom drew her shawl tighter around her shoulders. The night wasn't freezing, but October chill hung in the air. My own pantyhose-clad legs felt like icebergs.

"Dale's not here," a bass voice boomed above us. I jumped. I could just make out the silhouette of a man. From the bottom of the stairs where we stood, he looked colossal, only slightly smaller than the dinosaurs in the museum. Three yippy dogs, two white and one black, bounced around his legs.

"We're sorry to disturb you, sir. But my daughter was concerned about Dale." Mom made her way up the stairs, and I followed.

"He was here earlier." He glanced toward the street. "His car is gone now."

"Do you know when he'll be back?" At the top of the stairs, I could get a better look at Dale's landlord. He wore a sleeveless T-shirt that revealed bulging biceps and a "Jesus is Lord" tattoo. His long hair was pulled back into a ponytail.

"I'm having a hard time catching him at home. He's behind in his rent."

"You have no idea where he went?"

"No, but I can tell you where he has been. When he was late with rent, I called the Landlord's Association. Should have done that ahead of time. Landlord's Association blacklisted him. The kid's moved three or four times since spring semester—broken some leases."

"What was he like when he was here?" I pulled my drapey shawl around my shoulders to keep from shivering.

"He was quiet enough." One of the yippy dogs tugged on the big man's jeans. "Didn't have lots of friends."

Hearing someone was quiet and kept to himself was always a bad sign. Every presidential assassin was "quiet and kept to himself."

Across the street, a Jeep pulled into an open space. The driver's side door popped open, and Wesley stepped out. Oh great, what was he doing here? Had he brought Miss Merry Sing Along with him to torment me some more?

The giant man picked up one of the dogs and allowed it to lick his face. His hand nearly covered the tiny creature. His build was that of a professional wrestler. He had to be well over six feet tall. I'm five-eleven, and I had clear view of the underside of his chin.

I could feel my blood pressure rising as Wesley crossed the street. I set my jaw and ground my teeth.

"Wesley, how nice to see you," Mom chimed with a glance in my direction.

"What are you doing here?" I crossed my arms.

"You look nice, Ruby." His eyes traveled from my feet to my face.

His expression of appreciation made me want to melt. But I hadn't dressed up for him. "What are you doing here?" I tilted my head and took a step toward him.

"This might not be a safe situation. Honestly, Ruby, you should leave this to the police."

"I was just checking up on a student I was concerned about, that's all."

"He could be dangerous."

The Jesus tattoo man put his dog on the grass. "Look, I'll leave you two lovebirds to sort this out. I got to get up early for work tomorrow."

"We're not lovebirds," I snapped. Dale's landlord raised a bushy eyebrow at me. I spoke more softly. "Could I have a look around the apartment?"

Wesley stepped between me and Dale's landlord. "I think the police can take care of that."

I sashayed to the side to restore my full view of the landlord. "It's not a crime scene." I glared pointedly at Wesley. "I can look if I want to." I clenched my teeth tight to keep from yelling.

"Actually, you can't. I have to do an eviction notice. It's a violation of his privacy to let people root through his stuff until I can prove he isn't coming back for it. I think he was here today."

Wesley made a huffy noise. "See, Ruby. Law enforcement does need to be involved."

My hand curled into a fist.

"How are things on the police force, Wesley?" Mom stood close to me, grabbed my hand, and smoothed my fingers. "You'll have to come over for cake and coffee some Sunday after church." Mom was utilizing her hostess voice to defuse the tension in the air. It almost worked. "You're going to a different church now, aren't you?"

The dogs continued to yip around the landlord's legs. He crossed his arms and watched the verbal volley between Wesley and me.

"I don't want him over, Mother." I stepped away from the group. "And I sure don't need him to baby-sit me."

Wesley walked toward me. He pointed at his chest with his hand as he spoke. "I drove all the way across town because I was concerned about you, and this is the thank-you I get?" He reached out for my arm.

I pulled away before he had a chance to touch me. "You haven't earned the right to be concerned about me."

He backed up and put an arm around Mom. "I see you are dragging your mother into potentially dangerous situations."

Mom rubbed her fingers up and down her pearls. "Thanks for your concern, Wesley, but it really wasn't—"

I stomped back over to them. "There is nothing dangerous about this situation." I touched Mom above the elbow and pulled her toward me. "Dale isn't even home."

"You didn't know that when you approached the premises."

"Approached the premises? Don't use copspeak on me. What is your reason for being here anyway? This isn't about police business, and you know it."

Wesley threw up his arms and shook his head. "I can't believe you. I came over here because I was concerned for your safety." He combed his fingers through his short, wheat-blond hair.

"I don't need you to be concerned. Please go home." *Go home to Miss Vanessa Perfect Pants and your party. Go home, away from me.* I was finding it hard to maintain my mask of indignation and anger. A hint of hurt had crept into my voice.

One of the dogs stopped pummeling itself against the landlord's legs. Leaning on its back legs and tilting its head up, it barked at Wesley. Dogs are a pretty good judge of character.

Wesley's mouth fell open. He shook his head for several seconds. "Fine, that's what I'll do." He stepped away from the barking dog that was now lunging at him.

Wesley looked quite handsome as he stalked across the street with a scowl on his face. He yanked open the door of his Jeep, climbed in, and slammed the door shut. A moment later, the Jeep roared to life, and he sped off.

"He likes you," Mom and the landlord said in unison.

"He does not." My heart pounded in my chest, and every muscle in my body was contracted and tense. I scowled at my mother. "He likes being mean to me." Boy, did I sound like a whiny baby.

Both my mother and the landlord shook their heads. Mom spoke up, "Why else would a man drive across town at night?"

The Jesus tattoo man continued to shake his head at me. "Anger and affection. Love and hate. Everyone thinks they are at opposite ends of the spectrum. Fact is, one often disguises itself as the other. The line between them is thin."

"What are you, a philosopher?" Now he was getting on my

nerves. Everybody was on my nerves. *Curse these emotions.* I wanted to scream.

"An architect, actually."

"I don't know why he came over here." I paced back and forth on the sidewalk. "If he likes me, why doesn't he just say so?" *And if he likes me, what is he doing going out with Vanessa?*

"Sorry Dale wasn't here. If he doesn't come back in a couple of weeks, I'll put the paperwork through and see if the sheriff minds giving you a look around."

We said good night and walked back to the Caddy. Once she was settled in her seat, Mom took out her cross-stitch and head light as I drove through the dark residential streets.

"Wesley doesn't like me, you know."

"If you say so, Ruby." In my peripheral vision, I could see Mom pulling a long red thread through her cross-stitch.

"So don't go having that jerk over for cake and coffee."

"Fine with me." She almost sang the words.

"You know how I know he doesn't like me?"

"Do tell." Her mouth curled up as she jabbed her needle into the cross-stitch. Did she find me amusing? She was the one with a lightbulb on her head.

"He's seeing someone else. Vanessa, the one who sings at church."

"I know her. She's a nice girl."

"What are you saying?"

"I'm saying she's a nice Christian girl."

"Are you saying I'm not a nice Christian girl?" Taking one hand off the wheel, I patted my chest.

"I didn't say that, Ruby. You're a different kind of nice."

"What kind of nice am I?"

"The kind of nice that, according to you, Wesley Burgess doesn't like."

"That's right." I turned onto our street. The wheels of the Caddy rolled smoothly over the asphalt. "Maybe you could have Wesley over for just a small piece of cake and teeny tiny cup of coffee."

"If that's what you want."

"No, I changed my mind. No cake. No coffee. I'm not going to play 'steal the boyfriend' games with Vanessa. That would be mean and—unchristian."

"All right then. No cake. No coffee."

"God must have somebody in mind for me, don't ya think?"

"I don't presume to know the heart of God. I want that for you. I want you to meet someone."

"How about that biker architect guy? He had a Jesus tattoo. He was kinda cute."

"Are you trying to convince yourself you were attracted to him?"

I pressed the brake hard enough to make Mom's head jerk forward and back. The Caddy hummed in the middle of the street. I hit the steering wheel with my fist. "Ma, obedience is hard. Waiting for God to bring someone into my life tries my patience."

She reached over and patted my leg with one hand while rubbing her neck with the other. "I know. Believe me, I know."

"Sorry, I didn't mean to hurt you."

She continued to massage her neck. "Don't worry about it."

I shifted the car back into gear and drove the block and a half to our house. I turned into the driveway and killed the motor. We trudged up the stairs toward the house. I stopped on the walkway and stared into the living room. "Did you leave that light on in there?"

"I don't remember." She adjusted her purse strap on her shoulder.

Because of Dale rifling through my office, I was seeing intruders everywhere. After ascending the stairs, I opened the living-room door and stepped inside. I surveyed the couch, recliner, and the display cabinet full of Mom's garage-sale china and dolls. Even the magazines on the coffee table were in order.

Mom came up behind me. "I probably did leave the light on." She set her purse on the couch.

"You're right. I'm just a little jumpy because of everything that's happened lately."

A thud sounded above us, and my heart froze. I would have dismissed it as my wild imagination except that Mom looked up at the ceiling as well. Her cool hand touched my arm. A scraping noise, something being dragged across the floor, followed the thud.

"Maybe we should call the police," she whispered.

"What, and have Wesley come to our rescue? I can take care of this myself." I stalked into the kitchen to choose from our pathetic selection of knives.

"Don't let your pride get us killed." Mom's words pelted my back.

Another thud like something being dropped on the attic floor shook the room. Not exactly a quiet thief. Did we even have anything in the attic worth stealing?

The knives made a clattering noise as I spread them out on the counter. "We really ought to think about investing in a gun." Where was that knife I had used before?

"I don't like those things in the house." Her hand touched my shoulder. "Let's just call the police."

I held up a paring knife. Great, if our intruder was a mouse, I'd be able to take him on.

The noise continued above us. "Oh, all right, call the police, but say that we don't want Officer Burgess coming because he's such a tease."

My mom laughed—a sort of sputtering half giggle. Here we were, being besieged by thieves bent on stealing all the broken furniture and old clothes out of our attic, and she was laughing.

I laughed too, partly out of nervousness and partly out of how stupid I was being. "I'll call." He wasn't likely to be on duty anyway. He didn't have a uniform on when we were at Dale's place.

On the way to the phone, I saw the jacket. An old, navy, cotton windbreaker slung over a kitchen chair. "Mom." I pointed at the jacket and swallowed hard. Mom's jaw went slack, and her shoulders slumped forward. She swayed, then rested a hand against the refrigerator.

Jimmy had been wearing that coat when he'd shown up a week ago.

"I'm going up to talk to him first." *Darn him anyway.* Mom had been well on the road to recovery. And now he had to come back and mess everything up again.

"Let me go with you." She took a step toward me—eyes pleading.

"You stay here." I scooted a chair across the floor toward the fridge. I watched her sink into it with that look of dazed unbelief on her face. "I want to talk to him alone first. Then I'll bring him down."

She gathered the greasy coat into her hands and touched her cheek to it as I turned the corner in the hallway and headed toward the ladder that led to the attic.

Chapter Nine

The ladder was folded down. The scraping and banging above me continued. I placed my foot on the bottom rung. As I climbed, I prayed God would give me the self-control not to rip my little brother to pieces, 'cause that was what I felt like doing.

I popped my head through the narrow opening and glanced around. An old lamp had been plugged in and placed in the middle of the floor. Off in a corner where the roof slanted into a four-foot-high wall, Jimmy sat cross-legged, surrounded by stacks of paper, notebooks, and stuffed animals. He'd positioned another lamp, a kid's lamp with a Noah's ark scene for a base, closer to where he was working.

Outside the circles of light created by the lamps, the attic brimmed with boxes and old furniture. Two generations of women had stored stuff up here that was too beaten up to use downstairs and too filled with memories to throw away. The house had been Grandma's before Mom inherited it. Even though we had moved around a lot when we were kids, Grandma's house had always been home base. Mom brought me and Jimmy here for a month every summer so Dad could have more time to embezzle.

The only other possible source of light was a twelve-inch-square window cut into the slant of the roof. At this hour, the window was a black shroud.

Jimmy glanced at me, grinning. "Hey, Ruby."

Hey, Ruby? The guy disappears for almost a week, and all he has to say is, "Hey, Ruby?" He continued to smile at me. Jimmy suffered from big-teeth syndrome even more than I did. His lips were pulled back from his gums—a Cheshire cat effect. Maybe I'd get lucky and he'd just fade into the woodwork so I wouldn't have to deal with this whole mess. Honestly, I was pretty sure I loved my little brother—it was just that life was a lot easier before he showed up.

I hadn't been up in the attic in months, but I remembered it as being fairly tidy. Mom was one of those organize-and-label-everything kinds of people—a box for everything and everything in its box.

The mess in the room suggested Jimmy had been dumping out boxes, filing through the contents, and not picking up after himself. Junk littered the wood floor: children's toys, clothes, books, and piles of paper. The scene suggested a sort of frantic level of activity—as if he were looking for one specific thing.

Jimmy held decorated poster board in front of him, smoothing his palm over it. "Look. It's the collage I made in sixth grade. I can't believe Mom saved all this stuff."

What was up with this Mr. Casual act? "Where have you been?" I had stopped halfway up the ladder, with my waist even with the floor. I pulled myself up the rest of the ladder and crawled across the floor. I could only straighten up if I stood where the sides of the roof came together.

The smile faded from his face. "What are you doing all dressed up?"

"Where have you been?" I stomped toward him, hands on my hips.

He pulled a stack of paper toward himself and flipped through it. "I had some business I had to take care of." He bent his head and looked up at me.

"Business? We thought you were gone forever." I took a step toward him. "Would it have killed you to leave a note?"

Jimmy picked up a stuffed bear and held it to his cheek. "Look, it's Mr. Wipples." The bear was light blue with a bandanna around his neck, both eyes were missing, and he had a tear in his right arm. "Remember him?"

Any doubt I had about Jimmy not being my brother vaporized. Nobody but my real brother would know that bear was named Mr. Wipples.

I had wanted him to be an imposter. That would have been easier to deal with.

Irritation twisted my stomach tighter than I cared to admit. "Jimmy, you could have called. You could have left a note. Where did you go?" This guy was just not tracking with me. Whatever angry signal I threw out at him, he turned into a trip down memory lane.

"Sorry." His tone suggested offense at my being so confrontational.

"You had Mom worried to death." I crouched as I moved toward the corner where he'd set up shop. "You can't dart in and out of her life like that." I got down on my knees and looked right at him. "It's cruel."

He held up a ratty notebook. "Look, seventh-grade history notes."

I grabbed the notebook out of his hand and tossed it. "Jimmy!"

"I said I was sorry." He glanced around at the piles of stuff he'd dumped out. "I feel like a big chunk of my life is missing. I'm trying to get it back."

I felt half sorry for him. A piece of our childhood was missing—a big piece. I grabbed a doll's lacy dress and poked at the buttons on the bodice. "You need to at least tell Mom you're sorry."

He picked up the notebook and flipped through it. "Cool, the Battle of the Little Big Horn, and here's some Arizona history notes. Did you have Mr. Gregson for history?"

"Jimmy!"

He dropped the notebook. Perching on his knees, he shoved his hands in his pockets. "I was hoping to find some of Dad's stuff up here."

"Get downstairs and apologize." I bored holes through him with my eyes.

"I can't find any of his stuff."

No matter how emotional I got, no matter how many dirty looks and glares I gave him, he didn't pick up on it, didn't react to the emotion.

Jimmy crawled away from me toward another box. "She didn't burn it all, did she?" After ripping the tape off the box, he dumped its contents on the floor. The label on the box said "Court."

My insides felt like they were being stirred with a hot metal rod. I didn't like his evasiveness. And I sure didn't like the way he was accusing Mom of burning Dad's stuff. "We're lucky Mom managed to save the things she did." Dad had been the instigator of the crime that had destroyed our lives. I didn't care if I found a single tie or paperweight that had belonged to him.

Jimmy dumped the contents of a manila envelope on the floor. "It's the legal paperwork from the trial—receipts and stuff." He fingered each bit of paper, skimming the documents and holding the smaller pieces of paper momentarily before setting them aside. Something about his action was poignant—almost desperate. This was the only piece of "Daddy" he had.

"What are you hoping to find?" I didn't need to read the

transcript to know what it said. Mom and Dad had severed their trials. Mom had pleaded guilty, but Dad had defended his actions until the jury came back with the guilty verdict. He'd gone to prison justifying what he had done.

I could see him as they dragged him out of court; he ranted something about evil corporate giants and getting justice for the working man. Funny, he hadn't given any of the money back to the working man. We hadn't lived extravagantly, either. He kept most of the money in different bank accounts. I think for my father it wasn't about the money. It was about the thrill of seeing if he could get away with it; he was an adrenaline junkie, whose need to up the ante for risk-taking pushed him toward illegal actions.

Jimmy combed his hands through his brassy red hair. "Did you see him after he went to prison?"

"No." I had had no desire to see my mother or father after the trial. After I turned eighteen and was no longer eligible for foster care, I entered a new form of institutionalization—the university system. I'd lived from one relationship to the next and managed to hold it together enough to complete my master's degree.

"I went to visit him." Jimmy picked up a baseball glove and slipped his hand into it. "He was like half a man—like a ghost." He punched the center of the glove—hard. "Dad was an accounting genius. He had to die in prison like some kind of flunky."

Jimmy was failing to see the main part of this story—that our father had used his smarts to embezzle millions of dollars. I touched his ungloved hand. "He did it to himself, Jimmy."

"He deserved better. I think he was set up."

Jimmy had had fifteen years to manufacture some kind of fantasy that still allowed him to see Dad as his hero. Jimmy had been the much-treasured son, and I was just "the girl" to Dad. Maybe that's why he seemed to have some kind of blind spot where Dad's criminal record was concerned. I didn't want to argue with him—not now. "Why don't you come downstairs and talk to Mom? I'll help you look through this stuff some other time." I tugged on his shirt. "Come on; she's waiting for you."

Mom didn't have all kinds of hugs and cookies for Jimmy this time when he came downstairs.

⌒

Late October slipped into November. As the days ticked by, a cordial coldness settled into the house. Mom cooked for Jimmy, did his laundry, and changed his sheets, but I caught her giving him more than one sidelong glance.

I kept my office door at the university locked even if I just stepped out for a few minutes. None of Dale's former landlords knew where he was. He hadn't come to work at his library job. I'd given up on finding him. Maybe he had just quit school. I couldn't track down his mother or any other relatives. As far as finding Dale was concerned, the trail had run cold. The only way I could heat it up again would be to get into his apartment. I went about my routine of grading papers and giving lectures. Still, Aldridge's death tugged at my conscience.

To get my mind off that, I thought about Wesley a lot. Who was I kidding? I did still like him. But I didn't like the way he played games. I deserved better than to be some kind of girl-on-the-side when Vanessa wasn't taking up his time.

Late one Thursday afternoon, I sat in my office and stared at the colossal desk while my mind twisted into tangled webs. I still hadn't found the key ring Greta had given me.

Dale Cutler had wanted something in this office. What was the connection between him and Aldridge? Dale had signed up to take the class I was teaching back when Aldridge had been scheduled to teach it, and he had completed another class taught by Aldridge the year before—the scriptwriting class co-taught with the female film prof. Dale and Aldridge had known each other a little less than a year.

The last time I'd seen Dale that Friday, he'd said something strange: that he couldn't take classes in this building.

I needed to get another look at Aldridge's home office, and I needed to look at Dale's apartment. I doubted that Greta wanted to talk to me, but it was worth a try. I phoned her number and got lucky; Eliot answered.

After I explained the reason for my call, Eliot gushed apologetically, "I'm real sorry about the way Mom acted at the museum that night. She's dealing with a lot."

"I really would like to have another look around your father's place."

"Sure, if it will help prove Dad didn't kill himself. Mom hasn't gone through any more of his things. Why don't I meet you there with a key? What time works for you?"

I did a half twirl in my chair. "How about in two hours?" I hung up and did two full circles in my chair; not quite a ride at Disneyland, but fun.

I finished my paperwork in my office and tromped downstairs where I gave an Oscar-worthy lecture about logical fallacies and compiling bibliographies. Only four or five students fell asleep. There had been a time in my life when I thought I wanted to teach at a college. What was I trying to prove to myself by coming back to the U? I really didn't think it was about the money. Mom and I were doing okay with me working at the feed store. And it certainly hadn't been to prove that my faith had made me strong enough to deal with this kind of work.

After my performance in the classroom, I drove out to Aldridge's house.

Eliot was sitting on the front steps when I pulled up. He wore sweats, a baseball shirt, and a winter coat. He stood up when he saw me. For an athlete, he wasn't an overly muscular guy. His lanky frame made him more suited for basketball than baseball.

I strode up the sidewalk. He dropped the key into my outstretched hand.

"Make sure you lock up when you're done. Mom is convinced somebody is trying to break in. I don't know why. There's nothing to steal. She's already sold off all the valuable stuff." Resentment crept into his voice.

"Maybe somebody is looking for something," I thought out loud. *Maybe Dale Cutler.*

"I might come by later and pack some of his stuff up." He crossed his arms over his chest. "Mom is having a mental block when it comes to finishing that room." He turned toward the locked door of the house. "Too much of Dad in it."

I nodded. "I'll drop the key by when I'm done."

"No hurry. We got others. That one is for the back door." He stepped down three steps to the sidewalk. "I got to get over to the gym. See ya."

I turned the key in my fingers while Eliot's car started up. He waved as he drove by. *Nice kid.*

I made my way through the side yard. In the backyard, Greta had hauled away the barbecue, but everything else looked the same. The ancient gray tree had only a few dry leaves clinging to it. Though the day was windless, November cold saturated the air, warning that winter was on the way.

No little old lady was raking leaves in her backyard, but just in case some invisible busybody was watching the house, I made a big show of waving the key in the air before I stuck it in the lock. The last thing I needed was Wesley showing up to accuse me of breaking the law again.

The lawn was overgrown with browning grass. A wooden flowerbed featured some dried curled things and weeds still green with life. It was four-thirty and already getting dark. The sky acted like a veil—diminishing the light without completely blocking it out.

I twisted the doorknob and stepped inside. Leaving the door unlocked, I walked down the hallway. No matter how softly I went, my footsteps echoed through the empty house.

Before returning to Aldridge's office, I poked my head in the other rooms. Folded blankets and taped boxes occupied the bedroom—along with one lonely chair positioned by the empty closet. A few dishes were stacked neatly on the kitchen counters. I could see the empty fireplace in the living room. It had been cleaned out. Why had Aldridge built a fire that warm September day, the day he died? Was he burning something? Or had somebody else built the fire to burn something?

My eyes wandered up to the kitchen ceiling where an immobile fan hung. The papers had omitted the gory details of the hanging, but my guess was that the murder weapon hovered above me.

What had Wesley said? The only way to hang someone and make it look like suicide was to have them be unconscious or close to it. I wondered if there had been any trauma to Aldridge's head or evidence of him having ingested something that would knock him out. I wanted to know what the state lab had in their tox report, but I didn't want to have to ask Wesley.

Someone else at the police station would know, maybe Officer Cree. But that would involve the risk of running into Wesley, and I was trying to avoid him at all costs. Besides, I doubted they would release that kind of information to me.

My footsteps seemed to thunder across the floor as I stepped into the living room. Empty bookshelves were everywhere. All the windows were closed, and the air was still, like in a tomb. I stomped loudly across the floor—just for the company the noise provided. Just so I wouldn't feel so alone.

I ran my hands across the smooth wood of a bookshelf. I couldn't even feel dust. No paper clips, coins, or bookmarks had been left behind. No evidence that Theodore Aldridge had ever lived here, had ever thought the ideas inspired by the books on his shelf, had ever walked across this floor.

The ceiling fan loomed behind me—motionless. I retrieved the chair from the bedroom and positioned it beneath the fan. The chair, an antique wooden job with a torn leather seat cover, creaked when I put my cowboy boot on it.

I am five-foot eleven, which means that I never got asked to dance much in high school and that my nose was about three inches from the fan when I stood up straight. Of course, I didn't find a telltale scrap of rope. That would have been too much to ask for. The blades of the fan were plastic, made to look like redwood, and there was a nick on either side of one of them. The fan wobbled back and forth when I pulled on the blades. The screws that fastened it to the ceiling were loose. Evidence that a weight had been hung from it? Maybe.

I grabbed the key off the counter where I had tossed it and retreated back to the room that held the only evidence that Theodore Aldridge had lived in this house. I shoved the key in my pocket and checked the file cabinet. The gun was still there.

I didn't really know what I was looking for. Maybe the key I needed hadn't been on that lost key ring. It would be nice if I could find a frantically scrawled note that said "So-and-So killed me." Then I could call Wesley, and he could go arrest So-and-So. Wesley. Wesley. He sure popped into my head a lot. *Get over him, girlfriend. Get over it.*

I sat behind Aldridge's desk and knocked on the metal with my fist. I opened the desk drawer. Yep, there was a stapler and a pocket-sized book about rare book values. I swung around to the bookshelf and pulled the other book out about rare book values. I suppose if Aldridge had helped Cameron with the collection at the U, it made sense he would have reference books on the subject.

I turned my attention back to the desk. Underneath the paper clips and pencils rested an unframed photograph of Eliot in a base-ball uniform, kneeling in the grass. Eliot positioned his baseball cap on his knee and smiled at the camera. The photo was at least a couple of years old. Another picture showed Benjamin sitting on a couch, holding a book. Benjamin had an infectious smile that made me smile even though I was only looking at paper and chemistry.

The last photo was of Aldridge and Cameron and an older man

sitting outside on metal lawn furniture. The day was sunny with mountains towering in the background. The corner of the photo showed a sign that read Mountaintop Retirement Center. The back of the photo had neatly printed words, "Me with Xavier and Cameron."

My head shot up. Footsteps boomed down the hall. My heart froze. I had left the back door open. I let go of the photos. They drifted to the floor.

My first thought was that Wesley was coming back to arrest me again. Had the old lady with the rake been lurking in the shadows? *Not going to get me this time, Wesley. I came in through the door with a key—so there.*

The footsteps continued—evenly spaced, confident without being loud, clearly audible. Not the sound of a cop trying to be quiet to surprise an intruder.

I came out from behind the desk and darted toward the door. "Eliot. Eliot, is that you?"

The footsteps stopped.

I stepped out into the hallway. Sweat filled my cowboy boots. I could feel my heart ka-thudding when I put my palm on my chest. I swallowed hard. "Eliot?" I whispered. *Please, please, God, let it be Eliot.* I took a feeble step. *Bend knee. Lift leg. Plant foot.* I took another step. *Bend knee. Lift leg. Plant foot.*

The footsteps retreated. The back door opened and slammed shut. The screen door was still vibrating on the frame when I got there. I pushed the door open and raced down four concrete stairs. I glanced at the tree and out into the alley. Nobody was there.

I heard a car engine rev up on the other side of the house. I ran out front just in time to see a newer model blue Volkswagen screech around the corner and disappear. This had to be the lurker Greta had seen. My guess was it was Dale Cutler.

I ran to my Valiant. In a single motion, I opened the driver's side door, slammed into the seat, and turned the key. My Valiant is hardly a good chase vehicle. If a superbly handling car corners on a dime, I would say the Valiant corners on a large serving platter.

I pressed the accelerator with the enthusiasm of a child jumping on a water balloon. The car lurched forward. I turned the corner so sharply, my behind came off the seat. My leg muscles tensed.

Aldridge's house was only a few blocks from downtown. Five blocks ahead of me, the blue Volkswagen was the only car waiting at a red light.

If the guy was bothering to obey traffic laws, he probably wasn't thinking I would follow him. I sped up. The light turned green. The Volkswagen turned the corner onto Main Street and headed toward the edge of town. Traffic was light. All the downtown businesses were closed at this hour.

The sky had turned from gray to charcoal. I clicked on my headlights and turned the corner. A few cars coming in the opposite direction whizzed by. The Volkswagen had a clear shot to the edge of town and the highway.

I got within twenty feet of him. His red taillights glared at me. He sped up. I pressed harder on the gas pedal. The Valiant tops out at sixty-five. Old hotels, a theater, and countless art galleries whipped past my peripheral vision. I stayed within a hundred feet of him. The buildings thinned out. We passed a gas station and then a park.

I glanced in the rearview mirror and saw the flashing red-and-blue light. A rock dropped into my stomach. The needle on the speedometer inched past fifty. I was still in town, going fifty in a twenty-five-mile-an-hour zone. They'd probably take my birthday away for that kind of infraction. I had one flirtatious moment when I considered gunning it and chasing the Volkswagen. I did want to see who was in that car. But then that still, small voice spoke up. I had broken the law. I needed to live with the consequences and not make it worse.

I let up on the accelerator and pulled over on the street by the park.

Cars slowed down. People glared at me from their vehicles. I sank deeper into my seat. A minute ago, this street had looked abandoned. Now, the gawkers and the stare-at-you people were out in full force.

I glanced in the side-view mirror. All I could see was the upper half of a blue, almost black, uniform. A belt with all kinds of dangerous looking doodads attached to it hung around a trim waist. I did recognize a gun and flashlight.

"Driver's license and registration please, ma'am."

I knew that voice.

I closed my eyes and prayed one of those irrational prayers. I know they are pointless, but I think they must kind of amuse God. *Please, God, please vaporize me right now. Turn me into little specks of dust that just float away so I don't have to live through the humiliation of this moment.*

Of all the cops in this town, why did it have to be him?

Chapter Ten

The vinyl steering-wheel cover rubbed against my palms. I gripped it, adjusting and readjusting my sweaty hands. "You don't have to call me 'ma'am.' You know who I am."

All I could see through the window was his midsection, which consisted of an over-accessorized police belt. The belt turned forty-five degrees from me. He was probably looking at the gathering crowd of gawkers.

One woman on the sidewalk twenty feet in front of me had actually stopped walking to stare. She crossed her arms and drew her lips into a disapproving pucker. The gray bun on top of her head was pulled so tight her eyebrows were almost in the middle of her forehead. Her expression was such that I suspected she dipped her face in lemon juice every morning before she stepped outside to pursue her chosen occupation: finding things to disapprove of.

She continued to glare at me. Any minute now she was going to pull a pair of binoculars out of her gargantuan purse so she could get a closer look at my most embarrassing moment ever.

"Come on, Ruby. I'm on duty here," Wesley whispered. Then in a louder voice he said, "Driver's license and registration please, ma'am."

My hand trembled as I opened the glove compartment and pulled out the necessary paperwork to continue my journey down humiliation road. "I'm not making excuses, but I was chasing the guy who's been hanging around Theodore Aldridge's house. I think it was Dale Cutler, the kid I told you about." I swallowed hard and pretended I didn't feel my throat constricting.

Our fingers touched briefly as I handed him the papers. An electric charge traveled up my arm, fluttered around my neck, and warmed my cheeks. The whole thing was purely physiological. I couldn't help it if I still felt a physical attraction for him. You would think the fact that I was enduring the ultimate humiliation—being caught breaking the law by someone I cared for—would have doused some of those chemical biological responses. But no.

"Are you aware you were going fifty in a zone that is designated for twenty-five miles an hour, ma'am?"

"I know how fast I was going." I pounded the steering wheel with my palm. "Just write the ticket."

"I need your license too, ma'am."

I dug through my purse and handed it to him, being careful that our fingers didn't touch.

The dipped-in-lemon-juice woman strolled past my car. To say her eyes were glued on me would be an understatement. The shirt she wore had a gaudy print pattern that looked like a map to a vomit patch. Her disapproval bored into me—increasing the shame I felt. If it had only been a different police officer, this would have been easier to endure. *What are you trying to teach me with this, God?*

"I know I broke the law, Wesley. So write me a ticket." Now I pretended that bulb of liquid clinging to my lower lid was just my eyes watering. "Would you do one thing for me? Would you quit calling me 'ma'am'?" I wiped the tear away. No way was I going to let him see me cry. I sure wasn't going to use tears to try and get out of the ticket. I had broken the law, and I would live with the consequences.

"I'm sorry, Ruby." His pen scratched and whirled across his pad. I knew what these tears were about. It wasn't an attempt at manipulation. I wouldn't sink that low. The tears were about what I didn't have and all that I had lost. Vanessa had Wesley. His writing the ticket was a nail in the coffin of hope that there would ever be anything between us.

As he handed me the ticket, I could feel another tear forming. Why did God even put up with me? What a flunky I was. I couldn't articulate my faith to people, and I broke the law. I brushed another tear away.

"Honestly, Ruby, it's almost like you are trying to get in trouble so I'll have to show up."

The tone of amusement in his voice made me do a one-eighty. I gritted my teeth. *How insensitive . . . and arrogant. Yeah, right.* So his view of my actions was that I was deliberately getting myself tied to the train track so he could come rescue me?

I stuck my head out the window so I could see his face. "You're the one who showed up uninvited at Dale Cutler's old apartment." Funny how all the hurt I carried could become anger so easily. That Jesus tattoo guy was right. The line between love and hate was thin.

"You're the one who called me to your home on a false intruder call. Then you break into a house—"

"I didn't break in—"

"And now you're speeding. All in the part of town I patrol. How did you find out when I went on shift?"

"I didn't. How dare you accuse me of game playing—"

"Jeepers, Ruby, if you want to talk to me, why don't you just say so?"

I pushed the door open hard and fast so he had to step back. "You think *I'm* trying to manipulate ways to be with *you?* What was that call concerning Aldridge's bank account about? After you babbled away about official police business and me staying out of it. And then you go and call me—"

He was doing his give-nothing-away cop face, but I saw his cheek twitch. I had him.

The dipped-in-lemon-juice lady had actually stopped on the sidewalk. Her purse rested on her forearm, and her hands were neatly laced together over her stomach. She watched the interchange between Wesley and me with an open mouth.

I put my hand on my hip and raised my voice. "It's not television, lady."

The woman's eyes grew round, and she made a sort of huffy sound before strutting down the sidewalk, chin in the air.

"Ruby," Wesley scolded.

"She was staring." I pressed my back against the Valiant. "If I wanted your attention, I wouldn't have to get myself arrested. I don't play games with men anymore, okay? That died with the old me." My throat tightened again. "I really resent you accusing me of something like that." I took in a deep breath and squared my shoulders. No matter what, he was not going to see me cry. "Just because you still play games, doesn't mean I do."

He stood, feet shoulder-width apart, clasping his hands behind him. His expression continued to be neutral, but the precise line of his shoulders drooped slightly. He delivered his sentence in a monotone. "What do you mean, I play games?"

"I mean that you are making phone calls to me while you are with Vanessa. What am I to you, Wesley? Your backup in case things don't work out with her? Were you going to just string me along and tease me with your attention? Just in case? I won't be the girl on the side, and I sure don't want to be anybody's second choice. Those are old games that should have died with the old you. You're a child of God now. Act like it."

His jaw went slack, his lips parted, and even in the dim light of evening, I saw a veil descend over his eyes. "I can't talk about this right now. I'm on duty. I have to finish my patrol." He turned away slightly, then pivoted to face me. "I'm off in twenty minutes."

I crossed my arms. "I'll wait here for you."

He tapped the ticket I held in my hand. "You'll have to pay a fine."

"I know. I'll pay it."

He ambled back to his patrol car and opened the door. I turned and rested my arm on the roof of my Valiant. He looked everywhere but at me. He revved up the motor, craned his neck instead of using his rearview mirror, and zoomed past me. Noise from the car's engine vibrated in my ears as he disappeared over the hill.

I had said some pretty mean things. Was he even going to come back?

In the dimming light of evening, I trudged up the hill of the park toward the playground.

My fingers were sore from clenching and unclenching my hands. Why had I been so self-righteous—playing I'm-a-better-Christian-than-you-are games? My insides felt all stirred up. I needed to pray, to sort things out.

I plunked down into a swing, dug my toes into the ground, and pushed off. Cool air rushed around me. I tilted my head. My brain hit the back of my skull. Nausea stirred my stomach. Swinging was a lot easier when I was eight years old. I don't remember ever getting this dizzy.

Still, I continued. Legs out as I swung up, bent on the way down. I took in deep breaths and arced higher and higher. *Why was I so cruel to Wesley, God? Why can I be nice to everyone except the person I care about the most? What's up with that, huh?*

I swung up and down. *Why are my steps forward such baby ones? I should be a missionary in Africa by now, or at least I should be able to share my faith at work.*

The swing made an eek-eek noise as it arced. I took in another deep breath of air and pumped even harder, faster, harder, faster. The sense of my insides being stirred up disappeared. I jumped out of the swing and screamed, "Wheee!"

Landing hard on my feet, I tottered and fell backward. Relaxing into the wood chips, I stared at the dark sky. A million stars winked back at me. God wasn't keeping a tally sheet on me. He never would. I was doing that to myself. All I needed to do was keep talking to him, and good things would flow from that.

I scrambled to my feet and bolted for the slide, taking the steps two at a time. My muscles were limber, and my head was clearer than it had been in weeks.

The triangular beam from a flashlight emerged from the parking-lot area.

"Ruby, is that you?"

From the top of the slide, I could only make out Wesley's silhouette. How about that? He'd come back. His silky tenor voice carried across the playground. I zoomed down the slide, cool air rushing over me. I sat on the bottom of the slide, calm, cool, and confident, ready to handle whatever Wesley was about to say.

He made a crunching sound as he stepped on the wood chips. He angled the flashlight at my face. "Ruby." Weariness clouded his voice. There was a long pause, a deep sigh, and then he said, "You're breaking the law again."

I squinted and shaded my eyes against the glare. *"What?"* Of all the things I had anticipated him saying to me, that was not one of them.

"I thought you were going to wait down by your car."

"I wanted to swing and slide." *And talk to God.* I rose to my feet and stepped out of the intense light.

"Didn't you see the posted signs? Nobody is supposed to be in the park after dark." He readjusted the flashlight so it was shining in my face again. "I have to roust teenagers out of here all the time."

Again, I stepped away from the beam of light, shading my eyes and squinting. "Aren't you off duty?" A new brand of tension coursed through my veins. Why was he so fixated on pointing out every time I broke the law?

"Even when I'm not on the clock, I have to uphold the law."

"We can leave the park if it will make you happy. But my breaking city laws is not what we were going to talk about."

"I'm just concerned about you—about your spiritual walk."

How dare he turn this thing on me? How dare he. After I had pointed out his misbehavior toward women, he was going to play a game of one-upmanship. "My spiritual walk? *My* spiritual walk? I'm not the one still playing mind games with women. We're not talking about city laws—the laws of men."

A tiny, guttural, "Ah," rose from his throat.

"Just 'cause you go twenty-five in the twenty-five zone doesn't mean your walk with God is okay, Wesley. Does your fixation with the laws of men make you feel safer—make you feel righteous?"

"You . . . you might be right." The flashlight bobbed up and down, and then he turned it toward me again.

I bolted across the few yards that separated us and grabbed his hand at the wrist. "Don't you dare point that thing on me again. I'm going blind."

He tried to pull his hand away, and I gripped it tighter. I stood close enough to smell the perspiration that came from a long shift. He yanked on the flashlight. I held on to his wrist. He yanked harder. The flashlight fell to the ground.

Frustration welled up inside me. Why couldn't we get this thing resolved? My neck muscles knotted and my stomach clenched. All we had to do was stay away from each other.

He twisted his wrist out of my grip, and I hit his chest with the palm of my hand. "You make me nuts."

"You make *me* nuts." He poked his finger in my rib cage.

"You make me nuttier. I am such a rational person when you're not around. Why can't you just leave me alone?"

His hand cupped my shoulder. "Because I care about you." The warmth of his touch radiated through my shoulder, crossed my chest, danced up my neck.

I wrenched away from his grasp and stepped outside the circle of heat his emotion created. "But you're dating Vanessa."

He didn't say anything. He clasped his hands behind his back and tilted his head down.

"I thought so." I pulled each word up from the pit of my stomach.

"I won't be responsible for another Christian woman being hurt." In the past, I would have turned into a puddle of wax with that "I care about you" line. His attempts at seduction made me ill. Honestly, I'd rather be alone than have a relationship I couldn't show to God.

"I do care about you."

What a line. I wanted and expected more from him. Fury raged through every cell and molecule of my body. My toes curled inside my cowboy boots. I clenched my teeth so tight I thought they would shatter. I took two steps back, intending to walk away from him and his silly games.

He stepped toward me, grabbed my arm above the elbow. His face was very close to mine. The rhythm of his breathing, the steady intake and release of his breath, surrounded me. He touched my mouth with his finger.

I wanted him to kiss me. I wanted him to find me desirable. I wanted to be with him. I wanted to wake up next to him and watch him sleep. He held me there with the magnetic pull of his attraction for me. I could not move. I could not choose the right thing, even though my head knew what it was.

His fingers fluttered around my mouth and up to my temple.

I swallowed hard. I wanted all those things—but I wanted it to last.

With a deep sigh, he pulled his hand away. He ran his fingers through his hair and then rested his forehead in his palm. "Everything you say is true. I'm still playing the same old games. I'm still not treating women with respect. It's not just about sex. It's the whole way I look at women—like they are objects to be obtained. Do you have any idea what thoughts were running through my head . . . about you?"

"I can guess." *But only because the same thoughts were running through my head.*

"You're right. I'm playing the old games. I know what the right thing to do is, but I can't do it." He turned his back to me.

A year ago when Wesley and I had hiked into the forest, I had expected that we would have sex, and he had very kindly turned me down. His rejection of me, the biggest compliment any man had ever paid me, was the catalyst that brought me to Christ. He had treated me like a lady. I knew he was capable of doing the right thing. "Old habits die hard, huh?"

"I'm impressed with who you have become." He leaned down and picked up his flashlight. "I do care about you. You deserve better than me."

I sat down on the edge of the slide. I pulled my knees up to my chest and listened to his feet crunch on the wood chips and then pad softly across hard earth and fade into the night.

I shivered and drew my heavy coat tighter around me. The autumn wind cut through me, but that was not what the shiver was about. Here on this playground, God had just given me a whirlwind tour of my life. I saw how delightful talking to God was—*and* how easy it would be to give in to the temptation to sleep with Wesley. As long as a heart beat in my chest, I would never be beyond temptation. The conversation with God had to be constant.

The chill in the air signaled that a storm was coming. We'd warded off winter for some time. But it was early November, and we were past due for snow.

I rested my cheek against my knee. Warm tears welled up and slid down my cheek. I might spend my whole life alone, without the benefit of marriage or children. But that would be better than being separated from God.

I rose to my feet and trudged down the hill to where I had left my car.

$$\backsim$$

After going back to Aldridge's house to lock the door, I drove home. I slipped into my pajamas and crawled beneath my down comforter. I couldn't sleep. Jimmy's snoring in the room next door was unbearably loud. I grabbed my pillow and comforter and retreated to the living room. I could still hear his snoring, but it was a five rather than a full-volume ten. I put the pillow over my head and closed my eyes. I dreamed I was in a room lined with mirrors. A voice out of the darkness asked, "Where are your feet pointed?" I stared down at my bare feet and . . .

Pounding on the door broke through my dreaming. After I dragged the pillow off my head, I blinked. It was still dark outside. What was it with people thinking it was appropriate to wake me from la-la land in the middle of the night?

It couldn't be Jimmy this time. His snoring still wafted down the hallway. I sat up on the couch. The knocking was persistent and continuous.

Chapter Eleven

Still not completely coherent, I trudged across the living-room floor. I placed my hand on the deadbolt, preparing to push it open—then thought better of it. Only weirdos, criminals, and little brothers knock on doors at this hour. I turned on the porch light and peered through one of the four-by-six-inch windows cut in the door to see which category the knocker fell into.

It was a weirdo. Wesley. I was too tired to be angry or sad or anything.

I clicked back the deadbolt, turned the knob, and opened the door. A burst of cold air hit me. "Please make this quick." I rested my cheek against the edge of the door. My eyelids weighed roughly one ton each.

"Everything you said was right."

I opened one eye. Snow fell softly behind him in little blurred lines. The sky was black. He was wearing a short wool coat in a rich shade of blue. His hair was wet, and a thin layer of snow covered his shoulders. Had he walked here?

I opened the other eye. There he was. Six feet of gorgeous standing on my porch at an hour when only cats and bats are awake. In this light, his green eyes were almost gray.

"You were right, Ruby," he repeated.

I had waited all my life for a guy to say that to me, and when one finally did, I was so tired I couldn't process the information. "Right about what?"

"About me playing games. About me trying to catch you

breaking city laws, because . . . well . . . because I am having trouble with God's law."

My head felt like it had been stuffed full of rocks. I couldn't hold it up. Wesley's words were drowned out by the sound of the couch and comforter whispering seductively, *"Ruby, come back to bed. Ruby, come back to bed."*

"It's cold out here. Can I come in? Just to talk?"

"Can't we do this when I'm more awake?" I whined. The furniture was still speaking to me. I stumbled toward the couch. Behind me, I heard the door closing and Wesley's footsteps cross the wooden floor.

"I know it's late. But I've been pacing the floor all night. After I left the park, I went over to Vanessa's."

Oh, her again. I fell onto the couch. Half sitting and half lying down. My eyelids drifted over my eyeballs. I hate being woken up in the middle of a dream—even *that* dream. Something about the dream felt less scary. Where *were* my feet pointed?

"I broke up with her." Wesley's voice boomed above me. "Ruby, I'm pouring my heart out to you, and you're falling asleep. Come on, this is not easy for me."

My eyes snapped open, but a heavy fog still drifted across my brain.

He sat down on the opposite end of the couch. He touched the corner of my comforter. "Why are you sleeping out here?"

I sat up straight, blinking several times. "That's what's in your heart—asking me why I'm sleeping on the couch?"

His back stiffened. "No." He leaned a little closer to me. "Aren't you hearing anything I'm saying? Can't you at least be hospitable?"

"It's two in the morning." I grabbed my pillow, placed it on my stomach, and wrapped my arms around it. "What did you expect, tea and trumpets? I mean crumpets." The fog cleared and something he had said a moment before started to register. He had broken up with Vanessa. Electric charges zinged through my muscles.

"What is it with your sarcasm?" He stood up, boots pounding on the wood floor. His jaw was so stiff, I could see the separate muscles in his neck. "You are an infuriating woman."

Just as I was being drenched by warm fuzzy feelings, he was growing hostile. Why couldn't we get on the same emotional plane at the same time?

"You broke up with Vanessa?" I pushed myself up off the couch.

He ran his fingers through his hair. The rigidity in his shoulders softened. His eyes traveled from my feet to my face. "Nice pajamas."

I was wearing an oversized T-shirt I'd gotten at the second-hand store. It said "I love my—" and then showed a black-and-white picture of a Chihuahua. I'd never gotten within ten feet of a Chihuahua in my life. My pajama bottoms were a pink-and-lime-green striped flannel that Mom had gotten at a discount fabric sale and sewn up. I glanced down at my getup. *Now* who was being sarcastic?

When I looked at Wesley, I detected the glow of genuine affection in his expression.

"You find me amusing, do you?"

He walked over to me. "Among other things." He touched my jaw and neck with the back of his hand.

Oh, baby. I was totally awake, and every atom in my body buzzed with the electricity ricocheting around the room. "You broke up with her to be with me. I bet she wears matching pajamas to bed."

"I don't know. I've never seen them."

"That's good to hear." I shuffled my feet. "Wesley?"

"Yes." He looked at me with googly eyes, all round and twinkly.

"You're not going to *kiss* me, are you?"

"I'd like to." He leaned closer.

I took a step back to escape the force field of his attraction for me. "I don't want you to." I touched my mouth. "My teeth are all fuzzy, and I have morning breath—or middle-of-the-night breath. I want our first kiss to be minty fresh and special."

Wesley grinned. "Okay."

"God is giving me a second chance with this courtship thing, and I want to do it right this time." I was sixteen when I started living from one quasi-relationship to another. Maybe I could start over. What did healthy sixteen-year-olds do?

"I'd like a second chance at a relationship—or third or fourth," Wesley was saying.

"So court me. Try to impress my mother. Take me on a nice date . . . a real date. I expect you to show up at the door with flowers and a big box of chocolates." I was winging this. I got all my ideas about real dates with nice boys and girls from fifties television shows.

"Deal."

I leaned close to him and whispered in his ear. "We play within God's boundaries. No sex until the—" Whoops, he didn't need to know I was hearing the wedding march in my head. "Well, you know, only if—"

"I agree." His hand fluttered over my fingertips. "That won't be easy. We know what we're missing."

I melted in response to his touch. Wax woman was in the house.

I felt jittery and dizzy at the same time, like I'd just stepped off the Tilt-A-Whirl in time to be zapped with an electric cattle prod. Yeah, it wouldn't be easy. But I had endured too many broken relationships trying to make them work with my plan—it was time to try God's.

I thanked God that I was still a woman with normal healthy responses and pulled my hand away from Wesley's. I rested my open palm on my chest. My heart beat a mile a minute, galloping with the intense and persistent rhythm of a pony express horse. "You managed to maintain purity with Vanessa?"

"That's different." He sat back down on the couch.

I crossed my arms and stared down at his gorgeousness. "Different how?"

"I took a class at church with a bunch of other single guys. One of the things we had to do was write down a list of attributes we wanted in a wife. Vanessa fit the profile: pretty, been a Christian all her life, a virgin, sweet and quiet, from a good Christian family, sings in the choir, cooks for me."

"I'm starting to feel real insecure here. Please tell me she had at least one fatal flaw—that she picks her nose or something."

"She's close to perfect." He rose to his feet. "That was the problem. No matter how hard I tried, I couldn't work up an attraction for her. She was safe. It was easy to stay obedient."

"I'm not safe?"

"You're a fall off a cliff at ninety miles an hour."

Forget being compared to red roses, every girl wants to be told she's a car crash. "That's why you stayed with her? 'Cause she was safe?"

"I just kept hoping it would work, hoping there would be a

spark. She was good and decent, but it seemed like she was pursuing a Christian husband more than she was chasing God. She never expressed an opinion. She was always trying to please me, and that got on my nerves."

"Are you saying you like a woman with an opinion?"

"I'm here in this room with you, aren't I?"

"So why did you stay with Vanessa for so long?"

"Before I was a Christian, and even for a little after, the only relationships I'd known were purely sexual. I've acted on every impulse I've ever had—except with you in the woods." From where he sat, he reached up and touched my arm.

"I didn't realize." I was floored. Even a year ago, before I was a Christian, he had viewed me as special, worth waiting for.

He rested his head in his hands. "I didn't know what a Christian romance was supposed to feel like. I thought if I were totally numb—no passion at all—that must be what Christian romance was like."

He took my hand again. "Then I saw you that night coming down the steps of your mom's house, and I remembered—"

"What it feels like to be on fire, melting into a puddle of wax, and intoxicated all at the same time."

He gazed at me for a moment, narrowing his eyes like he was looking at something intriguing under a microscope. "What it feels like to be attracted to someone."

Maybe I'd overdone it with the metaphors.

"You looked pretty that night. Your hair was kind of soft and . . ." He made circular motions around his own head. "Kind of soft and out there."

Soft and out there. I'd have to write that one down. "Don't stop."

He continued. "Then, of course, you opened your mouth."

"Oh, quit," I said, barely putting up a protest. He still held my hand, pressing his thumb into my palm. I closed my eyes. That small touch was debilitating, intoxicating, wonderful. I opened my eyes. "So you're going to take me on a real date, right?"

"Yes." He let go of my hand. "Like we are teenagers and starting all over—only this time doing it right."

"I expect to be treated like a princess."

"Like Cinderella. A sassy Cinderella." He crossed his arms, leaned toward me, and whispered in my ear, "A princess." His whiskery cheek brushed against mine as he stepped back. His green eyes had a layer of clear glaze on them.

The moment was getting way too mushy. "I think I can whip you into shape." I punched his shoulder. An odd feeling I couldn't identify crept into my emotional database. "You should go home now."

"Yes, I should."

"Then you should call me in the next couple of days and ask me out on a date."

"Thanks for giving me a script." He walked toward the door, then turned. "Actually, before that. If you can get a picture of that Dale guy, we can take it over to Aldridge's widow and see if she recognizes him."

"You want me to help with the investigation?"

"Unofficial investigation, but yeah. I'd appreciate your input—your brains."

"Thanks." I felt warm and fuzzy all over. He liked my brains.

He waved good-bye, which was like a totally dorky gesture considering he was four feet from me. But because he was the one doing the waving, it was downright cute.

I watched from the big living-room window as he descended the stairs and strode up the sidewalk. He had walked all the way here from his house. I pictured him, arms crossed to keep out the cold, snow darkening his wheat blond hair . . . and the whole time he was thinking about me, the car-crash woman.

Jimmy's steady and persistent snoring and the low-level hum of the lights in the house served as background noise for the screaming fear that rose up in me. As I watched Wesley cross the street and disappear into the darkness, I knew what this exhilaration mixed with fear was about. My whole life, I had only played at intimacy. Uncommitted sex wasn't intimacy. Living together had allowed me to have the appearance of intimacy. But now God was asking me to get to know someone's heart and soul without the rose-colored glasses of sex. This was uncharted territory, and it scared the holy guacamole out of me.

I lay back down on the couch, pulled my comforter up around my neck. Could I work my life within God's plan? Was that even a remote possibility? I stared at the ceiling until I fell back asleep.

Chapter Twelve

Technically, the apartment is abandoned." The Jesus tattoo man, who'd told me his name was Robert, walked ahead of me down the stairs to Dale's apartment. He'd opted to leave his yippy little dogs upstairs. "I've got to call the sheriff to get this stuff hauled away. Laws these days favor the tenant. Sheriff said it was okay if you have a look. Long as you don't take anything." His "Jesus is Lord" tattoo rippled as he stuck the key into the lock and twisted. The door screeched open. "If we find a photo you can use, we'll have to make a copy of it. If Dale comes back, I don't want to risk him saying I took his stuff."

"You think he is coming back?"

"Kind of doubt it. Haven't seen him since that Friday you came by. He's behind on rent. It's going to take me a month to get the place cleaned out and rented again. The guy cost me a lot of money."

I stepped inside while Robert stood in the doorway. The main living area consisted of a kitchen and living room divided by a counter. An open door off the kitchen led to the bathroom.

"Look around but don't mess stuff up." Robert crossed his arms and leaned against the door frame. "If you find a photo, we can use my scanner upstairs, then put it right back."

Not that there was much to mess up. Dale hadn't taken time to unpack anything but the essentials. Open boxes with clothes heaping out of them rested on the burnt-orange carpet. Several pairs of jeans were thrown on the couch. Sweatshirts cluttered the floor. A shoebox and two coffee mugs rested on the counter.

"There's no bedroom," Robert commented. "The couch pulls out."

I wandered into the living room. Dale hadn't worked at making the place homey. He didn't even have the proverbial beer can collection most college students acquire. "Doesn't look like he was here much."

"I work long hours at the firm." Robert shrugged. "The guy was quiet. I really didn't pay much attention to if he was here or not."

Three unframed photos were pinned to the paneling. The first was a posed picture of an older woman, probably his mother, and a buzz-cut toothless kid, probably a little brother. The second photo was of Dale in chaps and cowboy hat, leaning against a fence. He was a few years younger, maybe a high school freshman. Even at that age, a look of weariness clouded his expression. The last photo was of Dale, Theodore Aldridge, and the female professor from the film department. They sat together in a pizza parlor with people milling around them.

The three grinned for the camera. Aldridge had one arm around the professor woman and the other around Dale. Two beer glasses, one empty and one full, sat on the table in front of him.

I pulled the pin out of the photo. "This is the most recent one. Maybe you can enlarge and crop it so just Dale is in the photo."

As I turned, I noticed the books and papers scattered across the coffee table. I recognized the paper I had given him a C on. On top of it lay the unsigned drop/add form. The corner of the form curled up. He must have dropped it off after I'd seen him that Friday.

I didn't see his long, olive-drab trench coat anywhere. I checked the only closet, which contained a stagnant pile of air and some wire hangers.

I returned to the coffee table. A library book about the values of rare books was set off by itself. I picked up the book. "This is probably overdue." It was the same book Aldridge had on his bookshelf. A typed screenplay titled "The Cowboy's Lament" sat on top of an American Lit book. The screenplay carried Dale's byline and was dated spring semester last year. I picked it up and flipped through it, then looked at the cover again. The instructors were listed as T. Aldridge and L. Philips. I glanced at the photo of the tight little trio. I wondered what L. Philips knew about Dale—or about Aldridge for that matter. "Could you make two copies? One with just Dale and one with all three?"

Robert stepped into the apartment and held out his hand. "No problem."

"Thanks."

⌒

Wesley and I pulled up outside of Greta Aldridge's house at the same time. I'd phoned ahead to let him know I had found the photo. My heart did a little pitter-patter thing as I pushed open the door of my Valiant and saw him. I must say he looked quite dapper in his leather jacket, jeans, and red watchman's cap. He wore buckskin gloves and a red scarf around his neck, Mr. Color Coordinated.

The temperature had dropped dramatically in the last few days. A thin layer of crunchy snow still lay on the ground. Even though we weren't on our official first date, I wanted to look nice—not an easy task considering I had to dress for the cold. I wore big, clunky moon boots, a long, puffy, purple down coat, and a lilac fleece hat. I couldn't find matching gloves, so I had one yellow fleece glove and an orange-and-brown thing Mom had knitted. The gloves kind of threw the whole outfit off, but I figured it was better than matching, ice-blue hands.

I sauntered over to Wesley and pointed toward a log home set back from the road. "That's it there—547 Hillcrest." I hesitated—waiting to see that look of adoration I had seen the night before. I stood with my hands at my side in my ever-so-fashionable wintertime look.

Wesley's glance traveled from my feet to my face. "Nice gloves."

"Hey, my hat and coat match." So much for how the fantasy of this relationship was going to go. Why did he notice the one thing that didn't match? Guess I better deal with reality.

Wesley crooked an elbow out for me.

I laced my arm through his, resting my hand on his forearm. Okay, so he wasn't a total dunce.

Greta's log home sat on a large lot outside of town, surrounded by a circle of young evergreens. Guessing from the distance between Greta's house and those around it, the covenants must allow for a house every two or three acres. The house had an upper story and an attached, two-car garage with forest green garage doors.

Greta's abode was a lot newer and more upscale than Aldridge's house in town. Either Greta made really good money as a counselor, her family had money, or she'd made him pay through the nose in alimony.

Both Wesley and I had parked outside the wooden fence. We walked together up the curving driveway, gravel crunching beneath our feet. I liked being this close to him, the strength he exuded, the pure maleness of him. I snuck a quick glance at his profile just to feel my heart do that leaping, somersaulting thing it did when he looked at me. I loved the way his long dark lashes nearly hid his green eyes when he glanced down at me. His hair was almost blond, but his lashes and eyebrows were dark. The contrast made his features that much more intense.

"You should do most of the talking," I said. Much as I was enjoying being close to him, I untwisted my arm from his when we came within a few feet of the house. "Greta doesn't like me very much."

"Do you think it was such a good idea not to phone ahead?" We took the single step up onto the concrete slab that stood in front of the big wooden door.

"This way, we have the element of surprise on our side." I scraped my boots on the welcome mat.

Wesley pressed the buzzer. We waited. I rocked back and forth, heel to toe, shoved my hands in my pockets, stared up at the sky. The section of sky above us was clear, but to the east a patch of foreboding, charcoal-gray clouds stretched over the city.

"How about tomorrow night for a date?"

I untilted my neck and gazed at the handsome creature in front of me. Now my heart did a full gymnastics routine. My aorta had just climbed onto the pommel horse when I swallowed hard and—sounding totally casual—said, "That sounds good."

"Pick you up at seven, take you to dinner."

"Remember, flowers and chocolate."

He leaned a little closer to me. "I won't forget."

When he was this close—close enough for me to see the gray-and-white flecks of color in his green eyes and smell his soapy cleanness—when he was this close, I wanted to kiss him all over his face. I resisted the temptation. If I wanted to date a gentleman, I needed to act like a lady. "Do you think we need a chaperone?"

Wesley's mouth curled up into a smile. "That's a little over the top."

"Okay, but I'm going to report back to my mom. Do you have someone you can be accountable to?"

"Maybe Officer Cree. He's a Christian. I trained with him before I went to the academy."

The big wooden door opened. Benjamin Aldridge came around the door and stood on the threshold. He looked at our shoes and said, "Hi."

"Hi, Benjamin. Remember me from the museum?" I had a clear view of the swirly growth pattern of his light brown hair.

He barely glanced up at me. "Yeah." He scratched his thin, bare arm, then tugged at the red T-shirt that was two sizes too big for him. A sprig of light brown hair stuck out on top of his head. Another strand to the side curled outward.

"Is your mom home? We need to talk to her."

"Yeah." He continued to stare at our shoes.

"Benjamin, you might want to let her know we are here."

Benjamin looked up at us and then pounded his forehead with a flat hand. "Oh yeah, right. I'll go get her."

Despite the cold, Benjamin neglected to close the door before he went searching for his mother. I didn't think it would constitute nosiness on my part to kind of crane my neck and take a gander at Greta's living room.

You can tell a lot about someone by looking around the place they live in. The big message of her living room was, "No dust or clutter allowed." Magazines were stacked precisely on a glass coffee table. I could see the corner of an off-white couch with puffy pillows trimmed in gold. Behind the sofa stood a china cabinet with smudgeless glass doors.

"Nosy Parker," Wesley teased.

"Not nosy, curious. There is a difference, you know."

"I had no idea." He touched my back. "Probably just with women there's a difference."

Before I had a chance to respond to Wesley's comment, Greta appeared in the doorway. Her smile faded quickly when she saw me. "I have nothing to say to you."

She wore a magenta button-down shirt, probably silk, and gray slacks. Her dark hair, with its contrasting blond streak, was pulled back into a tight ponytail. The narrow fringe of bangs created a precise line high on her forehead.

"Please." I stuck my foot in the door so she wouldn't have a chance to slam it on us without causing me bodily harm. "We just need a moment. I think I know who the guy is who's been lurking around the other house; a former student of your ex-husband's named Dale Cutler."

"We need you to look at a picture." Wesley stood behind me, placing a supportive hand on my shoulder.

From the side of the living room that was not within my frame of vision, I heard Eliot's voice. "Invite them in, Mother."

Greta craned her neck. "I thought you were watching the game."

Eliot came into view. He tucked his hand into the back pocket of his jeans. "Benny told me they were here."

"This woman all but accused me of murdering your father."

"Let them in, Mother. They might be able to find out who killed him."

Greta's jaw was clenched so tight, her chin pointed out. "He killed himself. You know that."

I sighed and rolled my eyes. *Great, I get to watch another episode of "Fun with the Dysfunctionals."*

"Mrs. Aldridge, we just need you to look at a photo," Wesley said.

Greta didn't glance in our direction. "You know full well your father killed himself. I am a trained professional. I saw the signs."

"Dad changed at the end of his life. He was trying to make amends. He found God, Mom. It's against those people's beliefs to kill themselves."

My whole body contracted. Those people? He found God? Holy katzenjammer! Had Theodore Aldridge become a Christian?

Without skipping a beat, Greta waved her arms. "Oh please, it was just a passing fad for him—like when he became a Buddhist until he found out he had to give up booze and women and material things."

"It wasn't a fad, Mom. He had changed. He wanted your forgiveness. If you weren't so filled with bitterness, you would have seen that."

Greta let out a gust of air and crossed her arms. "A man doesn't neglect his family for twenty years and then change in one day. . . ." Her head tilted down; her shoulders drooped. She seemed to be folding in on herself, losing energy.

Eliot towered over his mother by about a foot. "Look at the photo they brought." The vindictiveness had faded from his voice. He touched his mother's shoulder. "Just look at the photo, Mom."

I inched the photograph out of my coat pocket.

Greta snatched the picture from my hand. As she stood staring at the photograph, I noticed that her nails were bitten down to the quick.

"I never got a really close look at him. How tall is this Dale kid?"

I held my hand about an inch below me.

Greta looked at me for the first time. Her face sagged as if her skin were too heavy for her skull to support. The thick layer of foundation she wore didn't completely mask the dark circles under her eyes. "It could be." Greta shook her head. "I don't know. It's hard to tell. This kid looks skinny."

"He is about medium build."

Greta clutched the photo and bit her lower lip. "I only saw the lurker guy once or twice, and I never saw his face. He ran like a man carrying a few extra pounds."

I hadn't seen the lurker at all, only his car. "Dr. Aldridge never mentioned a student named Dale Cutler?" I needed to find out from Dale's landlord what kind of car he drove.

"He turned a lot of his students into friends and drinking buddies." Greta sighed so deeply that her shoulders moved up and down. "I'm tired. I'm real tired." She massaged her forehead. "I need sleep." She wandered out of view without another word.

Eliot glanced in his mother's direction and then back at us. "Sorry, this has been hard for her."

I dug through my purse. "I have that key for you, the one to your father's house. Thanks for letting me borrow it." I placed the key in his hand. "Eliot, did your dad become a Christian?"

Eliot leaned against the door. I saw dark circles under his eyes too. "Two weeks before he died, he apologized to me for missing all my games. I think I always disappointed him, because he was such a super brain and I barely got through high school. But he was trying to make things right."

"Was he going to church?" The news of Aldridge's possible conversion made the picture of his life more blurred, rather than bringing it into focus. If he had become a Christian, no one at the university had known it. Everyone there had characterized him as a brilliant scholar who loved a party.

Eliot shrugged. He stood back from the door and banged his fist against a flat palm, the same motion used to break in a baseball glove. "When I was sixteen, I gave up on my father ever wanting to be part of our lives. It's kind of like he died for me then. When he changed, I became hopeful that . . ."

"Did he know other Christians?" I doubted that Aldridge would have come to such a revelation on his own. But who could have told him about Christ? Far as I knew, there were no other believers in the department, and he didn't seem to have had much of a life outside of work. Maybe there had been a student who wasn't one of his drinking buddies.

Eliot shook his head. "Sorry, I don't know. I just know he took me and Benny out to dinner and told us he wanted to make up for all the years he'd missed. He was different; he was happy, really happy."

"Thanks for your help." Wesley held his hand out to Eliot.

Eliot nodded at me. "I better make sure Benny's not taking appliances apart again. He likes to do that." He closed the door slowly.

Wesley and I stood on the welcome mat. I stared at the swirly patterns carved in the wooden door. "That was more confusing than helpful. If it wasn't Dale I saw outside Aldridge's house, who was it?"

Wesley slipped his hand into mine. "I don't know. Why would Dale disappear if he wasn't up to something?"

"Do you think Theodore Aldridge really became a Christian?"

Wesley let go of my hand. "That's a question only God can answer." He turned to go, pulling me with him by touching my elbow.

"No, there's got to be someone who talked to him about Christ." I tilted my head toward the log cabin. "Do you think she had anything to do with his death?"

"She's definitely stressed out. But I don't think she would—" He kicked a rock with his boot. "State lab found some poison in Aldridge's bloodstream. The amounts are so small they have only been able to determine it's plant based."

"None of this fits, Wesley. He was a Christian, but nobody at the U knew. Greta thinks he was wicked to the core. He had a loaded gun in his house. He was getting cash payments for something over the summer."

"The older boy—Eliot—said that his dad tried to make amends only two weeks before he died. Maybe he'd just become a Christian a little before that."

"We need to find Dale. Even if it wasn't Dale looking for something in the house, I think he could help us. There's one more person who might know where Dale is." I held up the copy of the photo and pointed to the scriptwriting professor.

"Cozy bunch."

"That's what I thought."

I said good-bye to Wesley and headed toward my Valiant. I sat behind the wheel, staring at Greta's elegant log cabin. A shiver ran down my spine when I thought of the last hours of Aldridge's life. He passed out or came close to unconsciousness and then his killer had strung him up to make it look like a suicide.

I turned the key in the Valiant and pressed the reverse button on the push-button shift. The car chugged to life, and I checked my rearview mirror. Had the reason for Aldridge's happiness been the extra money he got over the summer, or had there really been a conversion? Who on earth could have been telling him about Jesus?

⌇

The next day, Friday, dragged on. My one class for the day wasn't until two-thirty and I sure didn't want to spend the morning pacing around my office. So, instead, I paced the floor of my bedroom and watched the clock. Mom was teaching craft classes all day at the senior citizens center, and Jimmy had been keeping himself busy rooting through the attic and sleeping. To his credit, he had gotten a part-time job at the animal lab on campus. He'd given Mom a nice antique pin, a sideways butterfly with pink-and-white crystals. I sensed he was trying to mend old wounds. Mom seemed to be warming up to him.

I sat down and reviewed my lesson plans and upcoming lectures and tried to catch up on my reading. Even with doing all that, it was only one o'clock.

To get my mind off Wesley and our impending date, I decided to cruise up to campus and try to locate Professor L. Philips. She was the one other person who might know something about Dale's whereabouts.

When I entered the building, I saw Donita standing at the end of the hall, unlocking the glass doors of the rare books cabinet. Both Aldridge and Dale had books about rare book values. Maybe Donita knew something about the school's collection that would connect both of them to it.

Behind her, Celeste the Cleaning Woman busied herself vacuuming the carpet. Earphones framed Celeste's round face. She sort of danced as she pushed the vacuum across the floor. Her mouth hung open as she pushed her tongue into her lower lip.

Several kids with backpacks and men in suits filed up and down the hall.

Donita was dressed in a black pinstripe suit with a light blue blouse. Other than the rhinestone frog on her lapel, nothing in her outfit said she was rebelling against conservative professorial dress. She'd even gotten her hair under control and pulled it up into a tidy bun.

"Are you in charge of this now?" I sidled up to her and tapped the glass part of the door.

"It's something to put on a resumé. Cameron agreed to it after much protest. He just bought these, the first ones since Theodore died." She held up two books. "Virginia Woolf's *Between the Acts*, first edition, a hundred and fifty bucks. Sir Arthur Conan Doyle's *The Hound of the Baskervilles*, four hundred dollars."

"That's all they are worth?"

Donita turned around and stared at the forty-odd books arranged in the display cabinet. "I think some of them are worth into the thousands. Cameron won't trust me with the values sheet. I'm only allowed to put the new books on the shelf."

Celeste's vacuum hummed in the background.

I wondered why Donita had dressed up so nice. "How are things going with your guy from AA?"

Donita slammed a book against the back of the display cabinet. "Fine." She pushed another book out of the way. I watched the shadow fall over her expression, like a cloud covering the sun. "Just fine."

"Didn't work out, huh?"

Donita touched her hair at the temple. Her slender fingers brushed over her ear. "I thought once I got sober, once I stopped seeing men through the fog of intoxication, things would be different." She made the comment almost as a joke, but she looked at me momentarily, and I realized what I had seen in her expression weeks ago. I saw the pain behind her eyes.

I took in a deep breath. More than anything, I wanted to tell her that she didn't need to live from one failed relationship to another, where the only choices were to be the one who got hurt or the one who caused pain. My briefcase felt weighty in my hand as I turned over words and possible phrasings. *What could I say to her? "I'm sorry it didn't work out?"*

"The big downfall to us moving in together was that there wasn't much room for my stuff with his wife and kid there."

Despite the heaviness in my heart, I laughed. She had this gift for taking the most tragic moment and seeing the funny side of it. "Maybe moving in together isn't such a great idea."

"Not with that guy," she joked.

"I don't know if living with a guy is ever a good idea."

She put down the book she held and waggled a finger at me. "I know what you're up to. I get this from the AA people all the time. I get to choose my higher power, okay? And it isn't your Jesus."

Smart cookie. Couldn't sneak up on her with the gospel. "You saw it coming, huh?" I tried to keep my tone light, but when I looked at her, it was like gazing in a mirror. I understood what it meant to be a romance junkie: living off the high of that initial attraction, finding a new guy when the high wore off or a crisis hit or he left. Always wanting more, always hungry, never satisfied. She'd been strong enough to beat the alcoholism, but had she just traded one addiction for another?

"Yeah, I saw you coming. You need to drop the Jesus babble. I am a Ph.D. I think I can figure out this relationship stuff on my own. I don't need Jesus—" she held up her fingers and made quote marks in the air, "to help me."

My tongue felt heavy as I struggled to find words. *Donita, it doesn't have to be this way. You don't have to hurt like this, and you don't have to pretend like it doesn't hurt.* "Don't you want to be married and respected and loved in that marriage?"

Donita let out a gust of air. "You think I'm going to find that in a repressive, sexist religion like yours?"

Donita was taking pleasure in slinging insults about my faith. More than one retaliatory comment ricocheted through my head. "That's not true, Donita, but trying to find a lasting relationship using the world's rules is like trying to build a house with artist's tools. I know that from experience." I paused, then added, with a little extra volume, "Has playing by the world's rules worked for you? Has it?"

My breath caught in my throat, and I wished I could take back what I had just said. Her insults about my faith had made me want to hurt her back.

Donita straightened her back and wrinkled her nose. "Maybe

in your little fundamentalist church world being oppressed and controlled by men is okay. But it's not my thing." Her hostile feminism was a way of protecting herself. She could push men away and accuse them of being sexist before they could hurt her. Her defense mechanism was effective in preventing the hurt, but it also made it impossible for love to get in. She turned her back to me and rearranged the books she had just set up.

I stared at her back until the pinstripes blurred. Her language and her posture were defensive—but I detected the undercurrent of pain. "I'm sorry I yelled. I'm sorry I said that. It was mean."

She turned back around. "Look, I like you. But I can't be around someone who's going to bombard me with Jesus talk. You need to respect my beliefs."

"Jesus is the reason I push air in and out. I can't not talk about him."

"Then I guess we are at an impasse. You're an intelligent person. I don't understand why you need that religious drivel."

There it was again, the assumption that if you were Christian, you must be dumb. I felt our fragile friendship explode into pieces. She only wanted to be my friend if I endorsed her destructive choices, and I couldn't do that. "I want you to find happiness, Donita, that's all. I just want you to be happy."

For several minutes, she pushed books around on the shelf without speaking. My heart pounded from the adrenaline produced by the argument. I took in a deep breath and closed my eyes. A still small voice told me not to leave yet.

She held up one of the books, brushing the binding with her hand. "That's funny. No one has been in here since Theodore. . . . You'd think the books would be dusty." She ran a finger along a shelf, then pushed one of the doors open and closed. "These cabinets aren't that airtight."

Donita's chosen strategy seemed to be to pretend she hadn't heard me say I just wanted her to be happy.

I felt myself shrinking from the underlying hostility still hanging in the air. I didn't want to make small talk about stupid books. "Maybe Celeste dusted in there or something."

"Are you kidding? Only Cameron has a key." Donita tilted her head in the direction of the administrative office where Cameron stared at us from behind the glass window. "We're being watched even as we speak."

"Oh." I smiled in his direction. He responded by coming out from behind the glass window, crossing his arms, and leaning against the doorframe.

Donita closed up the glass doors and twisted the key in the lock.

I indexed through a hundred things I could say to her. In the end, none of them seemed worth the effort. She didn't want to hear my "Jesus talk." I turned, walked past Celeste, and headed toward the stairs.

Donita followed me. "So what are you doing tonight?" Did I detect an unspoken apology in her words?

"Got a big date, actually."

She blinked several times. Her back straightened. "Really. Did *God* set up this date for you?" She emphasized the word "God" like she was punching something.

Whatever hope I had felt that she wanted to repair the damage done to our friendship, she'd dashed to pieces. "I hope so. We'll see how it goes."

Donita waved the key back and forth. "Better get this back to the warden."

She swung the key around on its string, creating a blurred circle. Then she leaned close to me and whispered. "I only do this because it makes the warden nervous. In a moment, I'm going to drop the key and pretend I can't find it. Just to watch the look on his face."

She let go of the key, and it flew four feet to where Celeste was vacuuming. My breath caught in my throat as the edge of the vacuum loomed toward the key.

Cameron's mouth formed a perfect O.

Celeste clicked off the vacuum a centimeter from the key. She pulled her earphones off and leaned over to pick up the key.

Without a word to Celeste, Donita grabbed the key and trotted across the carpet to give it back to Cameron, whose face had pruned up into a scowl. Donita gave me a backward glance, amusement coloring her expression. I patted Celeste on the back. "Thank you for getting that."

Celeste blinked several times, watching the exchange between Donita and Cameron. Her hand wrapped around the handle of the vacuum. She wore a plastic beaded bracelet. Part of her brown curly hair was held flat with a butterfly barrette.

Celeste smiled at me. "You're welcome." She pointed a chubby finger at Donita and shook her head, drawing her eyebrows together. "She's not nice."

"She's actually really nice and fun. She's just having a mean moment." Donita was going through man withdrawals, and she was taking it out on everybody.

"I'm sad for her." Celeste's mouth drooped.

"I'm sad for her too." I stared at Celeste's round face and large brown eyes. Donita had just treated Celeste like she was invisible, and yet Celeste responded with sympathy for Donita. "Celeste, I'm so glad you work here."

Celeste glowed. "Thank you." She wound the cord around the hooks on the vacuum, a faint smile on her face.

"Good-bye, Ruby. You're my friend."

"You're my friend too, Celeste."

I glanced down at my watch and saw that I had about a minute and a half to get to my class. Tightening my grip on the handle of my briefcase, I turned and hurried down the hall.

Chapter Thirteen

When class ended, I made my way across campus toward the Media Arts building, where I hoped I could find Professor L. Philips. The sky was dark, with no patches of blue. The wind cut through my coat and microscopic rapiers of snow jabbed my face and neck.

I crossed my arms over my chest, held my briefcase in front of me, and bent forward. I felt hollow, like the wind was blowing right through me. I was only too happy to take refuge inside the imposing red brick building. After standing and stamping in the lobby for a few minutes, trying to get warm again, I walked into the office and asked the girl at the desk where I might find Professor Philips.

"I think she might be in the theater reviewing some film. It's down the main hall on the left. There's a sign over the door that says Theater, but it's also room 133."

"Thank you."

I made my way down the hall, checking room numbers as I went. The theater was right where the girl had said it would be. I opened the door and slipped in quickly, so as not to let in too much outside light.

A six-foot-high grizzly bear lumbered across a movie screen at the front of the room. I could hear the mechanical click, click, click of a projector. A conical band of light shone out from the top end of the theater. I waited for my eyes to adjust to the dimness.

The seats illuminated by the light from the projector were empty. "Professor Philips?" I ventured. "Hello?"

The grizzly stood on his hind legs and roared. A light went on in the projection booth, and I saw Professor Philips's auburn hair. Bands of shadow covered her face.

The screen went black, and the door to the projection booth opened.

"What do you think of my footage?" Her voice had a pleasant, clear quality.

I glanced back at the white wall where the grizzly had been romping. "It looked good."

Professor Philips clicked on the theater lights and I could see that all five rows of chairs were empty. She was wearing jeans, hiking boots, and an off-white sweater with buttons at the collar. "I'm editing the footage for a wildlife film festival we're having up at the museum." Gold, wire-rimmed glasses fell about half an inch below her thin eyebrows. She had soft pink lips and a flippitydoo thing going on with her hair that was reminiscent of Marilyn Monroe. Despite the glasses and the casual dress, the impression Professor Philips gave was not of a forty-something professor, but of an aging starlet. The precise application of her makeup gave her an almost airbrushed look. She took a step in my direction and narrowed her eyes at me. "Are you one of my students from film history?"

"No, the secretary said I could find you here. I'm Ruby Taylor, and I teach over in the English department, Professor Phillips."

"Oh, you work here. Please, call me Lorelei." She reached out and grasped my hand briefly.

"I have a few questions about a student you had last year, Dale Cutler?"

The smile faded from her face. "I remember Dale. I had him

spring semester for freshman film project. He was in scriptwriting that same semester. Theodore really thought he had potential."

I picked up on an undertone of unspoken emotion when she said Aldridge's name. "Dale's missing. He's vacated his apartment. When was the last time you saw him?"

Lorelei studied me for a moment. She twisted a button on her sweater. Maybe it was just the dim lighting, but the reflection off her glasses made it hard for me to read what was in her eyes. "I've really got to get through this footage. The festival's coming up the weekend before Thanksgiving break."

She turned very precisely, like a model at the end of the runway, and headed back into the projection booth. I followed her up the sloped floor. While she rearranged round metal canisters and took a sip of her coffee, I stood in the doorway by the booth.

She set her coffee cup down on the table that held the projector. "I saw Dale a couple of weeks ago . . . maybe. I'm not sure. I do remember it was a Friday."

"What time Friday?"

"Late, it must have been ten o'clock when he knocked on my door. He was looking for a place to stay. I told him no. I don't even want the appearance of impropriety."

"How did he seem?"

"Agitated. Kind of looking over his shoulder. I gave him a cup of tea to calm his nerves and sent him on his way. Sorry I can't help you more."

"Did he say where he was going?"

"No, he didn't. He did ask me if I kept copies of freshman film projects, which I thought was a strange question. I don't have room on my shelves to save every student's project."

I stepped into the booth. "Dr. Aldridge was sort of mentoring him, wasn't he?"

Lorelei tossed her head and picked invisible lint off her sweater. "Theodore wasn't very close to his own sons. They didn't have a lot in common. Dale was sort of an adopted son."

She had a nervous gesture to go with every mention of Aldridge's name. I took a leap of faith in my deductive reasoning. "Were you involved with Dr. Aldridge?"

Lorelei slipped past me and turned off the theater light. Once she was back in the booth, she clicked the projector back on. Was she hoping I would vaporize so she wouldn't have to answer the question? A black bear with babies made an appearance on the screen, followed by shots of a massive moose grazing in a meadow, before she responded. "Yes, we were involved."

All of her face except for her chin was in shadow. Her words had been delivered with a completely neutral tone, which is almost always an indication of hiding deep emotion. I stood listening to the clicking sound of the film moving through the projector and wondered how far I could push Professor Philips before she would become hostile.

"This footage was not easy to get." Lorelei was a voice in the dark.

I glanced back at the screen: an eagle in a nest on what looked like a cliff.

"My crew and I had to climb a butte and wait through the night for her to come back." She laughed. "My crew is all twenty-year-old students. I have to work out to keep up with them."

"Bet you're in good shape."

"Strong legs and arms. Strong hands to carry all that gear." The eagle erupted out of the nest and flew toward the camera. The bird got so close to the lens that I flinched.

"Did Dr. Aldridge become a Christian before he died?"

Lorelei fumbled with things on the projection table. Something fell to the carpeted floor. "I really need to see what I have on this reel." Irritation had crept into her voice.

"Did he?"

I watched the eagle fly away, wings silhouetted against the early morning sun. The camera followed the bird until it was a dot in the marble blue sky.

I clicked on the projection booth light.

Lorelei stared straight ahead at the screen. She laced her hands together. "I think that eagle footage is my favorite." Even after the reel ran out, she stared at the white wall. "We had . . . we had . . . made plans to move in together. Then he told me he couldn't do that." Her hand fluttered at her neck. "He told me he had to get his life right with God." Again, her hand went to the button on her sweater.

"Do you think Dale had anything to do with his death?"

She grabbed another reel of film behind her. "I loved Theodore, and he hurt me." Her voice was thick with anger, or was it pain? She shoved the reel onto the projector.

Her mind was probably occupied with thoughts of how Aldridge had wronged her. She hadn't heard my question. "But Dale?"

"Dale and Theodore were close." After turning the projector on, she stepped toward me. "Dale was acting really strange the night I saw him." She studied me for a moment before hitting the light switch. "He seemed almost paranoid."

Except for the projector light, we were in darkness again. A countdown appeared on the movie screen.

"Dr. Aldridge was paying you a compliment when he said he didn't want to live with you. He was saying you were more to him than a warm body in a bed."

"It wasn't just about sex for us. We connected on an intellectual level. He respected my work."

"How many times have you said that about a man, and how many times has it not worked out?" I didn't know why I was getting into this argument—probably because I had failed to convince Donita. Maybe it was the fear that loomed around my own perfect date. Could be I was trying to convince myself that I could change the pattern of my own life. I spoke more gently. "I'm sure you wanted to be married—to have children."

"I have a thirteen-year-old daughter from a previous relationship." She continued to fumble with things on the projection table. Metal crashed against metal. "It's hard for a woman of my professional and educational level to meet a man in this town."

"From what I gather, Dr. Aldridge was happy at the end of his life. I would think you would have been happy for him."

Lorelei's hiking boots pounded across the floor. She flicked on the light. Her face was inches from mine, and I saw in her eyes behind the thin veil of the glasses that odd mixture of rage and deep wounding. She took time to form each word. "I . . . loved him . . . and he . . . hurt me."

She was close enough that I could feel her breath on my face. I took a step back. She straightened her back, not taking her eyes off me. She couldn't be happy that Aldridge had turned his life around before he died, because the change meant she lost him as a lover. She could only see things in terms of how it affected her. Nothing I could say to her would alter her interpretation of the relationship.

"Sorry to have taken up your time."

When I stepped out of the projection booth into the theater, a mother coyote lying on her side nursing a dozen pups flashed on the screen. I heard Dr. Philips's voice behind me. "The film festival will be fun. You should come—weekend before Thanksgiving."

"Maybe I will."

I shivered involuntarily as the theater door closed behind me. As I gazed through the tall windows that looked out on campus, I could see snow coming down in slashing lines. Standing there, I decided that the Christianese word I hated the most was "witnessing." *Like it's some little compartmentalized thing you put on a to-do list. "Get groceries. Clean the bathroom. Witness to three people about Jesus." Like they will just fall on their knees and cry, "I believe. I believe." The human heart is more complicated and obstinate than that.*

I buttoned my coat to the neck and dashed into the cold.

⌒

As it turned out, I only needed fifteen outfit changes before I found something that worked for my date. Getting ready took my mind off my talks with Lorelei Philips and Donita Hall. I had no emotional connection to Lorelei, but Donita probably wasn't going to come by to steal my chocolate anymore, and that thought bored a hole in my heart.

Mom and Jimmy served as fashion consultants. They sat in the living room, Mom in the rocking chair and Jimmy kitty-corner from her on the arm of the couch. With each outfit, I stomped down the hall, entered the living room, and did a couple of twirls for them. They either shook their heads or gave me a thumbs-up. I pulled clothes from my closet and from Mom's. She and Jimmy offered comments: "Looks like you're going to a funeral." "Too teenager." "Looks like you should be turning letters and listening to people buy vowels." "Hey, Mama, where's the Hell's Angel's rally?"

We laughed and joked, the three of us together in that living room.

I held up alternative footgear possibilities. With each outfit change, each round of laughter, I began to think that maybe things with Jimmy could be worked out. He was still rooting through the attic, looking for fragments of our father—some sort of connection to the past. But he wasn't disappearing without explanation. And today he'd given Mom another antique pin, a cameo with a mother holding a child. He gave me a thin gold bracelet. He must have gotten his first paycheck from his job at the animal lab. The gifts seemed to be his version of an apology. Hope budded inside me.

Snow was falling pretty heavily outside, so unless I wanted to freeze to death, I was limited in my wardrobe choices. It was six-thirty when I settled on a brown, fake-suede skirt and a purple sweater. I had no choice but to wear low-heeled boots. I didn't want to spend a fun date in the emergency room with my ankles swollen to the size of watermelons, so high heels were not an option on slippery sidewalks. The key to a successful date is to avoid the emergency room.

"You look good, Sis." Jimmy crossed his arms, smiling at me

from his perch on the couch. He'd gained even more weight eating all the stuff Mom had cooked. Because of the freckles and red hair, he would always have a little-boy quality to him, no matter how old he got. The pudgy cheeks only added to the effect.

"Thanks, Jimmy." I tugged on the sleeve of my sweater. "It's nice to get a guy's opinion." Things between us still felt strained, but we were making progress.

Mom patted Jimmy's hand and smiled at him. "Jimmy said he would go to church with us on Sunday."

"Good. All three of us can go." I must have been staring at him too long, because he uncrossed his arms and shifted down to a couch cushion. I looked away, shaking my head. Unbelievably high barriers still existed between us, but maybe we could be like a real family.

The doorbell rang. My heart ka-thudded and contracted at the same time. I couldn't get a deep breath.

Jimmy chuckled.

"Are you laughing at me?"

"Very deer-in-the-headlights look going on there, Ruby."

"Mom, he's teasing me. Make him stop."

Mom shook her head. "You two . . ."

The doorbell rang again. I actually thought about running and hiding in my room. The level of excitement and fear I felt was similar to standing in line to get on the Tilt-A-Whirl with a million questions racing through my head. Would I live? Would I die? Would I throw up? In a lot of ways, it did feel like I was sixteen again.

Mom pushed herself out of the rocking chair. "I'll get it."

While Mom made her way across the living room, I smoothed

over my skirt, touched my hair, and wondered if I had lipstick on my teeth.

Jimmy stood up and gave me the once-over. "Chunk of broccoli on your teeth."

I touched my mouth self-consciously and then saw the flash of light in his eyes.

"Ruby, it's the size of a brick."

Again, I touched my lips. "Stop." I punched him in the shoulder.

Mom opened the door and I heard her say, "Don't you look nice, Wesley."

I smoothed my sweater over my stomach; the nausea kicked in. I stood on cooked-spaghetti legs and reached out to touch the TV console for support. Mom stepped aside so I had a clear view of Wesley. He held a box of chocolates in one hand and a bouquet of flowers in the other.

"How's this for a start?" He lifted his gifts up even higher.

All I saw were those green eyes of his surrounded by a thick forest of lashes. *Oh, baby.* I swallowed hard, trying to find some moisture in my mouth. Honestly, I wanted to run to my room and lock the door. My heart pounded at a ferocious rate, threatening to explode out of my chest. It was exhilarating and mortifying at the same time—like being sixteen and innocent again.

Mom touched her neck with a flat hand and tilted her head in my direction. "Isn't that nice? He brought candy and flowers. So old-fashioned."

Like she needed to convince me this date was starting out well. So far, it was the stuff of a teenager's dream. I just hoped I could live up to Wesley's expectations. *Oh, God, don't let me blow this.*

Wesley was wearing a long, camel-colored wool coat. His hair was wet from the snow, dark, and smoothed back from his face. The vision of him made my toes curl in my boots.

I opened my mouth to say something intriguing and provocative, but I drew a blank.

Mom handed me her coat, a hooded number in navy wool with fur trim, another of her sewing projects. "Go on, you two. Have a good time. I'll take those." Mom reached for the gifts.

"I'll take the chocolates." I pulled the box out of her hand. "I might need 'em later."

A look of confusion passed between Mom and Wesley. I touched the box affectionately. They just didn't understand.

Wesley opened the door for me.

"Better have her back before ten, or I'll have to come beat you up, Wesley," my brother barked from the back of the room.

"Wesley, I don't think you've met my brother, Jimmy." I turned around and stuck my tongue out at Jimmy.

Wesley waved and then whispered in my ear as we headed toward the door, "You mean the guy who—"

"Came to our house in the middle of the night, yes."

I walked through the door, holding my box of chocolates. Wesley followed. His hand touched the small of my back as we made our way down the stairs. The porch swing creaked in the wind. Snow gusted around us in twirling funnel patterns.

I actually thought about pretending to slip so he would have an excuse to grab me around the waist to catch me. *Then we could have one of those wonderful look-into-each-other's-eyes-before-we-kiss moments. With the snow falling around us, it would be so romantic.*

I decided against that tactic because with my luck, I'd probably fall down and accidentally hit him in the face, causing his nose to bleed, and break my leg. Mangled limbs are not romantic. They don't serve nice dinners at the emergency room. The atmosphere is nothing to write home about, either. Besides, I might drop my chocolates, and it would look so tacky for me to fish them out of the snow.

We made it to his car without any accidents or kissing events. I reached out to open the passenger-side door of his Jeep.

"Um . . . that door is still broken. You'll have to get in on my side."

Wesley opened the driver's-side door, and I crawled across the seat, squeezing past the steering wheel—not an easy task in a skirt and long coat.

I settled in with my box of chocolates on my lap, and he climbed in behind the wheel. Over a year ago, we'd done this exact same thing. It had been summer then. His hand had brushed my leg when he threw the camping gear in the back of the Jeep as I crawled in. I remembered the sensation of electric blue snakes tingling on my skin where he touched me.

A year ago, I wasn't a Christian. A year ago, I would have slept with him if he had pushed for that. But things had changed. I was a new critter in Christ, and that made all the difference.

Wesley jammed the key in the ignition and smiled at me. I still felt the same intoxicating buzz when I was around him that I had experienced a year ago. But God was asking me to control my impulses, to honor Him, to respect myself.

Placing his arm over my side of the seat back, Wesley craned his neck and backed up. Was he ever going to learn to use his rearview mirror?

Wesley turned left and headed up the hill through the residential section of town. I adjusted myself in the seat and marinated in the spice of being close to him. I thanked God for pheromones and the biochemistry that occurs between people who are attracted to each other. *Cool inventions, God. Thanks.*

I filled Wesley in on the details about Dale I had garnered from my visit with Professor Philips. "Dale was hiding from or running from something. I know it was him rooting through my office that day. I smelled his cologne."

Wesley chuckled. "Nobody's ever been convicted based on a smell, Ruby."

"'Scuse me, Mr. Expert. I know what I know. Dale and Dr. Aldridge were involved in something together—beyond classes." *And it might have something to do with the rare books collection. I just haven't connected all the dots yet.*

"Could be. Kind of need some evidence though, Ruby." He gave me a gorgeous crooked grin. "Can't convict someone based on a woman's instinct."

"You're probably right."

Wesley pressed his hands into the steering wheel. "Do you like Mexican?" We passed the outskirts of the university.

"Sure." Actually, anything sounded good. I had been so caught up in the frenzy of getting ready for the date, I hadn't had my usual late-afternoon snack. My stomach growled. I touched my belly, hoping its demands for food weren't audible. How tacky and unfeminine would that be?

I smiled demurely at Wesley, one of those little ladylike numbers where your lips barely curl up—no teeth. I didn't want him to see any signs of aggression in me.

Wesley shook his head.

"What?" I said.

"That smile is so not you." After clicking his blinker, he placed both hands on the wheel.

The muscles in my lower back tightened. I gripped the chocolate box. We weren't even to the restaurant, and he'd already irked me. How did he know what was me and what wasn't? Couldn't he see how hard I was trying? I narrowed my eyes at him. *Read my mind, Tweedledee.* I took in a big bunch of air and spoke in a real sweet voice. "What do you mean it's not me?"

He glanced at me, arched eyebrows drawn together. Round eyes and an open mouth wrinkled the smoothness of his expression. "Ahh . . . nothing. I didn't mean anything by it."

I bit my tongue—hard. Why was I trying to deliberately self-destruct this relationship before it started? Intense desire to make the relationship work out was making it go all wrong. All the backwash of past relationships—the insecurity, the fear, the lack of trust—was right here in this car, controlling every word and reaction. In my relationships in my BC days—you know, before Christ—there had been two choices: to hurt or be hurt first. Like a puppy, I followed after men who mistreated me; and like a pit bull I shredded those who showed me any kindness. I glanced at the box of chocolates. Maybe we couldn't be sixteen again—there was too much history behind us.

But that didn't mean we couldn't make this work. *Okay, Ruby, backpedal, start over.* I patted his leg close to the knee. "I am really excited about tonight, my first date as a Christian." I gave him my normal smile, big grin, lots of teeth.

"Me too." He turned another corner. Up ahead in the field that separated the museum and the university, the red lights of a police car flashed. "Wonder what's going on there? Doesn't look like a traffic stop."

"Good thing you're off duty," I said.

"Good thing."

We drove past. No streetlamps and a thickening snowfall cut visibility down to about thirty feet. The car had pulled off the road and out into the field. A police officer dressed in a heavy jacket stood by another person—I couldn't tell if it was a man or a woman. No other cars were nearby.

"That's Sevee Cree's patrol car."

Wesley was actually looking in his rearview mirror. I rolled my eyes to the ceiling. He'd use the mirror to watch someone being arrested, but not to back up his vehicle.

"Officer Cree? The guy you trained with?" Shifting my torso slightly, I craned my neck. "Good thing you're not on duty." Our perfect date was slipping away in increments.

Wesley slowed the Jeep down to a crawl. "Yeah, good thing I'm not on duty." He pulled over and turned the Jeep back around. "Cree might need my help."

A heavy weight pressed into my chest. "You're not working. Please don't sabotage this date." We had just narrowly avoided my attempted sabotage.

He parked in the field about twenty yards from the patrol car. "What if someone is hurt, Ruby?"

I pressed my lips together. I didn't want to be selfish, but wasn't this Officer Cree's job? It was like Wesley didn't want this date to work.

Cree glanced in the direction of the Jeep as we pulled up. I could see now that the person he was talking to was a woman: head tilted down, shoulders bent forward. Officer Cree touched her upper back. She looked up, shaking her head. Her hand touched her face and then fell to her side.

Wesley clicked open his door. "You might want to hang back a little bit." He touched my shoulder. "I'm not sure what this is about."

After he climbed out, I slid across to the driver's side so I would have access to the only working door in the car. I reached out for the door handle. Tension started in my fingertips and worked its way up my arm to the back of my neck. Of course, if Officer Cree needed help, Wesley should help. Still I felt gypped that he had made this a priority over our date. Was he hiding behind his job to avoid the hard work of a relationship with me?

Wesley trudged across the field. A fairly large dog came out of the shadows and sat down at the woman's feet. The woman's long hair coiled in the intense wind.

I pressed open the door, stepped down, and pushed my way through the tall grass. Wesley had joined the others and the two officers were conferring with their heads close together. Cree pointed across the field toward the museum. The woman wiped her eyes—either tears or watering from the wind. I couldn't tell at this distance.

Wind cemented against my ears. Snow came down in sharp, wind-driven needles. I slipped my hood on my head. Crossing my arms over my chest, I took a few more steps toward the officers. Wesley held up his hands in a stop signal.

Cree touched the woman's shoulder and pointed toward the patrol car. In an instant, the dog bounced around the group of people, barked, and took off across the field. The dark museum loomed in the background.

The woman spun around, planting her feet shoulder-width apart. Her body bent forward. Gloved hands balled into fists. "No, Felix, no." To say her scream was bloodcurdling was an understatement. Her voice, heavy with dread, cut through the wind, stinging my ears with more intensity than the snow.

Cree pulled a flashlight out of his belt and took off after the dog. The light bobbed across the field.

I ran up to the woman and Wesley.

In one complex motion, the woman pulled the hair away from her face, wiped her eyes, and placed a flat hand on her chest. "I don't want him to touch it. I don't want Felix to touch it." Her voice swelled and vibrated with emotion. "Stop him."

About forty yards away, Cree stopped and fixed the light on the dog and the object of the animal's pursuit. The dog circled around a lump on the ground and half jumped at Cree, barking loudly and sharply. Cree steadied the flashlight.

I saw it. The familiar long, dark coat.

I took off across the field. Maybe Wesley screamed at me to stop, but I didn't hear anything.

I was breathing heavily by the time I reached Cree and the body.

"Felix, go." Cree pointed back toward the patrol car and the woman. "Felix, go."

Felix bounded up and down, paced back and forth—barked.

"Ruby, you don't need to see this."

"Turn him over. I think I know who it is."

"I don't want to disturb anything. This could be a crime scene."

The body was on its side. "Give me the flashlight then."

"Ruby, why—?"

"Give me the light." The intensity of my demand told him not to argue.

He handed me the flashlight. I circled wide to the other side of the body. The flashlight bobbed in my hand. I threw back my hood and leaned closer.

One hand, immobile like marble, was drawn protectively to the face. In the circle of light, I saw the full lips and narrow eyes. I noted the scars above the eyebrow where the earring studs had been. His cowboy hat had fallen halfway off.

Not far from the body, I saw the shiny metal of the key ring I'd gotten from Aldridge's house.

My stomach contracted. I stood up. In the November cold with snow stabbing my face and neck, I said, "I know this kid. He took those keys from me." My stomach churned. My limbs became lead-weight heavy. I turned toward Officer Cree. "This is Dale Cutler. He was a student of mine."

Chapter Fourteen

I don't know how we ended up at the café that time forgot. I remember Wesley saying that I was too upset to take home, and then after some time passed, he said, "We have to eat something."

I have a vague memory of the cold glass of his Jeep window as I pressed my forehead against it. Hot air from the car's heater blew against my legs. I clutched my box of chocolates and tried not to revisit the images of Dale frozen in that field.

At some point, my grip on the box lightened a bit. I shifted in my seat so I could look at Wesley. "Okay, I'll eat something. But I don't want to talk about what happened tonight."

The café that time forgot was actually called Joe's. I know that because there was a plastic revolving sign in the parking lot. I crawled out from Wesley's side of the Jeep. He took my hand as we walked across the parking lot. Through the thick gloves, I couldn't feel much of anything, but I appreciated the gesture. The only other vehicles in the parking lot were two beat-up pickup trucks.

The restaurant itself was a trailer that had been converted to a place to eat. The contractor hadn't knocked himself out doing the remodel. It looked exactly like a double-wide sporting a "No Shoes, No Shirt, No Service" sign.

"Where are we?" I couldn't see much beyond the lights of the parking lot, but the impression I got was that we were not surrounded by lots of buildings and businesses but by rolling hills and mountains. The snow had stopped, but the temperature hovered around freezing.

"Frontage road, about an hour outside of town," Wesley said.

"Oh," was all I could manage. After leaving Officer Cree and the distraught woman, Wesley had apologized profusely about ruining our date. When I met him a year ago, he owned a roofing business. Roofing had been just a job. Being a cop seemed to consume him. Even when he wasn't at work, he was thinking about it. Maybe his workaholism was a way of avoiding the hard part of life: relationships. "Was that your first dead body?"

"No." His hand brushed over my hair. "Thought you said you didn't want to talk about this." His tone indicated that he didn't want to say more.

"I changed my mind." The way I process things is to talk about them. I needed to process. "I imagine you come across a lot of them in your line of work." Whether he admitted it or not, he also needed to process what had just happened.

He gestured that I should step in ahead of him. "A few," he responded.

I took the two metal steps up and entered Joe's. "Guess you just get used to it."

"No, you never get used to it. Can we talk about something else?"

The air inside the restaurant was warm, heavy, and grease scented. What would have been the living room and dining room had been gutted. Three tables and a round booth done in brown vinyl occupied the space. Static-filled Johnny Cash songs from a portable radio and the sizzle of the grill provided the auditory atmosphere of this fine dining establishment.

"I'll take those." Wesley pried the box of chocolates out of my hand. I hadn't even realized I had hauled them with me.

Two people occupied the restaurant. A very old woman flipped a burger behind the counter, and a very old man sat hunched over a table, nursing a cup of coffee. The elderly gentleman had taken his red and black checkered hat off and set it on the table. I've seen linen skirts left in suitcases that had fewer wrinkles than the old man.

The old woman turned around and smiled at us. "Well, look what the cat dragged in." She slapped her hip. "Wesley Burgess, I haven't seen you in a coon's age."

"Hi, Adele."

"Have a seat, honey. I just got to get Randy his burger."

Wesley led me toward the booth. I slipped in, and he sat next to me. He whispered in my ear. "She'll push the potato salad real hard. Whatever you do, don't eat the potato salad."

I glanced around. Maybe it was just Randy and Adele, the kind of good, down-to-earth people they were, but this place made me homesick for more hours at the feed store. With my limited hours, I wasn't getting to see all our regular customers. "You know this place, do you?"

"My dad used to treat me and my brother after a long day of harvesting. They have the best milkshakes in the world here."

"You grew up on a ranch?" I realized I knew very little about Wesley's background. I had never met any of his family. I grabbed one of the menus tucked behind the napkin holder. Only five items were listed: cheeseburger, steak dinner, fried chicken, grilled cheese sandwich, and spaghetti with meatballs. The menu, which had coffee-stain rings on it, looked like it had been typed on an old typewriter. The *e* in each word was slightly elevated.

"Dad's place is about fifty miles from here."

"I'd like to meet your family."

Wesley scooted away from me. He pulled out way more napkins than we could ever use and then spun the silver napkin holder on the table. "My brother is okay, but my father is a little—a little strange."

"Is he a hit man for the Mafia?"

"No." He picked up a napkin and tore it in half.

"Has he done hard time? He can't be any more bizarre than my family."

Wesley half laughed. "Dad kind of has—fantasies. He thinks he invented things."

"He doesn't think he invented the Internet, does he? 'Cause, you know, Al Gore did that." I tore open a sugar packet, tilted my head back, and poured it on my tongue. *Yummy.* The weight of the events of the evening lightened a bit.

Wesley continued to shred his napkin. "No, my dad thinks he invented 'Take a Penny, Leave a Penny.'"

"'Take a Penny, Leave a Penny'? I don't think anybody invented that. It just appeared on the planet." I twisted my empty sugar packet and spoke in an ominous tone. "Maybe it was dropped here by aliens."

"My father thinks he invented it and never got the credit. He believes other strange things—sees conspiracies in historical events."

"Like the second shooter on the grassy knoll?" I threw my twisted-up sugar packet at him, hitting him in the shoulder. "Lots of people believe that."

"Dad's conspiracies are a little more elaborate and unique." He picked up the sugar packet and threw it back at me. "We didn't have TV growing up, so he read all the time. He knows a great deal. You can talk to him like he's a normal guy. It's just that every once in a while, he drops one of his paranoid conspiracies into the middle of a conversation."

The sugar packet fell on my sweater by my neckline. "I still want to meet him."

Wesley reached over for the sugar packet. His fingers brushed my neck. "Maybe I'll introduce you to him."

His touch turned me into molten lava. I pulled myself free from the laser beam of his gaze.

Adele placed a burger and fries on Randy's table and pulled ketchup and mustard out of her apron. Randy grumbled a thank-you.

She plodded over to our table. Adele had a slight hunchback, and the order form shook in her hand. "What can I get you kids? Got a fresh batch of potato salad." She pulled a pencil from behind her ear. She had a slash of blue eye shadow across each lid, accented with some slightly crooked false eyelashes.

"I think we'll have milkshakes and some of your fried chicken," Wesley said.

"Would you like fries?" She leaned a little closer to us. "Or potato salad." Her eyes twinkled, and she lowered her voice an octave.

"Fries, please." Wesley and I spoke in unison.

Adele shuffled back to the kitchen, and I saw her take the chicken out of the refrigerator. From this distance, it looked like the stuff was already cooked.

"What's wrong with the potato salad?" I spoke under my breath.

"Strange spices," Wesley whispered back.

I rested my head on the table. "I don't feel much like eating."

My stomach still churned from what I had seen. Flirting with Wesley provided only a brief distraction.

"You have to eat something." Wesley opened the candy box and pulled out a square of dark chocolate. "Have a chocolate appetizer."

I still rested my head on the table, but I turned so I could look up at Wesley. "Is this how you pictured our date going? A little crime-scene viewing before a time warp visit to Joe's?"

"No, I wanted to take you to a nice place. I'm sorry. We shouldn't have stopped. Cree could have handled it on his own." He shoved the chocolate toward me. "You'll feel better."

I placed the candy on my tongue and bit into it. It tasted like Styrofoam. "He was just a nineteen-year-old kid." I chewed, hoping the dullness would fade from my taste buds. I could barely discern the caramel and dark chocolate.

"Still think he had something to do with Aldridge's death?"

"I'm sure he was the one rooting through my office. Those were Aldridge's keys next to him." I sat up straight. "I shouldn't have hounded him like I did. Maybe he would have told me more." I hit the table with my fist. "What was he doing out there in that field?"

"He may have been dumped there. Could have been natural causes, drug overdose—anything really. Won't know until the coroner looks at him. If there is something suspicious, the pathologist will drive down from Lewisville and take samples for the state lab."

"Dale acted so suspicious. What was he running from if he didn't kill Aldridge? He knew something. I think it might have something to do with the rare books collection in the English department." My hand balled into a tight fist.

Wesley rubbed my back. "We don't need to talk about this." He twirled the pepper shaker. "I sure know how to show a girl a good time, don't I?"

"Of the top ten things that could have gone wrong with this date, finding Dale dead never came to mind."

"What did come to mind?"

"You would realize you didn't like me. You'd act like some macho, burping pig at dinner, and I would realize I didn't like you. The food would be bad. We'd get in a car accident, and my hair would be messed up. The one place I didn't want this date to end up was the emergency room."

Wesley chuckled. "You're kind of a pessimist, aren't you?"

"You mean to tell me that you didn't think of disastrous things that could happen?"

"Just one."

"You mean we would end up in bed?"

He nodded. "Didn't you think of that too?"

"Been there, done that, they don't make a T-shirt for it. We're going by God's playbook, remember?"

Adele sat down two milkshakes in tall glasses. She returned a minute later with the metal cups the shakes had been mixed in. I smelled the precooked fried chicken sizzling on the grill.

Wesley shook his head and combed his fingers through his short hair. "I appreciate your resolve. It helps me." He stirred his shake with his straw. "It helps to have someone to talk to about work too."

I took a sip of my milkshake. The chilly thick liquid slid down my throat. "Lot different from roofing, huh?"

"I'm thirty years old; I needed a job with a future. Being a former marine and a seasonal roofer who skis all winter doesn't make you qualified for much else." He jabbed the milkshake with his straw. "I just didn't expect it to be this consuming."

He continued to stab at his shake intensely—deliberately. His lips were drawn into a tight line.

I covered his hand resting on the table with my own. "You can talk to me about it all you like. But, really, God is the one who will offer you more help."

Adele set the chicken and fries down in front of us and placed her hands on her hips. She wasn't going to leave until we took our first bite and gave her a thumbs-up.

I bit into the chicken and nodded my approval. Satisfied, Adele wandered back to Randy's table and sat opposite him. They didn't say anything to each other. Instead, she pulled a deck of cards out of her apron and laid them out on the table.

I suppose there are advantages to not being able to taste anything. "There is nothing special about this chicken." I spoke quietly, so Adele wouldn't hear. "Why do you come here?"

"The milkshakes." He held up the silver cup. "And the pie. She makes them from scratch."

Gradually, my stomach unclenched itself. By the time we got to the apple pie, I could taste the tartness of the Granny Smiths. Undercurrents of the ugliness of what I had seen earlier still tugged at my conscience. Maybe Dale and Aldridge had been into something related to those books. Dale still didn't deserve to die like that.

Right before we left Joe's, Wesley pulled a chocolate from the box and placed it in my hand. "It's mint," he said with all sorts of heady intrigue in his voice.

Didn't fool me a bit. I hadn't just fallen off the turnip truck. I had said that I wanted our first kiss to be minty fresh, and he hands me a mint chocolate. Duh. No, I didn't just fall off the turnip truck. I was pushed.

Wesley threw twenty dollars on the table and waved good-bye to Adele, who had gone back to her kitchen. Randy had fallen asleep beside his half-eaten hamburger. His snoring had served as musical accompaniment while we ate our pie. Yeah, this place had atmosphere, and plenty of it.

Adele waved a soapy hand at us from the sink where she washed her pots and pans. "Come around more often, there now, Wesley."

Outside, the clear, night sky glittered with stars. The storm had faded, leaving a thin layer of snow on the ground. The air was cold and crisp. Wesley grabbed my hand and led me toward the Jeep.

"Done with that mint yet?"

I rolled the chocolate around in my mouth, over my tongue. My heart pounded out primitive jungle rhythms. My skin felt hot and tingly all over. "Working on it."

Wesley stopped beneath a light and turned to face me. He let go of my hand—eyes wide with anticipation.

I swallowed the last tidbit of chocolate and looked up at him. He leaned closer.

Mint flavor flooded my mouth. My face flushed with warmth. He touched my arm just above the elbow. Even through the thickness of a coat and sweater, I could feel the pressure of his touch. If we were limited to brief kisses and hand holding, I didn't want to rush things.

I pulled off my gloves and held up my hand, fingers apart, in front of my lips. "Why can't hands do what lips do?"

Wesley straightened his back. "What?"

"It's a line from Shakespeare. Actually, the reverse of a line. Romeo wants to kiss Juliet, so he says, 'Why can't lips do what hands do?' We all know how they ended up. So . . ." I grabbed his hand at the wrist and slowly pulled his leather glove off. "Why can't hands do what lips do?"

Wesley let out a low "Huh."

He placed his hand flat against mine, pressing hard. Slowly he traced the outline of my fingers with his fingers and then circled his thumb over my palm. I closed my eyes. His glove fell to the snowy ground. I interwove my fingers with his. In the crispness of evening, we swayed beneath the light, relishing the sensation of physical proximity.

"Why can't hands do what lips do?" He squeezed my hand tighter.

Without opening my eyes, I whispered, "Why not?"

He threw back my hood and pressed his lips close to my ear. "I'm sorry this date wasn't perfect. We'll try again."

I opened my eyes and memorized the way the warm glow from the light covered him in gold shimmer, the way shadow rested beneath his cheekbones and strong chin. "I'd like that." And I memorized the luminescence of affection glistening in his eyes. "I'd like that a lot."

◠

In the days that followed our less-than-perfect date that ended okay, I found it hard to concentrate on work. Everything I read was boring, boring, boring. I found myself thinking about our regular customers at the feed store—and missing them.

Every lesson plan failed to hold my interest. The only thing that competed with thoughts of another date with Wesley was Dale's death. I sat in my office, grading papers on a Tuesday night and wondering if his fate would have been different if I had been kinder to him. *Would he have told me what had gone on between him and Aldridge? If I had tried to build some sort of relationship with him, would he be alive today?*

I straightened a pile of papers. Nobody at this university had grown closer to God by my presence. I simply put in my time every day and went home. Over and over, I had asked forgiveness for becoming a closet Christian in the face of disdain for Christianity. I had checked out a dozen books on apologetics, looking for the precise argument to rebut the pessimism I encountered. I looked for something clever and intellectual with which to convince Donita. Nothing helped.

I gave a paper a B and set it on the done pile. We were nine days away from Thanksgiving break. I massaged the tight muscles at the back of my neck. After that, only a few weeks until the semester ended. It looked like I wasn't going to get a renewed contract, which was fine with me. I had to fulfill my commitment here, but I was anxious to get back to the feed store. I still couldn't figure out why I had come back to the U anyway.

Outside in the hallway, I heard the squeaky wheels of Celeste's cleaning cart making its way up the hall. She hummed a melody I couldn't quite place. What was that song?

I read through a personal essay written about how scary it was to move from small town Montana to the "big city" of Eagleton. Eagleton was a whopping fifty thousand people. I suppose it was a dramatic adjustment if you had grown up in a town of a thousand.

Celeste moved toward my door, still humming. What was that tune? La-la-la-la-la. I set the big-city-is-scary essay aside and slumped in my chair, hands on my stomach. The problem was that I had read other versions of that essay five times already. I knew they hadn't cheated, but they all said the same thing. The other theme that popped up all the time was "the party life is great." A giant case of groupthink was going on with my freshmen. I was tired of student essays. I pulled my Bible out of my briefcase and set it on the desk. I sat up straight. The words in my Bible were blurry. Had I even asked God if I should take this job? In my BC days, academic achievement had been the source of my identity. There were a dozen other jobs I could have gotten to make financial ends meet. Why had I come back here?

The squeaky wheels of Celeste's cart grew louder.

"Hi, Celeste," I called.

She popped her head in my door. "Hi, Ruby." Her thick fingers gripped a mop. "I gotta do the bathroom floor."

Hours alone had made me hungry for conversation. Donita wasn't coming by to chat anymore. She actually seemed to be avoiding me. I pushed my goodie bowl across the desk. "You want some chocolate?"

"Sure." Celeste stepped into my office, took a candy, and peeled the silver paper off the chocolate. She swayed side to side, still humming the tune I could not quite place. Her brown hair was more fuzzy than curly, surrounding her round face in a nice, even, half circle. "You're reading your Bible," she said brightly.

"Yes, yes, I am." I didn't care anymore who saw me reading it.

"You love Jesus?"

"Yes."

"I gave Theodore a Bible." Celeste made audible chewing noises as she ate another piece of chocolate.

"You?" Slow realization spread through me. All this time, I had assumed that another professor or a brave and articulate student had told Aldridge about Christ. I pictured them having C. S. Lewis-type discussions—bouncing theological arguments back and forth. "Oh, you."

"I told him Jesus loved him." She hung her head and folded her hands in front of her. "And he cried. Theodore said he was a bad man and Jesus could never love him." Celeste put her face very close to mine. She touched my wrist. "That's not true. Jesus loves everybody." She nodded her head for several seconds to make her point. "Everybody—He loves everybody."

Her fingers tapping my wrist were lighter than ladybugs on my skin. She straightened up and continued. "We sang songs together every night. Then he got to go to heaven to be with Jesus."

I stared into Celeste's round bright eyes. "Your faith is so simple—so clear."

She hummed the same tune for a couple of bars and then began to sing the plaintive words of "Jesus Loves Me."

That was the song I couldn't quite place. Jerking and stumbling through the words, I joined in. I could be so stupid sometimes. Intellectual argument hadn't won Aldridge over—kindness had. Everyone else around here had endorsed his destructive choices, but Celeste had seen the needs of his heart.

Intellectual argument wasn't going to win Donita over either. But I had thought it would. Now I knew why I had come back to the U. I wanted to genuflect one last time in front of my old idol, my intellectual ability. Coming back to this job was about me feeling big and important in the world's eyes, and I had been willing to hide my faith for that. Now that verse about a dog returning to his vomit made sense to me.

Celeste's clear voice rang through my office. "You know this one." Brightness and cheer surrounded her words.

"I should know it, Celeste. I should know it." People don't comprehend God with their head—they comprehend with their soul.

Celeste continued to sing, and I mumbled along. She sang me two more songs and threw in hand motions as an added bonus. After she finished, she pulled a piece of paper from the large pocket in her smock. "I have to do the bathroom next. Gail always makes me a list so I don't forget."

She showed me the list, written in large block letters. Celeste's supervisor had printed the five things that this precious woman needed to get done tonight. Celeste needed to add one thing to that list: "Restore the foundation of Ruby's faith."

"I guess I better get back to my work too." I glanced at the pile of ungraded papers.

"We can sing again some night if you would like." She stepped out of my office and picked up a bucket that was hooked to her cart. Her arms wrapped around the bucket so it pressed into her belly.

"I'd like that, Celeste. I'd like that a lot."

Celeste glanced down the long hallway of offices. "When I go by each door, I pray for that teacher. The names are on the doors, you know." She added matter-of-factly, "Some I can't read. Daddy came with me one night and pronounced all the names for me." She touched her forehead. "But I forget. I'm not smart like you."

"Celeste, you are smarter than I will ever be."

Every day, Celeste came faithfully and cleaned up the messes other people made. She did it quietly, without complaint, without recognition. The rest of the people buzzed through this building full of ideas, trying to make themselves significant with intellectualized plans to make the world a better place. But only this beautiful, simple woman cared enough to notice that Theodore Aldridge was hurting. Only she took the time to tell him he was dearly loved by the creator of the universe.

Celeste still clutched her bucket. "I have to do the bathroom now."

"Thanks, Celeste. You have a good night."

"You too, Ruby, my friend." Celeste sang, "Yes, Jesus loves me" all the way down the hall. The bathroom door creaked open, and the song grew dim.

Chapter Fifteen

The receipt I had found in Jimmy's room felt hot and heavy pressed against the palm of my hand as I stalked across campus toward the animal lab where he worked. The drive from the house to campus had been an angry blur. I'd gritted my teeth so hard my jaw hurt. I'd parked the Valiant, pressed the receipt into my palm, and slipped my glove over it.

But now, every time I felt the paper press into my hand, my muscles contracted and I couldn't see straight. I stopped in the middle of campus beside a sculpture made of computer monitors with broken screens stacked on top of each other inside an iron frame.

Icy cold stabbed at my skin when I slipped my glove off. The receipt was poison next to my hand. I shoved it in my pocket and made my way up the slippery sidewalk of Bridger Hall. Once inside, I checked the board. The animal lab was in the basement.

I went down the stairs two at a time. My boots echoed on the metal steps in the concrete stairwell. I had never been to the animal lab, and I was quickly getting the impression of going into an underground bunker or a cave. By the time I made it to the last stair, I no longer could see any natural light. Ailing fluorescent lights fizzed and sputtered over my head. A moldy odor hung in the stagnant air. The walls and floor were concrete. I passed metal doors with frosted windows covered in mesh. Each door held a label: Supply Closet, Professor David Hammet, Animal Experiment Lab. I twisted the doorknob and stepped into the humidity of the animal lab.

Rows of cages containing furry critters, mostly mice, lined the walls. The place smelled of sawdust and urine and underneath that a less detectable antiseptic or ether scent. The squeaky-squeak hamster exercise wheels, the heater gusting eighty degree air into the facility, and approaching footsteps swirled in a dissonant cacophony. Sweat trickled past my temple. I took off my gloves and unbuttoned my coat.

A steel gray door in the corner of the room opened. A woman in a lab coat appeared. "I thought I saw someone on the cameras," she said. Thin and middle-aged, she had straight stringy hair and plastic-framed glasses that had gone out of style ten years ago. Underneath the fluorescent lights, her skin held a jaundiced tinge.

Her comment caused me to glance toward the ceiling. Cameras were mounted in two of the four corners.

She shoved her hands in the pockets of her lab coat. "It's a security measure. We've never had any trouble, but the animal rights people are always looking for an opportunity." She stepped toward me, lowering her voice. "Why are you here?"

"I'm looking for my brother, Jimmy Taylor."

"Oh." She nodded her head up and down a few seconds too long, still giving me the hairy eyeball. "He's back in the cat lab. Third door on the right."

"Thanks." I stepped toward the door, but she blocked me.

"You have the same red hair as him—only a little lighter."

She seemed to be trying to confirm that indeed I was who I said I was. "Yes, our father was a redhead."

"He's very charming, your brother." Nuances of affection permeated her words.

Not what I wanted to hear right now. The word "manipulative" came to my mind. Jimmy had inherited our father's dangerous charisma. I smiled for the infatuated, jaundiced woman. "He has his moments."

She laughed and stepped out of my way. It took a degree of pulling for me to open the heavy metal door. I could still feel her staring as the door eased shut behind me. My footsteps echoed on the concrete floor. The hall smelled of urine and bleach.

The first room I walked by looked like command central. Through a large window, I saw several security monitors showing empty hallways and rooms with cages. Command central contained a desk, a microwave, stacks of books, a computer, and a microscope. Bags of animal feed lined either side of the room.

On one of the monitors, I watched Jimmy in black and white as he poured food into dishes with cats bustling around him and rubbing against him. The image was stark and grainy, lots of black and glowing white, not many shades of gray.

In front of me, the hallway split on either side. I walked straight ahead until I came to the third door on the right. I pulled the receipt from my pocket. For the first time since I had found it in his jacket pocket, I looked at it without having the muscles in my lower back tighten. My long walk through animal death row had calmed me down.

I pushed the door open. Jimmy sat in the middle of the floor. Two cats had settled on his lap. Another rubbed against his knee.

"Sis, what are you doing here?"

I held the receipt in front of me. "I found this in your jacket pocket. I wasn't snooping. Mom asked me to do laundry. I was cleaning out your pockets."

One side of Jimmy's lip curled up. "I can't see it from here."

"It's a receipt for a men's clothing shop downtown. I found a dozen more of them in that jacket of yours that hasn't been washed since you moved in." After I found the receipt, I *had* snooped. Under his bed, I had found a box full of antique jewelry. I had a feeling he hadn't bought the jewelry he had been giving Mom. An odd assortment of teddy bears, some of which had a metal button in their ear that said Steiff, and a stack of comic books in plastic sleeves were also stashed under the bed.

He shrugged. "So I need to clean my pockets out more often."

"What's interesting . . ." I swallowed hard and stared at the receipt. "What's interesting is the date. You've been in town since March. You didn't show up on our doorstep until October."

One of the cats, a calico, crawled on Jimmy's shoulders. He stroked its paws. "They kill these cats, you know, after they're done with the experimenting. I had a cat when I lived in Jackson Hole. I kind of miss her."

He was doing that evasive thing again—never answering me directly. "Jackson Hole. Is that where you lived before you came up here—in March? Or have you been here even longer than that?" Anger swirled around my toes and up my legs until a stabbing tightness in my lower back and stomach made it hard to take a deep breath. "Why didn't you get in touch with us sooner? You didn't come in on the bus, did you?"

Jimmy slipped the cat off his shoulders and settled it gently on the floor. After coaxing the other cats off his lap, he stood up and turned his back to me. He pulled a damp rag from a bucket he had on the floor and wiped the inside of one of the cat dishes. "I suppose they would just die in the animal shelter where they get them from anyway."

"We are not talking about the cats." Fortunately for my little brother, my intense frustration had turned my legs to marble. My paralysis made it impossible for me to walk the four feet across the room and shake him real hard.

He picked up one of the cats, a gray tabby that was smaller than the others. "They're not abused while they are here. They are well fed. Got lots of toys." He nuzzled his face against the tabby, which licked his chin. "All the stuff in the world doesn't matter if you are just headed toward death." His voice faltered. "I don't like working here," he said in a hoarse whisper. "But if I don't care about them, who will?"

A white cat with a patch of orange around its eye rubbed against my leg. "Why, Jimmy? Why did you hang out in town for months before finding us? Why did you come so late at night?"

The cat continued to rub against my leg. *Darn it.* I could feel my anger melting with each purr of the feline. I kneeled down and gathered the cat into my arms. The big lug must have weighed twenty pounds. The cat purred so loud that his body vibrated against my stomach. Somehow it didn't bother me that rats and mice had experiments performed on them, but cats?

The critter was sucking all the anger out of me. This time, I asked the question with only a deep sigh. "Why, Jimmy? Why did you come back here at all?" I sat down on the floor, and three more cats made their way toward me.

The tabby squirmed, and Jimmy put him down. "We moved around so much when we were kids. I always thought of Eagleton and Grandma's house as home. We came here every summer— took that trip through Yellowstone."

Finally, an honest answer from him. "Why not get in touch with us sooner?"

Jimmy's smile drained from his face. From the forehead down to the eyes and then across the mouth, the brightness disappeared. Again, he turned his back to me. This time, he picked up a Dustbuster and ran it across the carpet on the cat hotel and scratching posts. Two more cats, a black-and-white one and a long-haired orange critter, rubbed against my knees.

The shrill keen of the vacuum dominated the airspace. Jimmy had made it impossible to continue a conversation—something he had done on purpose, I was sure.

Gently pushing aside assorted cats, I rose to my feet, still gripping the now-wrinkled receipt, evidence of my brother's deception. Yet he had managed to wiggle out of a clear explanation. Jimmy was good at that.

I needed answers before I went to Mom with this. Jimmy sure wasn't going to tell me anything else. I stalked over to him and clicked off the Dustbuster. "You *are* coming home tonight, right?"

"Sure."

"Don't leave again. It will break Mom's heart. Please."

Jimmy stared at the floor and then clicked the Dustbuster back on. I moved toward the door. Over the mechanical buzz of the vacuum, he glanced at me and nodded, reassuring me. Whatever he had done, I would never forgive myself if I drove him away.

I hadn't told him the half of what I had found in his room. Faced with the fullness of my suspicions, he might leave again. I needed more evidence before I made any accusations.

As I slipped out the door, he revacuumed an area he had already gone over several times. I heard the Dustbuster shut off just as the heavy door closed behind me.

I walked back to my Valiant. One more time I pulled the receipt from my pocket. I had a choice to make. I could simply pretend I hadn't found the receipts. Things were good between Mom and Jimmy right now. Why did I have to rock the boat? Why? Why? Why? If he was into something illegal, the pain would only be worse for Mom down the line—and for me because I had allowed myself to hope for a "normal" family.

I clicked the door handle of my Valiant, which of course was jammed. I kicked the door hard with my winter boots. The first time was to unjam the door. The next three times were to expel the frustrations I felt. My kicking became highly stylized. By the fourth kick, I was doing a sort of a sideways karate jab with my leg.

Out of breath, I stood back from my car. I thanked God that I owned a car with a hard steel body and ancient paint job. *Better than hundred-dollar-an-hour therapy,* I thought.

"Car trouble, Ruby?"

Cameron Bancroft stood on the sidewalk, looking oh-so-dignified with his long brown wool coat, unbattered briefcase, and shiny leather boots.

I put my hands on my hips. "I fixed it."

"Not the best place to park."

I clicked open my door. "I was in a hurry." I could read the subtext in his expression and words. He thought I was nuts. I didn't care. Even if the pay was better than the feed store, I didn't want to work here anymore. I'd done enough genuflecting at false idols for a lifetime. I just needed to keep my commitment and get through the rest of the semester. "See you around."

I slipped behind the wheel and turned the key. The Valiant made an obnoxious roaring sputter when it started.

Cameron took two steps back on the sidewalk. I gave him a little wave and pulled out of my space. In the rearview mirror, I could see him still standing on the sidewalk, staring in my direction, coughing from the exhaust fumes. What was he doing on this side of campus anyway? The English offices and classrooms were up the hill.

I drove through town. *What should I do? Ignore what I found out about Jimmy, or try to find out more?* The deception about when he came into town and the stuff under his bed suggested there might be more serious things he wasn't telling Mom and me.

I hit the accelerator hard and did a sharp turn toward home. I didn't like living with a lie. I couldn't pretend.

I drove back to the house and pulled a recent photo of Jimmy off the bulletin board. In it, he sat at a table, holding a pair of scissors next to a man in a wheelchair, whose head tilted sideways. I had shot the picture from above, looking down at him. He smiled for the camera. We had helped Mom teach her craft class to developmentally disabled people. It had been a fun afternoon. We were doing the kinds of things a real family did together: helping the community, hanging out together. It was probably all a lie.

I shoved the picture in my purse and grabbed one of the comic books from underneath the bed. I pulled one from the middle of the pile, making sure to straighten them so Jimmy couldn't tell they'd been disturbed.

The comic book shop was about ten blocks from our house. I found a parking space right in front. Inside, two skinny teenage boys stared at a computer screen and swirled joysticks, pushing buttons at a frantic pace.

An older, but equally gawky kid stood behind the counter sorting and resorting a stack of cards. The kid was maybe seventeen. He had curly brown hair, glasses, and a large nose. When he looked up at me, his muddy eyes, magnified by the glasses, filled most of the lens.

I slapped the comic book on the counter. "Is this worth anything?"

The cards the kid was sorting had medieval looking characters on them. Without stopping the shuffling of his cards, he glanced at the comic book. He did a double take on the comic book, stared at me, and took a step back. His mouth fell open. The cards fell out of his hand and all over the floor and counter.

He pointed a bony finger at the comic book. "That's a . . . that's a . . ." His breathing became erratic and wheezy.

One of the kids playing the video game, a pimple-faced blond, jumped up and ran over to the wheezing teenager, who continued to point at the comic book. "He's asthmatic." He ran behind the counter and proceeded to open and empty drawers. "He's asthmatic. You triggered an attack." The blond teenager located the inhaler by the cash register and handed it to his friend.

The older kid pointed at the comic book while he shoved the inhaler in his mouth.

The blond picked up the comic, read the title, and dropped it like it was on fire. "Ho . . . ho . . . holy . . ." His eyes grew huge, and his hands fluttered spastically. "Holy moley. Oh, holy moley cow! It's a . . . it's a . . ."

"So it's worth something?"

By now, the third kid was alerted to the drama and raced over. While his two cohorts continued to gyrate behind the counter, he picked up the comic book. This one managed to hold onto it. "No way. No way, dude."

"It's valuable?" I was asking such a simple question. I hadn't expected to have the added bonus of the dance floor show before I got my answer.

The calm kid wrinkled his freckled nose at me. "It's a No. 1 *Batman*, 1940 edition, first appearance of Cat Woman and Joker."

"So ballpark, how much is it worth?"

The blond kid behind the counter had calmed down enough to answer. "Like ten thousand dollars." He pounded his hand on the counter. "Ten thousand, dude."

The asthmatic set down his inhaler but continued to slap his chest with a flat hand.

The third kid, the freckle-faced one, looked up at me. "Where did you get it?"

I pulled the comic out of his hand. "I have a brother who's in the business." I stepped toward the door. "He asked me to come down here."

The asthmatic reached a trembling hand toward me. "Can I— can I look at it one more time?"

They all stared at me like children gazing at a Christmas tree for the first time: glassy eyed, open mouthed. "Sure." These kids probably would never be the prom king at their high school. I felt an affinity with them. High school is a few years behind me, but I am convinced whatever label was put on you in high school haunts you for the rest of your life. I was delighted that Loner Poetry Girl could give the Geek Club a thrill just by letting them hold a rare comic book.

I handed the comic book to the older kid. The other two gathered close. Slowly, delicately, he pulled the comic out of the plastic sleeve. All three of them oohed and aahed in unison. He turned the pages carefully while his cohorts gazed and whispered the occasional "Wow."

The older kid put the comic book back in the sleeve and handed it to me.

All three of them thanked me in unison.

They stared and waved at me through the glass door as I pulled away. I hoped all of them invented something cool for computers and made a million bucks.

Even though the police station was a fifteen-minute drive away, I did a decade's worth of thought on my way. No reasonable scenario made it possible for Jimmy to have bought the comic book. He didn't even have money for a car. His job at the animal lab probably didn't pay more than minimum wage.

My brother was a thief. If I was going to tell my mother, I needed something more solid for evidence than a comic book. Jimmy would talk his way out of the facts I already had.

Once inside the police station, I grabbed a visitor's pass from Cindy behind the glass and phoned Wesley's desk number.

"Officer Cree."

"Sevee. It's Ruby. Is Wesley in?"

"He's off shift. We share this desk."

"Can you come out and get me?" I glanced down at the photo of Jimmy. "I have an important question to ask you."

"Sure, get your visitor's pass."

A few minutes later, Sevee came through the locked doors and led me past rooms labeled "Interrogation 1" and "Interrogation 2" to a set of carrels, each with a computer in it along with personal photos. At the back of the room, a middle-aged woman worked on a computer behind a wall of glass, which I suspected was bulletproof.

Sevee sat down at his computer. "What do you need?"

"If I—" I cleared my throat. My voice sounded shaky. "If I had a picture and name, could you tell me if someone is a convict?"

Sevee tugged at the collar of his uniform. "Not really."

I rested a hand on the gray, five-foot-high wall of the carrel and squeezed hard. "You must have access to a database or something."

Cree tapped a few keys on his computer, and the screen returned to a screen saver: a generic picture of lakes and mountains. "I do, but that kind of information is private." He looked right at me with dark, chocolate brown eyes.

"How do I find out?" I stepped into the carrel and leaned close to him.

"Once somebody has been sentenced and judged, it's public record. Affidavits are public record. You have to have a good reason for wanting the information. You could petition the Clerk of District Court."

My hands balled into fists. "That could take months. I need to know now. Can't you just peek for me?"

Cree stared at me for a moment, nodding and half smiling. "No, Ruby, I can't just peek." He rose to his feet and grabbed a chair from another carrel.

He pointed to the chair, and I sat my ornery little behind down. "Sorry. Of course, I don't want you to break any privacy laws."

Cree leaned back on the chair and crossed his feet on the desk. "Why don't you tell me what this is about?"

"I think my brother is stealing stuff. I'm just wondering how long his criminal record is."

"You could check the newspapers. If he was charged with or convicted of something, it would be in the paper."

"Far as I know, he's only been here since March."

"Where did he used to live?"

"I think he said something about having a cat in Jackson Hole."

His chair creaked as he sat up straight. "There you go."

"Thanks." I stood up. Wesley and Sevee hadn't made a huge effort to decorate their carrel. There were two postcards with pictures of motorcycles and a photograph of a frosty-haired man with Wesley and another man with graying temples. Judging from Wesley's long hair, the photo was at least five years old. I didn't see anything that told me something about Cree's personal life. "What kind of name is Sevee anyway?"

Sevee took a gulp from his coffee cup. "I never liked my name much, so I go by my initials, S. V."

"Which stand for?"

Sevee stood up and cupped a hand on my shoulder. "I'll tell you on your and Wesley's wedding day."

"Don't hold your breath."

Cree nodded his head at me, in that knowing, half-smiling way he had. He sat back down at his desk and tapped keys until the file he'd been working on appeared on the screen.

I had no idea where Wesley and I were going. Maybe Sevee's prayer line to God had less static on it than mine.

"Ruby." He clicked a few more keys. "If you go down to the

evidence room, the tech can sign those keys out to you so you can try them in your desk. Wesley put the paperwork through for you."

"Did they figure out what killed Dale?"

"They've been waiting for the body to thaw out. He didn't freeze in that field. Someone had him on ice for quite some time. Shouldn't be long now."

After swinging by the evidence room and getting the keys, I returned my visitor's badge and headed down the stairs. I really wanted to see if one of those keys worked, but I had more pressing business to deal with right now. I tossed the key ring in my purse and drove to the public library. Starting with February, I worked my way through local sections of various Wyoming newspapers. I had to go back a whole year before I found that Jimmy had been charged with writing bad checks. He'd served a short sentence. Eagleton was quickly becoming like Jackson Hole, a hangout for the rich. That's probably what brought Jimmy back up here—not because he wanted to be reunited with his family.

I made copies of the news stories.

The sadness I felt was almost unbearable. All my suspicions had been confirmed. Now came the hard part—telling Mom.

I found her in the big solarium of the senior citizens center. She was teaching her Seniors and Tots painting class. The class was designed for older people and their grandchildren, or any kid who wanted to hang out with senior citizens, to learn to paint.

All the students, maybe twenty of them, stood beside their easels. Snowy, silver-haired, or bald older folks each stood next to a smaller person with a kid-sized easel. The setup was very orderly. Adult. Kid. Adult. Kid.

Mom had arranged a still life of silk flowers in a rusty watering can with my red and turquoise cowboy boots beside it. She loved using my boots in her paintings.

"Now make sure your brush strokes are light, not forced. Just relax." Mom waved her own paintbrush in the air as if she were conducting. "Loose wrist. Relaxed hand."

The winter sun shining through the large windows of the solarium warmed my cheek. Outside, a crystal layer of snow glistened on the lawn. The whole place was bright and open. Off-white linoleum shone as if it had a layer of glaze on it.

I clutched the comic book and the newspaper stories. The clock told me Mom had five minutes left of class. She moved from easel to easel, offering encouraging words to each artist as they packed up their supplies.

When she got toward the back of the room, she saw me and waved. My expression must have given something away because the glow faded from her face.

Her brows furled, and she shook her head. As usual, her long, salt-and-pepper hair was braided and twisted into a bun on her head. She moved around the room with the ease of a ballet dancer.

"Go ahead and finish up with your class," I said.

My timing on this could not have been worse. I should have waited until she got home at the end of the day. I just hated having unsettled business, and I wasn't sure what Jimmy would do now that he knew I was onto him, even though he had promised to come home. Hopefully, he still had that small sense of commitment to his family.

Mom instructed the class to finish up. Several people were still dabbing paint onto their easels when Mom came to the back of the room. "What is it, honey?"

"Is there some place private we can talk?"

"There's nothing going on in the kitchen right now." Mom touched my arm above the elbow and steered me toward a swinging door. "Has something happened to Wesley?"

"No, he's okay."

"What is it, dear?" Mom moved toward a table with an industrial-size coffee maker on it. "We usually have some coffee or tea . . ."

I placed my hand on one of the kitchen's steel counters. "I don't want any, Mom, please." I spread out the papers and the comic book on the counter. "It's Jimmy."

She turned to look at me. "Jimmy?" She said his name pleasantly enough, but her hand rubbed the underside of her chin— something she always does when she's nervous.

I tilted my head toward the stuff on the counter. "He has a record."

She stepped slowly toward the counter and tilted her head to read. Her shoulders drooped. Her rigid spine crumpled. "Are there outstanding warrants? Did he do his time for this stuff?"

"Far as I know."

She stood closer to me. "I have a record, Ruby. Much worse than anything Jimmy did. It's in the past. God forgives."

"I don't think it's in Jimmy's past. I found boxes of jewelry under his bed. And that." I pointed to the comic book.

Her hand moved to the crystal butterfly on her shoulder. The one Jimmy had given her. Her mouth twitched. "He told me himself he was interested in antiques. He's probably been buying with the money he earns at his job."

Why had I thought I wouldn't meet with resistance when I laid out the facts for her? "He's got a minimum-wage job, Mom. There was a lot of jewelry in that box. That comic book is worth ten thousand dollars."

"He is your brother. He is my son. With the Lord's help, we straightened our lives out. Why can't you believe that Jimmy has done the same? He's going to church. God answered my prayer. He brought Jimmy back."

"What if he is dangerous, or—" Really, all his crimes were white collar. I didn't think my brother was violent.

She grabbed my arm in that special place just above the elbow and pressed hard enough to cause me discomfort. "He is my son."

I looked down into her probing blue eyes. Nothing I could say— no amount of evidence—would erase her maternal blind spot. "I think we need to watch him a little closer."

She loosened her hold on me. "I have a class to teach."

I could still feel the pressure of her thumb on my triceps. A gentle reminder that I had crossed a line—betrayed my own flesh and blood. "I hope I'm wrong, Mom. I really do."

She let go of me and turned toward the door. Her soft-soled "practical shoes" hardly made any noise on the linoleum. I gathered my pages of evidence together.

"He is your brother." Her voice was almost a vapor—a ghost-like whisper.

She pushed the swinging door open with her shoulder and left. After the door stopped swinging, I followed her.

All the easels were abandoned in Mom's teaching area. The room was empty. I stared at my mother's back as she clipped a fresh piece of paper onto an easel, dipped and dabbed her brush, and touched it to the canvas. Her narrow fingers and delicate wrist were a whirl of motion. She worked the brush across the canvas, mixing, dabbing, remixing.

A blood red rose emerged beneath the rapid, light brush strokes.

Chapter Sixteen

Jimmy kept his word and came home for dinner that night. Over our bottomless pit of reheated casserole, we limited our conversation to weather, the glory of childhood trips to Yellowstone, and the funny things Mom's students did in her classes. Neither Jimmy nor Mom made any mention of the receipts, the jewelry, or the news stories that revealed Jimmy's past.

The elephant in the living room broke all our furniture and left footprints on the floor. We just kept chatting away above the bellowing and stomping of the angry beast. Had it been anybody else, my mother would have gently confronted, would have tried to work through things. She would have sought out the truth. But with her son, she was happy with an illusion.

The only bright spot of my day was that Wesley called and said he could take me out the next night, which was Friday.

By the time Jimmy left for work the next morning, a tightening anxiety had enveloped my torso. The sensation was familiar, an anaconda suctioning around my stomach and chest, lessening the amount of air I took in with each breath. The trigger for the respiratory problem was always the same. I prefer life when things are moving forward, when conflicts are being resolved. If I couldn't make that happen, I had trouble breathing.

By late afternoon, when I returned from teaching my class, Jimmy still hadn't come home from work, even though he had said he only had to work half a day. I paced the rooms, checked the clock, and tried real hard to fill my lungs with air. Then I checked under his bed. The jewelry, bears, and comic books were gone.

I had three hours until my "perfect" date with Wesley. This time, I wouldn't need hours of preparation and a hundred outfit changes.

My initial motivation for driving back up to campus was to look for Jimmy. I found a parking space. The campus was quiet. Thanksgiving break started partway through the next week, and the student population had already thinned because so many took the whole week off.

Murky layers of charcoal clouds covered the sun. By five it would be dark. I had gone digging into Jimmy's past because lack of resolution bugs me. I needed an explanation. The one thing I didn't want was for Jimmy to disappear again. I didn't think Mom's heart could take that. Besides, we didn't have any more room in our freezer for frozen casserole.

A few people milled across campus, mostly making a beeline for the library or the bookstore. My boots crunched in the snow. A patina of ice blanketed the concrete steps that led up to Bridger Hall. I planted each step with precision, pushed open the door, and made my way down the corridors and stairwells that led to the animal lab. All the way down, I prayed that Jimmy had just stayed late at work to finish up some job. Maybe the cats had shed an extra large amount of fur.

Jimmy wasn't in the lab. Instead I found a woman with clear, pale skin. Brown braids flowed out from beneath a Rastafarian hat. "I didn't see him when I came on shift." She flipped her braids over her shoulder. "Some of his work wasn't done. The mice were fed, but I had to clean their cages."

"You didn't see him at all?" My feet seemed to sink into the floor. The heavy, invisible weight on my chest suffocated me. *I did this. I drove him away. Why couldn't I just pretend?* The girl set her bag of pellets on the table. She tilted her chin. "I didn't see him at all."

"Thank you."

I slowly took the stairs out of the cave while visions of Jimmy leaving again danced through my head. Mom would descend into total paralysis. I should have kept my mouth shut until I had more to go on. I just plain should have kept my mouth shut. I had let my anger control me. At the very least, I shouldn't have said anything to Jimmy. Woulda, coulda, shoulda.

As I came out of Bridger Hall, even shallow breaths required substantial effort. At this rate, I'd be ready for a respirator in the ER by the time my date started. I scanned the campus around me. Older brick buildings stood beside new ones with solar panels. I had no idea where he would go if he left home. Was he still on campus somewhere?

In my peripheral vision, I could see Truman Hall up the hill. *Might as well make this a useful trip.* Somewhere in my subconscious, a little voice told me to wait to see if Jimmy showed up. I had a textbook I needed to get out of my office for my lesson plan, and I hadn't had a chance to try the key ring Wesley had gotten released from evidence. That would kill some time.

I trudged through the snow. Only a few lights were on in the three-story building. I had been issued a key to one of the outside doors, but when I tested the door, it was open.

I sprinted up the stairs toward my office. The tightness around my torso decreased. Maybe if I couldn't resolve things with Jimmy,

I could at least put an end to finding out the mystery of what was in that desk drawer.

I noticed a light on in the main office. I poked my head in, peering past the empty secretary's desk. Cameron Bancroft sat hunched over a stack of papers. He acknowledged me with a nod of his bald head.

I bolted past the rare books display, past Donita's office. My key clicked the lock, I pushed, and the door to my office swung open. I pulled Aldridge's keys from my purse and filed through them. I tried the first one that looked old-fashioned enough to fit with the age of the desk. Too big. I tried a second and third one. On the fourth try, I found a key that fit perfectly, but no matter how hard I turned the key in the lock, it didn't budge. Something wasn't right. This had to be the key. I pulled the key out of the hole and turned it over in my fingers.

I stared at the desk for five minutes. Locks. Keys. Keys and locks. Benjamin Aldridge had said that his dad had given him a book on locksmithing. If Benjamin was into locks and Aldridge had bought him books on locksmithing, maybe good old Dad had taken a look at the book before he gave it to his son. Maybe the desk didn't open with a standard key.

I pushed my chair back and glided all the way around the desk. Then, lying on my back, I inched underneath the locked drawer. At the back of the drawer, fresh-cut wood contrasted with the older wood. When I touched the fresh-cut area, a sprinkling of sawdust fell on my face. The carpet felt itchy against my back as I lay there thinking.

If Aldridge had rigged this up to be opened a different way, he must have told somebody. Who could he trust? Benjamin or . . .

I wriggled out from under the desk, scrambled to my feet, and raced down to the main office. "Cameron, what is Celeste's last name?" Cameron's eyes were glassy. He'd probably been staring at the computer screen for a long time. "Who?"

"Celeste."

"Is she an adjunct?"

"No, she cleans this building."

"Oh, Celeste the Cleaning Woman. I have no idea. Check the Rolodex on Marge's desk."

The Rolodex? Someone needed to introduce Marge to the concept of a computer file.

I found only one Celeste in the Rolodex, and her last name was Stewart. I dialed the number from the secretary's phone. As the rings started, I could feel Cameron staring at me. I turned. He stood in the doorway of his office, rubbing his eyes. His vest was unbuttoned. He pulled his loose tie off and wiped his brow with the back of his hand.

"Why do you want to reach her?"

I looked past Cameron into his office. My heart rate increased. A male voice on the other end of the telephone line said, "Hello."

I hung the phone up. "Guess nobody's home." Without taking my eyes off Cameron, I stepped back toward the door. Blood drummed past my ears.

Cameron wrapped his tie around his hand. "Why did you want to talk to her?"

"I just wanted to ask her what kind of cleaning products she was using. I seem to be having a little bit of an allergy attack. I thought maybe something she was cleaning with was doing it. I don't suppose you have the key to the cleaning closet so I could just look myself?"

"Cleaning staff does. Secretary might." He snorted. "There's no reason why I would need access to cleaning products, now is there?" Cameron lumbered back to his desk and sat down. The glow from the computer screen made his face icy blue. "Budget balancing. Always a pain." He grinned at me, showing lots of teeth. Then he turned his attention back to the computer after running thick fingers through his nonexistent hair.

By the time I'd left the secretary's office and sprinted toward my own, my heart was hammering out a primitive rhythm. Adrenaline coursed through my veins, and my mind raced.

I had left my keys and purse scattered across the floor of my office. I closed the door behind me and leaned against it. I took in a shallow, raspy breath. Cameron had a long, black coat, similar to Dale's, similar to the person Greta had described lurking outside the Aldridge's house. And Cameron was on the hefty side. Greta had thought the man she'd seen at the house was carrying a few extra pounds. I could hear Wes's voice in my head: You can't convict someone based on his wardrobe selection. And if I had been wrong about Dale? Then Wes would ask me in that low silky voice of his what Cameron's motive was.

I swallowed and half filled my lungs and stomach. Once outside my office, I glanced up and down the empty hall. Twice I dropped my keys. My hands weren't moist with sweat; they were swimming in it. I wiped them on my coat and stuck the key in the lock—my hands trembled so badly it took three tries.

I ran through the hall past Donita's office. I stopped at the rare book collection. *Motive? Something to do with these books.* I had to get that drawer open to confirm what I was thinking.

I bounded down the stairs, glancing over my shoulder more

than once. I pushed open the doors and raced toward the Student Union where I would have the protection of lots of people.

My pulse thudded in my neck as I checked the white pages. The number I had just dialed was listed under Joseph and Maureen Stewart. The phone rang three times. A male voice answered. "Hello?"

"Hi, um, is Celeste there?"

"May I ask who's calling?"

"I am Ruby Taylor. I work with Celeste up at the university. I'm her friend."

I heard a muffled cry of, "Celeste. Phone for you." Then footsteps.

"Hi?"

"Celeste, it's me, Ruby." Two women milled past me on their way to the ladies room.

"Hi, Ruby. You called me." Her voice was singsongy.

"Celeste, I need information about Theodore's desk. Did he tell you if there is a special way to open it?" I closed my eyes and clenched my teeth. Maybe I should have allowed for a little more small talk before I hit her with my request.

Silence filled the air for several seconds.

"I'm not supposed to tell. Theodore said not to tell anyone but a policeman."

"Somebody hurt—somebody killed Theodore." I thought of the loaded gun he had kept in his file cabinet. "He knew somebody might hurt him, so he told you how to open the desk, right?"

"I can't break my promise to Theodore. It's wrong to break a promise."

"If I brought a policeman, could you tell me then? Could you tell the policeman how to open it?"

I could hear Celeste breathing, inhaling and exhaling. Her voice trembled when she spoke. "I tried to tell a policeman. Theodore said if anything happened to him, I was supposed to tell the police." She took in an audible gulp of air. "When I . . . when I . . . went to the police station, they . . . they thought I was telling a story." She sobbed. "Because I'm not smart. I would never lie," she cried. "I would never lie."

Celeste sobbed into the phone. *Poor girl. I should have talked to her in person.* "Oh, Celeste, I'm so sorry I—"

A male voice roared across the line. "What are you doing, making my daughter cry?"

I pulled the phone away from my ear. "No it wasn't me, she—"

I could hear Celeste sobbing in the background.

"Just who do you think you are anyway? Do you get some kind of cheap thrill out of making her cry? She is the most kind, most decent—"

"No, sir, please, I was just—"

He hung up. I stood at the pay phone with the receiver pressed hard against my ear. *Now what?*

I rested an elbow on the shelf below the pay phone and tapped the receiver against the cradle. From where I stood, I could see the graying sky through the large windows of the Student Union. *What is this gift I have for totally alienating people when I'm trying to be nice? First Greta Aldridge, and now Celeste.*

People milled through the corridors of the Student Union. From the eatery around the corner, dishes banged and order numbers were called over an intercom. The air was heavy with smells of nacho cheese, burgers, and grease. On a couch about twenty feet away, a male student snored.

It would be stupid, downright moronic, for me to go back to Truman Hall and try to get that desk open. I didn't think I'd given myself away to Cameron, but it didn't make sense to take any chances.

I checked my watch—less than two hours until D-day, my date with Wesley. I picked up the phone and dialed his number. He answered after the seventh ring.

"Hi, Wesley."

"Ruby, hi. Is everything okay? Are we still on for tonight?"

"How about you meet me a little early at . . ." I glanced down at the address by Celeste's phone number. "At 921 South Fifth. And wear your uniform."

"Wear my uniform? Is this some kind of weird game?"

"No. I think I can get some answers about Aldridge's death. But I need your help. The person who has information only wants to talk to a police officer."

Wesley didn't say anything, but I could hear the sound of gears turning in his head. Smoke was probably coming out his ears from the effort it took to process my strange request.

"Please, Wesley, humor me. The woman will be more likely to give me the information if you are in a police uniform."

"Okay, but we'll be done by seven? I made a reservation at that French place downtown."

I was dressed in jeans and cowboy boots. I wouldn't have time to change, and he had picked out a nice place to eat. "Yes, by seven. No problem."

I hung up with this awful feeling in my gut that we weren't going to make it to dinner. I'd gotten on his case for sabotaging a date, and now I was about to do the same thing.

My car was parked at the far end of the lot. It hadn't mattered when I parked there in mid-afternoon daylight that the place was not well lit. Now, as my feet pounded the concrete of the sidewalk, I wished I had paid attention to the location of the streetlights. I saw Cameron behind every tree. Every shadow was suspect.

I heard footsteps. When I glanced behind me, a stocky man with a backpack flung over one shoulder stopped twenty feet from me. He shoved his hands in his pockets while I stared at him. Slowly, he turned and disappeared into the mass of cars.

I dug in my purse for my keys while I kept walking. The instinctive fight-or-flight adrenaline kicked in. My heart hammered away. As I fumbled through my purse, I told myself that the physical reactions I was having to the darkness were just the result of my overactive imagination. My foot slid on the ice, but I righted myself.

There was no reason for Cameron to follow me. Other than his ownership of a long coat, no evidence existed to suggest his guilt about anything.

My foot slipped on the ice again, stretching my inside thigh muscle to a painful length. My toe pointed up, and I slid on my heel. Both legs became airborne. I landed on my behind.

My purse lay four feet in front of me. I glanced around to see if anyone had witnessed my clumsy moment. My thigh muscle burned. I crawled toward my purse and pulled it by the strap toward me. On hands and knees, I patted the sidewalk, feeling for anything that might have fallen out. My fingers touched the cold metal of my keys.

I heard footsteps, rapid and growing louder. I scanned the murky silhouettes of the cars but could detect no movement. The footsteps continued toward me.

I rose to my feet and bolted the twenty paces to my car. I got the key in the door lock on the first try. Again, I scanned the lot. The footsteps stopped as suddenly as they had started. Underneath my heavy winter clothes, I was sweating like a . . . well, like a pig. My heart threatened to go Alien on me and burst out of my chest.

I clicked my door open and stood for a moment in the crisp, evening silence. I didn't hear any more footsteps. A car should be starting up about now. I couldn't bring the vague outlines of the vehicles into focus. Visibility was less than twenty feet. Now I was getting all the deep breaths I could use and then some. It would have been nice if I could have exhaled without that wheezy intensity that bruised my stomach and lungs.

I opened my door and slipped into the driver's seat. I reached for the ignition, then glanced down at my empty hand. *Duh! No key.* I rested my forehead on the steering wheel. In my self-produced panic, I had left my keys in the car door.

With a heavy sigh, I lumbered out of the car, pulled off my glove, and patted the area around the keyhole until I touched cold metal. What I would give for Mom's purse. She probably had three flashlights in that gimungous thing. *Gimungous. That's a Donita word.*

Later, I would recall sketchy details of what happened next. I remember that someone slammed me hard into the door. Hard enough to shut it. I don't know if it was from the force of the push or because I slipped on the ice, but I hit my head severely enough for the darkness to grow even blacker.

I also vaguely remember the sound of my car starting up and someone driving away. I may have created that memory just to fill in blank spots in my brain caused by the trauma, or perhaps I was still conscious enough at that point to hear and comprehend the familiar sputter of the Valiant starting.

I do remember one thing with crystal clarity. I remember thinking as my body hit the snow, *Dear God, it's cold out here. I could freeze, just like Dale.* I remember the chill seeping into my bare hand and the thought that floated across my brain: *Ruby, you should put a glove on that. Your fingers will turn blue, and they will have to cut them off.*

Chapter Seventeen

She had a mole between her lip and nose. Not a dainty Cindy Crawford beauty mark either. It was gimungous. *I'm really liking that word.* Her face was so close to mine that the mole was really all I could see, a round brown dot to focus on. Her breath smelled like burning plastic.

"Pupils are the same size," she said to me. Or at least I thought she was talking to me.

My first coherent thought floated through my brain—I grabbed it. The thought went something like this: *She's a doctor. You would think she could afford to have that thing removed.*

"I don't want to have it removed, Ms. Taylor."

Could she read my mind? I must have said that, not thought it.

Again, she put her face very close to mine. "Can you squeeze my fingers?"

It was then I detected her expensive fragrance, the kind I can only afford to walk through when the perfume girl at the mall sprays it on passersby. "I don't know. Can you squeeze lemons?" Had that come out of my mouth?

I heard a chuckle and a deep male voice. "Sounds like she's back to her sassy old self. I'd say she was okay, Lorraine."

I knew that voice. Where did I know that voice from? If I could just see where the voice had come from . . . but all I could see was Lorraine's big face right in mine again.

"What day is it, Ruby?"

What was up with all the questions she was asking me? Lorraine had lots of wrinkles around her eyes. I twisted my head to the side to see around the good doctor. My homing devices were starting to kick in. I knew that voice—it meant safety and strength.

"You had quite a fall, Ruby." A different voice, female.

It was my mommy. Only her face was all distorted. She had a huge nose and tiny, slanted-back eyes, like I was seeing her through a wide angle lens. And she was holding—a cat. *A cat?*

Help, I'm trapped in a Salvador Dalí painting, and I can't get out.

Her warm fingers touched my cheek.

Mommy.

"Quite a blow to your head, dear."

The cat yowled—a toe-curling bellow.

"That thing will spread germs." Dr. Lorraine straightened up and put her hand on her hip.

Mom drew the cat protectively to her chest. "I couldn't leave the poor thing at home. I sure couldn't leave her in the car. She was so frightened and cold when she showed up in my yard."

That was my mom, always rescuing the orphans. The cat, a black critter with white around the rim of one eye, nuzzled into Mom's neck.

"You got a little frostbite here." Dr. Lorraine held my fingers in her dry, cold hands. "Not too bad though."

"Good thing I found her when I did." It was that male voice again, only this time it came attached to some strong hands— hands that took over the holding of my frostbitten fingers. *Can hands do what lips do?*

I gazed up into heavily lidded green eyes. *Ooh-la-la.* "Hi, Wesley."

He laced his fingers in mine. "Hi there."

He was dressed in his policeman's uniform. I stared at his badge. The sight of the uniform opened a floodgate. The whole gamut of what I had planned for the night flowed through in one giant wash of memory. "Celeste," I said. I bolted into a sitting position. A hot ball of pain exploded at the front of my head. "Owww!" I lay back down.

"Shhh, shhh. Don't try to move." Wesley touched my cheek. I could hear Dr. Lorraine giving instructions to my mother. Their voices were nothing more than background noise. I was enjoying the soothing sound of WKI Wesley, easy listening radio. His voice made me sleepy and warm and mushy all over. My eyelids felt heavy.

"I went over to Celeste's by myself. Sounds like Aldridge put a mag lock at the back of the drawer. It's triggered by a switch. Celeste told me where the switch was." He traced my jawline with his finger. "You need to quit harassing Celeste."

My eyes shot open. "I wasn't harassing her. She's my friend."

"Her father seemed to think you made her cry." Wesley pulled the heavy blanket up around my neck. "When you didn't show up, I got a funny feeling."

"Cop instinct?"

"No, care-about-you instinct."

His affectionate remarks were warming me up faster than the thermal blanket. "That's nice," I cooed.

"I went up on campus to look for you. By the time I found you, you had a little hypothermia. I carried you to my car."

"We carried me to the car."

"We?" Wesley grinned. "Yeah, something like that."

"Just like a knight in shining armor." My eyelids felt really heavy. *That evil Dr. Lorraine must have given me something. Darn her anyway.* I needed to stay coherent for this romantic moment.

"You were shivering pretty badly. I wrapped my coat around you, brought you here, and called your mom."

Nuts. The one place you didn't want a date to end up was in the emergency room, and that's exactly where I was.

Sadness that made my muscles heavy started in my neck and trickled down to my toes. "You were being gallant, and I missed the whole thing because I was unconscious." The trauma or whatever Dr. Lorraine had given me loosened my tongue. The filter I normally ran all my feelings through wasn't functioning. I was saying exactly what was on my mind—exactly what I felt.

"Sorry. I tried to wake you," said Wesley.

"You were being a prince of a guy, and I missed the whole thing." I didn't know what the doctor had given me, but it wreaked havoc with the control systems I had on my emotions.

Wesley leaned over and kissed my forehead. "You are Cinderella, my sassy Cinderella," he whispered in my ear and then stood up. "Ruby, you're crying." He touched the rim of my eye with a delicate fingertip.

"Am I?" Warm tears trickled past my temple. "I want to make this relationship work, but I don't how. I just know how to ruin relationships." I really had to get that emotional filter fixed. I was being way too honest.

Wesley's fingers traveled down my face. He cupped my chin and jaw in his hands. The heat of his touch radiated through me. His Adam's apple moved up and down. He drew his dark arched eyebrows together, forming a tiny vertical ridge between them.

"Me neither. Other than saving sex for marriage, I don't know how you make things work long term."

"I thought being a new critter meant I got to start over. Like I could be sixteen again and do it right this time. But the past keeps breathing down my neck. It's kind of like we are both programmed to ruin relationships out of habit."

He nodded. "Out of habit. With our history, we practiced for divorce, for breakups, not for anything permanent."

"Sorry I sabotaged our date."

He nodded, then took my hand and squeezed it tight. "We're even on that score. Third time's the charm?"

"I don't know." But I did know. I was bent on wrecking the thing I wanted most. Where relationships were concerned, I had a first-strike philosophy. Because I was so afraid of being hurt, I destroyed the relationship before it got to that point. My head cleared a little bit. "We're going about this all wrong. We're doing exactly what we did with other relationships; we're dating."

"What else is there to do?" Wesley squeezed my hand tighter.

"Do things together with other people around—no dating. I need to meet your family."

Wesley stared at me without saying anything. Maybe he wouldn't accept my proposal.

Mom stuck her head into the frame of my vision. "Ruby, honey, the doctor doesn't think there is any long-term damage. We're supposed to watch you for twenty-four hours—wake you while you sleep—to make sure you don't slip into a coma."

"I need to go back up to campus." I lifted my head about an inch. Evil Dr. Lorraine had put lead weights in my brain.

The cat crawled out of Mom's arms and onto my stomach.

Mom tugged on the blanket, straightening it. "You're supposed to rest."

I could feel the cat's purring through the blanket as it settled on my chest and belly. "Wesley will go with me. I need to go back up on campus. What did that doctor give me anyway?"

"Nothing, dear. It's the hypothermia; it makes you drowsy." She patted and squeezed my shoulder.

"I can't be drowsy. I need to get up on campus. I need to get that drawer open." With considerable effort, I propped myself up on my elbows. My head hurt, but this time I was ready for the hot coal of pain. "Wesley, will you help me?"

"I suppose if I don't go with you you'll just go by yourself." He turned and looked at my mother. "At least that way someone will be there to catch her if she blacks out." He still hadn't answered my proposal about us just doing stuff together. At least he was willing to help me with this.

Dr. Lorraine reached for the cat. "Germ spreader. It has to go." The feline's hackles went up, and it released a low, guttural warning. Dr. Lorraine shrank back.

I petted the cat's head. "Guard kitty."

Dr. Lorraine's shoulders stiffened, and her nostrils flared in and out. "I'm releasing you into your mother's care, Ms. Taylor. Please take the cat when you go. We'll have to wash down this whole unit."

The doctor stalked away down a long corridor. A nurse standing behind the counter talked on the phone. All the curtains were pulled shut so I couldn't see the patients behind them.

After a good fifteen minutes, I worked my way up to a sitting position and eased my aching body off the gurney, wobbling as I stood up. Mom helped me into my coat while Wesley steadied me by holding my arm.

Wesley went ahead to get his car so I wouldn't have to walk across the lot, injured damsel that I was.

On our way out of the ER, I leaned close to Mom and asked, "Jimmy come home yet?"

Mom shook her head. The cat snuggled underneath Mom's ratty old brown coat with its head sticking out by Mom's neck. The look on Mom's face siphoned the marrow from my bones and twisted my stomach. The fluorescent lights made her skin appear pale and bluish. Her mouth twitched. Everything about her face—the slack jaw and lidded eyes—suggested fatigued defeat.

"He's coming back. He wouldn't do this again." My voice lacked conviction.

She met my gaze, and to her credit, she didn't blame me for Jimmy's disappearance. I would rather she attack and blame me. Her vulnerability just made me feel guilty all over.

"If he doesn't come back, I'll find him, Mom."

Wesley pulled up with the Jeep. I pushed open the big glass doors. "You want us to wait while you walk to your car?" Cold air swirled into the ER.

"I parked close." She nuzzled her nose against the purring cat. "I'll be fine." Her words rang with insincerity as if she were reading from a script.

"You sure?"

She nodded.

"I won't be long. Just go home and have some tea. I'll be home." I yanked on the door handle of the Jeep and then remembered that the passenger-side door still didn't work. With a groan, I hobbled around to the driver's side and climbed awkwardly across the seat.

"Sorry," Wesley said. "I gotta get that fixed."

As Wesley and I pulled away, Mom still stood at the big glass doors. The cat had crawled out of her coat. She cradled it like a baby, stroking its belly.

When we neared the campus, I rooted through my purse for the keys to Truman Hall. "Where was my purse when you found me?"

"Over your shoulder. Why?"

"My car was gone, right?" I didn't trust my own memory of the event.

Wesley nodded as he pulled into the university parking lot. "Some kid was probably waiting in the lot—looking for an opportunity." He glanced at me as he pulled into a space. "What are you thinking?"

"Cameron Bancroft has a long coat. He's built like Greta described. I think he and Aldridge had something going on with that rare books collection, and somehow Dale's connected too."

"Meaning?" Wesley found a parking space in the visitor's lot. He clicked the key to kill the motor.

"Say Cameron's using the money he got from that old guy to buy the books. But then he fences the books and replaces them with cheap look-alikes. Aldridge is in on the deal. That's why over the summer he had that extra cash. Then he becomes a Christian, has a crisis of conscience, and decides to turn himself—and Cameron—in. So Cameron kills him."

"That's a good story. Just one thing is missing."

"What?"

He leaned closer to me. "Evidence."

I touched his whiskery chin. "I know; women's instinct only counts in Agatha Christie novels." We had a moment where he got all gooey-eyed on me, real soft focus. Gooey eyes are usually a prelude to a kiss.

Wesley looked away before I did. He turned his back to me and opened the door of the Jeep. Yeah, we had some things to talk about. But now wasn't the time.

I crawled out on the driver's side while Wesley held the door for me. I still felt lightheaded.

The sky was pitch black as we walked across campus on the icy sidewalks. "Maybe Cameron was trying to scare me or hurt me. He took the car. Maybe he thought I was going to the police."

The night was windless and cold. Light shone from the windows in the library and the student union, but many of the other buildings were dark. It was nearly nine o'clock on a Friday night—hardly high-traffic time.

"How does Dale fit into this picture?"

"I don't know." I massaged my neck. My head still throbbed from the accident. "He had the same book about rare books. A professor might not know how to black-market something like that. They needed a fence."

We circled around Truman Hall to the door I had a key to. I clicked the lever on the doorknob.

With Wesley taking up the rear, we made our way up the dark stairwell. I slipped off my coat and hung it over my arm. Our feet rhythmically hitting the carpeted stairs was the only sound in the building.

When we reached the top of the stairs that led to my office,

Wesley put his hand on the middle of my back. I so appreciated his strength, his desire to protect.

We walked toward the rare books display. "Those are the books I told you about."

Wesley touched the wood frame of the display case. "I need something more solid before a judge would issue a warrant to get an expert to look at these closely."

I continued down the hall. Wesley followed.

A single light had been left on by the main office, which was locked. Cameron was gone.

"Just down this way." I found the light switch for the hallway. Wesley stood behind me as I shoved the key in my door. I hit the light for my office. I scanned the desk, the bookshelf. Everything looked as it had when I left.

"They use mag locks in security systems, usually for doors." Wesley stepped into the office. He kneeled on the floor beside the desk. "The magnets have six hundred to twelve hundred pounds of pressure—no way could you get them open by pulling on them." Carefully, he opened one of the side drawers and lifted the false bottom. He grabbed the flashlight off his policeman's belt. "See, he ran the wire from the back and installed the switch down here."

Without a word, I reached in and clicked the switch. We worked well together, even if we were stumbling through our romantic relationship. Ruby and Wesley: ace crime fighters—courtship goof-offs.

Again without prompting, I reached up and pulled the locked drawer open. My whole body contracted with anticipation as I stood up.

"You do the honors," Wesley said.

I peered inside. Lying on the cedar wood lining was a book, a collection of Edgar Allen Poe's short stories.

Wesley put his head close to mine. "A book?" He touched a black box at the back of the drawer. "Transformer. The lock only needs twelve volts."

Already the heaviness of disappointment threaded around my limbs. "Makes sense. He's a professor." I was hoping for a little more. I picked up the volume. "Why go to all this trouble to lock away a collection of short stories?" I looked at the top of the book where a bookmark poked out. "It's gotta mean more than it looks like it means."

"What, like some kind of secret code? Ruby, this isn't an episode of *Murder She Wrote* where the dead person leaves a cryptic message behind. Maybe someone already got the important stuff out of the drawer."

"You were never a lit major. Of course he would do it this way." I opened the first page of the book. "It's a first edition. Cameron said something about an old guy at that dedication. That's where they got the money for the collections. His name is on the bookcase down the hall. You know, in memory of blah, blah, blah."

"Blah, blah, blah?" Wesley seemed mildly amused by my broken steel-trap memory. He mimed taking out his notepad. "I'll just write that down."

"Now look who's being sassy and sarcastic. The old guy had a weird-sounding name." I opened the book to the page that was marked. Aldridge had placed a neatly folded piece of paper by the story "The Telltale Heart." I stood up and started to look around the room. "Tell me Wesley, did you take any literature classes at all in your life?"

"I was in the marines, remember?"

"So you probably know how to light a fire with toenail clippings, live on bugs and dirt for days, and kill the enemy using only elbows as a weapon, but you, dear sir, don't know why it matters that he marked 'The Telltale Heart.'"

Wesley shook his head. "Good thing I have you here." He took the book out of my hand. "Why don't we see how loose these floorboards are?"

I raised an eyebrow, impressed with his literary knowledge.

"I had no TV growing up. While my father was doing research on the next conspiracy he could be paranoid about, I was reading all the classics our little public library had."

I moved to a corner of the office on my hands and knees. "Glad to hear it. I was afraid I was attracted to a muscular thug." I peeled back the carpet and felt for loose boards.

Wesley was already checking the other corner not occupied by the desk. "The dead body in that story was hidden under the floorboards. In the main character's deranged mind, the heart of the corpse beat so loudly it convicted him of his guilt." Wesley tore back more carpet.

"Exactly." My voice contained an unexpected tone of surprise. I had treated him like six feet of gorgeous, only responding to surface things. There were layers to Wesley I didn't know about. My attraction for him clicked up a notch, beyond the physical. I liked his brains.

He stopped poking at the floor, sat back on his heels, and looked at me. "You know, Ruby, not everyone who's knowledgeable about something has letters behind their name. Some of us had an informal education."

Wesley was doing that thing where he stared at me, but it was like he was looking beyond me, underneath me.

"I know that. I've been arrogant," I said.

Wesley gazed at me a moment longer and then returned to his work. "I think I found it."

As he lifted the board, I crawled across the carpet. I pulled away another board, which created about an eight-by-six-inch hole. We worked with our shoulders pressed together. I relished his physical proximity more than anything, craved it like chocolate. At the same time, I knew it was the most destructive force in the universe. *What's a girl to do?*

I cleared away the scraps and peered down into the hole. "See, Wesley," I gave him my best raised-eyebrow I-told-you-so look.

He grabbed his flashlight off the floor and turned it on.

I reached down into the shallow hole and pulled out the contents of Aldridge's "telltale heart," wondering whom it would impugn.

Chapter Eighteen

The contents of Theodore Aldridge's "heart" didn't exactly beat loud enough for the D.A. to write up an indictment. His secret hiding place contained a Bible, a well-used baseball, and a smooth, flat stone. Below that were detailed pencil drawings of various household items: computer, phone, washing machine. Each drawing had a cutaway that showed the inside parts of the object. At the bottom of each drawing, written in precise, carefully formed letters, was the word "Ben."

I pulled out a spiral notebook that functioned as a journal. I leafed through it. The journal started on September 6, the day Aldridge became a Christian, and ended September 19, the day before he died. Each entry ended with the words "Jesus loves me—that's all I know and all I need to know." The last entry consisted of only the date. Aldridge had placed the notebook in his hiding place in anticipation of coming back the next day to make another entry.

My throat tightened as I leafed through the entries. Aldridge had had only thirteen days as a new critter in Christ before his past caught up with him. But it had been time enough to let his sons know he loved them.

I scanned his notes. They chronicled his meeting with his sons, his attempts to talk to his ex-wife, his breaking up with Lorelei Phillips. On one line he wrote, "Celeste tells me that when I mess up I can start over. Her faith is so simple, so straightforward." Nothing in the journal alluded to Cameron Bancroft or any crime.

Underneath the journal was a video labeled, "Dale Cutler: Freshman Project."

The date on it was for spring semester the previous year. Lorelei Philips was listed as the advisor.

I shrugged.

Wesley shrugged.

"The media room is probably locked, but there's a classroom downstairs with a VCR in it. I have a key for that."

"Hope there's something on the tape." Wesley leafed through the journal. "I don't think this stuff is worth turning in for evidence."

I opened the fresh new pages of the Bible. Aldridge hadn't had much of a chance to read this before he died. The contents of the drawer were his hidden life—the secrets he kept. He hadn't told many people about his new faith. Of the first people he'd told, Greta hadn't believed him and Lorelei could only see his conversion in terms of how it affected her. I wondered if that negative reaction had made him hide his faith. Video in hand, I rose to my feet.

Wesley followed me as I padded down the dark hallway. Truman Hall didn't feel like Truman Hall without lights, people, and ideas circulating around. The locked doors and dark hallways held a sense of foreboding that the daylight and noise hid. Now, even our footsteps were muffled by the carpet.

At the top of the first flight of stairs, Wesley's fingers touched my elbow. I heard a click. A cylinder of light washed over the stairs. "Be a pity to have to pick up pieces of you at the bottom of the stairs." Wesley held the flashlight by his ear.

Below, I could see the carpeted stairs and the hallway covered in industrial-strength linoleum. Some of the classroom doors were open.

"Yeah, you probably wouldn't put me back together right anyway." I tromped down the stairs.

After I unlocked the door to the classroom, I switched on a single light that hung over the VCR, turned on the TV, and shoved in the tape. I sat in a desk next to Wesley. With the exterior of a coffee shop as background, the credits indicated that Dale was the writer, director, and editor of the project. I recognized the coffee shop as one not far from campus.

The first scene showed the interior of the coffee shop. The plot of the short film involved a young man and woman who were in the process of breaking up. The scenes were shot inside and outside the coffee shop, and as the woman drove away down the street. For the exterior shots, the larger campus buildings loomed in the background.

We watched the full fifteen minutes of film. As the ending credits rolled, Wesley said, "There's nothing here."

"Dale must have given it to him for a reason. Dr. Philips said he asked her if she had a copy. Aldridge hid it and told Dale where it was. That's why Dale was rooting through my office. It must be important."

"All the stuff under the floorboards was personal. Maybe he kept this film because Dale was like a son to him. Everything that was precious to him was there."

"Then why hide it so cryptically?"

Wesley rose to his feet. "It's just a teenybopper love story, Ruby. There's nothing there." He squeezed my shoulder. "I'm going to go get our stuff upstairs, and we'll go get something to eat."

"Let's do takeout. I need to get home to Mom. I'm a little worried about her." Again, our visions of a perfect date fell dismally short of reality. Somebody else had our table at the French restaurant.

As the tap, tap of Wesley's boots on linoleum faded, I pressed the play button and watched the tape again. This time I stood up, my nose not more than two feet from the screen. The interior coffee shop scenes must have been filmed during business hours. From time to time, people in the background glanced at the camera self-consciously. Maybe the story wasn't significant. Maybe it was something in the coffee shop or on the street. I rewound the tape and watched the coffee shop scenes again. It was in the rewind that I saw the flash of coppery red.

I stopped the tape, rewound, and hit play again. A table in the far background caught my eye. I paused the tape. The closer I got to the screen, the more I saw nothing but dots. I stood back about three feet. My forehead throbbed where it had been smashed into my car door. The aftereffects of the hypothermia still made me weak and drowsy.

I stared at the paused video screen. A numbing paralysis overtook my body, and my gut turned tight, tangled somersaults. Even with the white lines created by the pause button, I recognized the twosome in the booth. They'd been filmed in profile: Cameron Bancroft, recognizable because of his girth and bald head, on one side of the booth, and my brother, in all his red-headed glory, on the other side. They were at the edge of the screen, so they probably weren't aware they were in the camera shot. I hit the play button.

People walked in front of them, they slipped in and out of focus and were on screen maybe a minute and half, but if I concentrated only on them, I could clearly see Cameron push a book across the table. A few seconds later, Jimmy pulled money out of his wallet, counted it, and gave it to Cameron. My brother, the fence.

Someone watching the video, concentrating on the main action, wouldn't notice the exchange. But Dale viewing the film frame by frame as he edited it had seen it. Had he given the film to Aldridge not realizing that he was involved?

I heard Wesley's footsteps behind me.

"I think I know why this tape was hidden."

Wesley didn't say anything.

"I was right about Cameron." I wasn't quite sure how Dale had recognized the act between Jimmy and Cameron as criminal. Unless Aldridge had already confessed to Dale. That had to be it. Aldridge must have told him in the days before he was killed. "See for yourself." I hit the play button.

Wesley was silent. He didn't step toward the television screen. I turned slightly . . . then stopped.

"Maybe another time. We should get home." A quiver crept into my voice. I pressed the eject button, grabbed the tape and swallowed hard. Someone was standing behind me—and it wasn't Wesley. I didn't turn around. My heart thudded in my ears. I sensed his presence, could hear him breathing in and out.

My skin cooled as perspiration seeped through my pores. I closed my eyes and tried to remember the layout of the room. If I dashed toward the door, could I make it up to Wesley?

I turned slowly. The only light in the room was the small fluorescent above the VCR. In my peripheral vision, I could just make out the profile of a person—probably male.

"Enjoy the movie?"

I recognized Cameron's voice.

I looked sideways without moving my head. I had a straight shot to the door. Wesley had to be on his way back by now. I just needed to buy some time.

"How did you know I was here?"

"Been keeping an eye on you since you chased me out of Theodore's house. Figured you'd find what I couldn't." He took two steps toward me.

I leaned in the direction of the door, but my feet were glued to the floor. I pressed my thumb against the tape and leaned even harder.

Cameron took another step toward me. His hand was out. "I'll take that and anything else you found."

I just hate the awful wheezy breathing that comes with total panic. "What else do you think we found?" For someone whose heart was pumping with the erratic tenacity of a Mexican jumping bean, I sounded remarkably calm.

"Just give me the tape."

I managed a single step toward the door.

"Your boyfriend's not coming for you."

A punch in the stomach couldn't have taken the air out of me faster. He'd hurt Wesley . . . or worse.

I turned to look full at Cameron's silhouette. He still had his hand out. Light reflected off his bald spot. "I'll lose my job, the department. I love this university. No one has to get hurt. Maybe we can talk about a permanent teaching appointment for you."

So that was his strategy—to bribe me with a job offer. Good thing I was totally disillusioned about the institution of higher learning.

I raised my arm as if I were about to give him the video. *Ha! Did he think I'd give in that easy?* Fueled by anger over what he might have done to Wesley, I dashed toward the door.

Darkness in the hallway disoriented me. With Cameron's footsteps pressing on my ears, I ran toward where I thought the stairs were. Cameron was no Joe Athlete. Any other time, I could have outrun him easily. But my muscles were mushy and weak from the incident.

My inner compass told me I'd gone too far. Why hadn't they put some windows in this dungeon? I found a wall to guide me, but I wasn't sure exactly where I was going. The sandpaper texture of the brick scratched my hand.

Cameron's heavy footsteps and raspy breathing helped me keep track of him. He was in worse shape than I was. *Thank you, God.* I slipped into a small alcove. Sweat trickled down my temple. I shoved the video inside my shirt in my waistband.

Cameron clicked on lights as he traversed the hallways. His slow footsteps crescendoed. Light flooded through the hallway where I crouched. If I stayed here, he'd find me. If I ran, he'd see me. Choices. choices. The empty hallways functioned like an echo chamber. It was hard to tell how close he was.

The footsteps stopped.

Where was Wesley? Certainly Cameron wasn't able to overpower an ex-marine who had police training. Maybe Cameron was lying. Maybe Wesley was examining the desk or reading or going to the little boy's room. *Yeah, right! And maybe lemon juice doesn't hurt when you pour it in a paper cut.* Cameron had found some way to disable him, or Wesley would have been here by now.

I couldn't wait for a rescue. Inhaling deeply, I rose to my feet.

I could see the exit doors. I sprinted toward them. Cameron raced after me. He was closer than I thought. Right on top of me.

The doors loomed in front of me. Thirty feet. Cameron's wheezy inhale and exhale was oppressive—like he was breathing in my ear, inches from it. Two sets of feet pounded on the linoleum. I kept my focus on the double metal doors. Twenty feet.

I felt a tug at my collar, then a tightening around my neck. I gasped for air as my throat was constricted. He was choking me with my own shirt. I swung around. His face was inches from my own. The acidic odor of perspiration and cologne mingling made me dizzy. Bad smells as a weapon—there was a concept.

Cameron spoke with clenched jaw. "Give me the tape." He pressed his sweaty hand against my neck, then yanked on my shirt.

I kicked him hard in the shins with my cowboy boots. He made the sound a poodle makes when it's stepped on. He let go of my shirt, but the kick didn't have the doubling-over effect I had hoped for. His fingers snaked around my forearm. So I kicked him again— a little higher up. I'm a lady, mind you, but sometimes the occasion calls for very unladylike behavior. This time, he made the sound a rottweiler makes when it's stepped on—*and* he doubled over.

I propelled myself toward the door and out into the freezing night.

Chapter Nineteen

I had already had frostbite one time tonight. I really wasn't in the mood for a repeat performance. Both the Student Union and the library were dark. At this time of night, I wouldn't find any crowds of safety to run into.

My boots pounded on the sidewalks. Icy patches slowed me down. My lungs felt like they'd been scraped with long fingernails. My bare arms tingled from cold.

Behind me, the doors of Truman Hall burst open, and Cameron took a clear trajectory in my direction. I needed a place to hide.

I could circle back to Truman Hall, hope I found an unlocked door, hope Wesley wasn't completely incapacitated. No, not a good option. Cameron knew Truman Hall too well.

Don't ask me why. I suppose it's because human instinct is to gravitate toward the familiar. The only other building on campus I knew the layout of was Bridger Hall, where the animal lab was.

I veered from the icy sidewalks onto the more stable snow. My arms had goose pimples the size of golf balls. My breath came out in vapory puffs. Hopefully, some overly ambitious grad student was working late. One grad student. That's all I needed—one grad student who had left the doors unlocked.

Cameron zigzagged toward me. I had maybe fifty yards on him. I bolted up the steps of Bridger Hall, hoping the darkness would provide a degree of cover. I pulled the handle of the door. *Please open. Please open.* The door separated from the frame, and I took in a deep breath. It squeaked as I pulled it toward me. I cringed.

On a campus this quiet, almost any noise was noticeable.
I opened the door about ten inches and slipped inside. The last
sound I heard was Cameron's approaching footsteps.

I crouched and peered out the tiny window by the door.
Cameron headed up the sidewalk that led to Bridger Hall, but he
stopped and glanced from side to side. *Please, God, make him go
somewhere else.*

The second floor was completely dark. Where was that ambitious grad student when you needed him? I made my way down
the stairs. I was more likely to find an exit in the basement than
on the third floor.

When I got downstairs, I found the animal lab door ajar. I
pushed it open.

"Hello?" There had to be someone here. If the lab was worried
enough about sabotage from activists to have a security system,
certainly they wouldn't leave the door unlocked.

The videotape pressed into my rib cage. I could hide it here
and come back to get it. If Cameron did find me, it would be better if I didn't have the tape. I pulled it out of my waistband.

I gripped the cassette and stared at the rows of rodent cages.
Those cages were probably cleaned every day, but I had no desire
to retrieve a tape with hamster doodie on it.

Several hamster wheels squeaked as I left the first room. *Late-
night workouts with Richard the Rodent. Come on, ladies, get those
tails up, move those paws.*

After opening the heavy door, I made my way down the hall
toward command central. Through the window, I noticed a shelf
of videotapes beneath the monitors. I slipped inside the office.
The security system must function similar to that in a convenience

store. They kept the tapes for a period of time before recording over them.

I tore Dale's label off and found a replacement in a desk drawer. I wrote today's date on it and put it at the back of the shelf so it would be a while before it was grabbed for reuse. I ripped a tiny corner of the label off so I could distinguish it from the others when I came back for it.

I saw motion out of the corner of my eye and turned my attention to the monitors. All the little critters were quiet except for the cats. Four, maybe five, cats wrestled with each other and climbed up and down their carpet trees. I could have sworn there had been close to ten cats there when I'd confronted Jimmy. Maybe they'd already been done away with.

I placed my fingers on the screen. "Poor kitties."

Something moved on another monitor. In fuzzy black and white, I saw Cameron enter the rodent room. With my heart hammering, I thought about diving under the desk. No, too obvious a hiding place. Instead, I ducked behind a stack of food bags in the corner by the door. A shelf above me that held smaller bags of food created a shadow that covered me. The corner where I crouched was dark, and I had a clear view of the monitors. In order to fit, I had to pull my knees up to my chin.

The image on the monitor was murky—shades of gray bled into each other. It was Cameron's round build and bald spot that told me it was him. Besides, who else would be skulking through the animal lab at this hour? He did a half turn in the rodent room before heading toward the door that led to the office where I was hiding and the other animal rooms. He disappeared off screen.

I heard the hall door click open.

As he stepped across the threshold, he popped up on a monitor that covered the hallways. I watched him as he turned toward the door that opened command central. The room got colder, and light flooded in.

From my vantage point, I could see him from the knees down. His feet tapped across the floor. I saw his knees bend as he checked under the desk. He spent some time standing still, occasionally saying "Hmm," and jingling the keys and coins in his pocket. *Must be watching the monitors.*

My legs cramped. I really wanted to stretch them out. Each breath I took seemed outrageously loud to me. But Cameron just kept watching *Animal Lab Adventures.*

Apparently, the images on the monitors were enormously entertaining, because he spent roughly half a century viewing them while my calves and thighs twisted tighter. He was probably formulating some new class in his head—Animal Lab Videos 101, an in-depth exploration of the cultural merit of fuzzy images of animals doing nothing. Why not? Everything from the back of cereal boxes to pornography were considered good texts for academia.

Being pretzeled in this dark corner with nowhere to go and my limbs cramping up like macramé gave me way too much time to think. I pondered how much the academic world and I didn't fit each other anymore. I thought about how much I missed working full-time at the feed store. I desperately wanted to get back to my going-nowhere job.

I bent my stiff neck back slightly. My head still burned from the carjacking incident.

Cameron coughed and turned in my direction.

I pressed my lips together and held my breath. My stomach growled. I hadn't eaten since lunch.

He took three steps toward my corner. Blood drummed past my eardrums. The cramping in my legs had become painful. Screams of agony compiled themselves in my empty stomach, preparing for launch.

Come on, Cameron, just go. Go, go, go.

I gritted my teeth. *Go, please, go.* Pain, red hot and burning, pulsated through my legs.

Cameron stepped toward the door and slipped through, closing it behind him.

I waited. *One Mississippi. Two Mississippi.* I tilted my pain-racked neck toward the shelf above me. *Three Mississippi.* Cameron's footsteps faded. He was headed away from the rodent room, away from the only exit. *Four Mississippi.*

With a heavy sigh, I stretched out my legs. I massaged my calves before crawling out from behind the feed bags. When I peered through the windows of command central, I couldn't see Cameron. He was out of range of the monitors as well.

I eased the door open and crawled toward the next door that led to the rodent room. Footsteps. More coughing. He was coming back.

Adrenaline pulsed through my veins. I straightened my legs. My guess was this was Cameron's first tour of the animal lab. Because I knew the layout of this place better than he, I could navigate my way to the door faster than he could in the dark. I flicked off the hallway lights.

The footsteps stopped. "Hey—"

I scrambled through the door and placed two animal cages on

the floor—a little something for Cameron to stumble over. I memorized the path to the door before hitting that light switch too. I had almost total blackness for cover.

Cameron opened the door to the rodent room. As I sneaked into the hallway, I heard the impressive mingling of metal, surprised mice, swear words, and pudgy human flesh. I felt along the cold concrete until I found the stairs.

I dashed up the stairs and out the door into the crystal cold night. Moonlight gave the snow a cool blue glow. I crossed my arms over my chest and leaned forward. The temperature had dropped twenty degrees.

A police car with Wesley standing beside it was parked in the middle of campus between Truman and Bridger Hall. Wesley saw me and raced toward me.

I slowed down. My muscles got heavier with every step. I hadn't eaten since lunch, my head throbbed, and I was really, really tired.

Wesley gathered me into his arms. "I was worried about you."

I pointed toward Bridger Hall. "He's in there. Cameron is in there. He tried to hurt me."

Wesley led me toward the patrol car. His soft grip around my frozen arm buoyed me. I shivered. After he radioed the other cop searching the campus to look in Bridger Hall, he opened the back door of the cop car and sat me on the seat.

Without a word, he retrieved a blanket from the trunk and wrapped it around me.

"Where were you?" I had meant for the question to sound demanding, but my words were weak with no punch at all to them.

He kneeled in the snow and looked up at me. "Someone locked me in your office."

"Cameron."

His hand touched my cheek. "I removed the ceiling tiles and crawled over to the next office, used the phone to call for backup. By the time I got outside, I had no idea where you'd gone."

I really wanted to be angry at him for not coming to my rescue, but all I felt was gratitude. Whatever happened to us, right now, I was glad he was here. Glad he was in my life. I slipped off the seat into his arms. His fingers touched my hair, my neck. The emotional impact of all that I had been through hit me.

My brother was a criminal. The video proved that beyond a doubt. I was going to have to tell Mom. We couldn't play pretend anymore. Cameron had probably killed two people over some old books.

I sobbed into Wesley's neck. This night had been too much. I was exhausted, my head hurt, and my stomach growled. He stroked the back of my head, making soothing sounds.

"The whole time I was running from Cameron, I kept hoping you would show up."

"Looks like you handled yourself all right." Nuances of admiration threaded through his voice.

"I just hate being dependent on you. Needing you scares me. I'm afraid I'll lose myself."

"That's a lot of personality to lose." Wesley touched my lips with his fingers. "Everything about this relationship scares you, doesn't it?"

I relished the glow of affection I saw in his eyes.

"You mean you're not afraid?"

Wesley lowered his eyes.

He was terrified. The plumbing around my heart froze up. I

could barely speak the words. A glacier moved through my aorta. A prayer that was more of a plea erupted in my brain. *God, will we be broken forever—will we always be afraid of true intimacy?* It occurred to me that without the blinding intoxication of physical intimacy, what was naked in the relationship was not our bodies, but our souls—that's what was scaring me. If Wesley saw the real me, without the emotional distortion of sex, would he still like me? I had to know. "What about we back off? Just spend time together without dating."

Wesley stroked my cheek with his thumb. "I—"

A rush of static came through the radio on Wesley's shoulder. He clicked a button and talked into it. "Go ahead."

The message Wesley got over his radio was filled with static, but it sounded like the other cop hadn't been able to find Cameron. He clicked off his radio.

"No sign of him, huh?"

"They did find lots of mice running around. Ruby?"

I held up my hands. "What? You think I had something to do with rodent escapees?"

He shook his head. "Let's go gather up that stuff for evidence." He rose to his feet and held out an arm for me.

I wrapped my hand around his muscular forearm.

I went back for the video with a police escort—just in case Cameron was hiding somewhere.

Wesley drove me back to the station in his Jeep so he could type up my statement. On the way, I called Mom on my cell and told her to meet me there to give me a ride home. I didn't tell her about the tape with Jimmy on it. It would be better if that news came when we were in the same room. I dreaded having to show her the tape, but maybe it would penetrate the wall of denial she had built about her son.

Wesley stopped at a drive-through and got me two tacos—a far cry from the meal he had planned for our "perfect date." As we drove toward the station, we didn't say another word about giving up on our proposed romantic relationship. Instead, we focused on what we were good at, examining other people's crimes.

Dale was searching my office for the tape. Aldridge must have told him it was there before he died. But Cameron thought the tape was in the house, or he was looking for the keys. Dale saw Cameron in Truman Hall the day he tried to drop my class. That's why he said he couldn't take classes in that building anymore.

"You know," I said, holding up the videotape, "would you kill two people because they found out you were making a thousand extra bucks a month?"

"That's what those books were worth?"

"That's what Donita, a teacher in the English department, said. Cameron tried to hurt me. He's capable of violence, but it just doesn't seem like an extra thousand a month would be worth killing two people over." I took another bite of taco.

"He'd lose his job, his reputation, probably just do short term or no jail, and he'd have to pay the money back. If that status is all you have, wouldn't that be worth killing for?"

"I don't know." Cameron had tried to bribe me with the offer of a permanent job. Maybe that's why Aldridge was getting a cut of the money. Bribery and favoritism seemed to be Cameron's strategy, not murder. The taco tasted like curled-up balls of cardboard. I set it on the dash and gazed out the window. The bank clock downtown said it was 11:00 P.M. I pressed my head against the side window of Wesley's Jeep. Bits and pieces of neon flashed by in my peripheral vision.

I took another mealy bite of taco and longed for a hot bath, a plate of chocolate, and the chance to climb under my comforter and sleep until Jesus came back. Right now, I didn't feel much like living my life. The upside of all this was that my life right now made me look forward to heaven.

I hoped God wasn't too disappointed in me. This obedience stuff was hard. I glanced over at Wesley's gorgeous profile. Even in winter, his skin was tan. Yeah, this obedience stuff was hard.

My eyelids felt heavy.

Honestly, life didn't get any easier when I became a Christian. But I knew I didn't want to go back to the despair of my old life.

Tightness slipped from my muscles. Wesley's car glided toward the police station. The fog of sleep drifted across my brain.

When I slept, I dreamed . . .

Chapter Twenty

I was in a dark room with a wall of mirrors around me. Soft light filtered in from some indiscernible source. A voice that came from all directions at once asked, "Which way are your feet pointed?"

"What?" I glanced down at the shredded rags I was wearing and my bare, dirty feet.

"Which way are your feet pointed?" The voice was relentlessly gentle and began funneling in from a single direction instead of coming at me from all sides.

"Toward you, dummy."

"That's good, Ruby. That's very good. That's where they need to be."

Again, I looked down at my attire. The weight of disappointment settled on my shoulders—pressed on me. My clothes were smeared with dirt and garbage. Rancid odors assaulted my nose. I slouched. My head, my limbs—they all felt heavy. Just me having a major bad hair, bad wardrobe day.

Now the voice resonated from inside my chest cavity and at the same time seemed to come from a loudspeaker and was also very close to my ear: from three directions at once. "Can you see what I see? So beautiful."

I tilted my head and gazed in the mirror: me in all my tangled, red-headed glory dressed in clothes that had been stomped on and run through a paper shredder. I even had dirt smears on my face. "What's to see?" Unbearable sadness weakened my knees. I crumpled to the floor. "I don't like these mirrors," I whispered.

"Look again."

"I don't want to." I rested my cheek against the cool, dark floor and closed my eyes. "I don't want to look."

"Look again." The voice was soft but persistent, like waves pounding on a shore. "Lift your eyes, child."

Reluctantly, I raised my head—opened my eyes. *Me again. Just ragged me.* Something flashed in the mirror behind me. I turned around. *Just me again in the other mirror. Same old me.* Out of the corner of my eye, I caught a glimpse of glittering sparkle. Had I just seen a robe of diamonds?

The vision, however brief, made my head tingle. The sensation ran down my face and neck, past my heart, and into my veins. Simultaneously, warmth washed over my skin and seeped into me. The heaviness I felt vaporized.

Heat burned the center of my hand. I opened my fingers. In the middle of my palm, a bright hot jewel glistened.

The rhythm of a gentle waltz swirled around the room, beat against my eardrums, played inside my head. Muscles in my legs, arms, and back were warm and limber. I thought, *I can dance. I could dance, you know.*

The steady rhythm of the music stopped. I opened my eyes.

The Jeep glided to a stop as Wesley pressed the brakes. Murky lights glowed on the Eagleton Police Department sign.

"Must have been a good dream." Wesley's voice filtered through the cottony fog of diminishing unconsciousness. "What?"

"You were smiling. It must have been a good dream."

"I think it was." A circle of heat still burned my hand where the jewel in my dream had been. *How weird.* "It didn't start out good, but it got better. For a long time I was afraid to finish it."

Wesley pushed his door open. "Was I in it?" He smiled his goofy crooked grin.

"Sorry." I shrugged.

His jaw dropped slightly. Was he actually disappointed that he hadn't made a guest appearance in my dream? There was something sweet about that—sweet and arrogant at the same time. Like my every waking and sleeping thought was supposed to be of him. *Please.*

After trying the passenger-side door and remembering it didn't work, I crawled across the driver's seat. I gave Wesley's elbow a reassuring squeeze as we walked up the sidewalk to the station house. "Even if you're not in my dreams, I am glad you are in my life."

"In your life, but in what capacity?"

That's the question you need to answer, dear Wesley. Would he want to be a part of my life if there was no dating, no sex, just us getting to know each other? What a risk I had taken in making my proposal. My feet were pointed in the right direction. A year ago, I would not have valued myself enough to say such a thing. In my BC days, my relationships had been about trading sex for attention and time. I had grown.

Scant amounts of snow drifted out of the dark sky as we made our way up the steps. Mom was waiting inside with her visitor's pass clipped to her coat. She held a cat in her arms, only this one was a calico. Hadn't the one at the hospital been black and white? She looked tired.

Wesley led us through the door, past the interrogation rooms, into the cops' carrels. For a Friday night, it was surprisingly quiet. The jail was in a separate part of the building, so we didn't pass any drunks or angry criminals. Two or three cops in uniform milled through. Others sat at their computers, typing.

Mom found a seat on a bench and sat down with her cat. The harsh lights of the station house made the lines and wrinkles around her face and mouth more prominent. Her cheeks were devoid of their usual rosy color. Her blue eyes had lost their luster. She stroked the cat's head.

"Didn't that cat used to be black and white?"

The cat nuzzled against her cheek. "This is a different one. Six more of these little precious orphans have shown up at my door."

"Really?" Now I knew that Jimmy hadn't left town yet. Just when I was ready to brand my brother a total criminal, he did something kind like free some cats from certain death. He had dropped them off at Mom's because he knew she would take care of them. I wondered if catnapping was a misdemeanor or a felony. I could tell the police where to find Jimmy. He would try to engineer an escape for the remaining cats before the night was over.

Wesley sat down in front of his computer.

"I have to make a statement and then I can go, Mom." I took a deep breath. "I need you to watch a tape." Better for Mom to deal with it now than to hear about his arrest on the news.

"What kind of tape?" She stood up and shrank away from me. "What are you talking about?" On some instinctive level, she must have known what was coming.

I swallowed hard. "Mom." She stiffened when I touched her arm above the elbow. Her gaze was unwavering; her mouth tight. "I found a tape that shows Jimmy fencing some antique books. The guy he got the books from probably killed two people."

"How can you say these things about your brother? He's been going to church."

"Church attendance doesn't make you moral. Ask Wesley.

He gets to arrest drunk deacons all the time. You know that, Mom."

She shook her head, backing away from me. "He's my son," she whispered. "You didn't hold him after you pushed him out of your body. You didn't look down into his precious newborn face and dream dreams for him."

The cat wiggled in her arms, clawed her shoulder. She seemed oblivious to the pain the clawing must have caused. She pointed a finger at me. "You didn't watch him grow, see all the talent and charisma he had. You didn't hold him when he had a terrible fever and wish that the fever could be in your own body instead. You . . . you didn't envision bright futures for him."

The calico leaped from her grasp. As its feet hit the floor, its tail fluffed up. The cat hissed at a passing police officer and pressed against Mom's leg.

As she spoke, Mom backed up until a distance of five feet lay between us. Her voice had become shrill enough so that a few people raised their heads and glanced in her direction.

"And you, Ruby, you didn't ruin his chances in life by being a criminal yourself."

"No, Mom." I rushed toward her, tried to put my arms around her. "He made his choices." Her frail arms pressed against my chest. Her head rested under my chin.

She pulled away from the hug. "It's my fault. Send me back to prison. Send *me* back. Let my little boy go." She pounded her chest with an open palm. "Send *me* back."

"No, Mom, no. It's not your fault."

Mom collapsed onto the bench by the door. Over and over she said, "Send *me* back. Send *me* to prison. Send *me* back."

By now, Wesley was alerted to the drama. I held up a hand, indicating that I could handle things, which was probably a lie. He nodded and returned to the work at his desk.

A female cop brought me a blanket. I kneeled on the floor and wrapped it around Mom's shoulders.

"I don't want to look at that tape." Her voice was hoarse. The calico cat jumped up on the bench beside her. Mom's shoulders bent forward. She turned her head away from me so I saw her face in profile: the tiny upturned nose, the little white scar on her chin, and the weary eyes.

I wrapped my hand over hers. "Okay, you don't have to look at the tape." I didn't need to torture her. Everyone in the world deserves at least one person who will be on their side no matter what they do. Usually that one person is called Mom. God created maternal love. Who was I to argue with it?

"I don't want to see the tape," she repeated, then closed her eyes. "I know what's on it."

I kept my hands close to hers as she rocked back and forth, and that stupid cat crawled into her lap. Orphans and misfits always seemed to find their way into Mom's life.

She squeezed my hand. "Go get your work done. I'll just wait here." Her voice was a vapor—no strength to it at all.

"You sure?"

She nodded. The worry lines in her forehead were distinctive, along with that deep furrow between her eyebrows. I couldn't bring myself to leave.

"Go, Ruby." She patted the back of her head and then tucked a strand of hair behind her ear. "I'll be okay."

"All right." I walked across the floor to where Wesley sat at a computer. I kept glancing over at Mom to make sure she was still breathing.

The female cop who had brought the blanket came back and very gently placed a paper cup in my mom's hand. Steam rose from it. Mom wrapped both hands around the cup and bent her head toward it. The cat settled in beside her, resting its head on her leg. Mom's hand fluttered up to the butterfly pin on her coat collar.

Wesley had all the stuff we'd found in Aldridge's hiding place laid out on his desk, ready to be put in an evidence locker. He spoke as he typed. "Already sent a unit to Cameron's house. Of course he wasn't there. His wife didn't know where he was. Any theories on where he might hide?"

I shrugged. "He probably left town by now."

He pushed a pile of stapled papers toward me. "Coroner's report. Dale's body was moved. It had been on ice for a while before he was tossed in that field. Guess what he died of?"

I stared down at the report, which was only slightly easier to read than Chinese. "Cause of death—poisoning."

"The only reason they were able to figure out what was in scant amounts in Aldridge's bloodstream was that it was in lethal quantities in Dale. The plant was oleander."

"Oleander. The flower?"

"Every part of it is deadly. The air even gets poisoned if you burn it. Whoever built a fire in Aldridge's fireplace threw enough oleander branches in there to knock him out. Maybe they intended to kill him, or maybe they were going to string him up all along and just needed him unconscious."

I stared down at the first-edition Poe and opened it again to where Aldridge had marked it. "Maybe Cameron was an exotic gardener." I pulled out the piece of thick paper that was used as a marker. "There's something that doesn't fit."

"What's that?"

I unfolded the paper. "The motive, remember? Cameron has a big ego, but I don't think he's irrational. The penalty for killing two people would obviously be way harsher than that for selling those books."

Wesley leaned back in his chair and ran his hands through his hair. "How big was Cameron's ego? Sometimes fear of loss of reputation makes people do irrational things."

The paper was a smaller version of the photo I had seen in Aldridge's house—Cameron, Aldridge, and Xavier Konrad outside the Mountain Top Retirement Center. Nothing was written on the photo, front or back.

I stared at the photograph. Donita had said that Cameron knew he was going to get the bundle of money for the department but didn't know until after Konrad died that it would all have to go toward the books. Cameron was obsessed about the fiscal health of the department. "What if . . . the reason Cameron killed Dale and Aldridge was because they found out about a different murder that Cameron committed—at Mountain Top?" I pointed at Xavier Konrad in the photo.

"So Cameron kills the old guy, thinking he's going to get a bundle of money to do with as he pleases. I don't recall anything unusual about Konrad's death. No cops were sent to investigate. Nothing suspicious."

"How easy is it to kill some old guy and have it not look like a murder? Just give him too much heart medication. Unless the guy had a bullet hole in his head, no one would question his death."

"We'll send a detective over to Mountain Top tomorrow." Wesley narrowed his eyes at me. "You don't need to go over there. The police can deal with this." He stood up and stretched.

I gave him my best who-little-ol'-me? look—wide eyes, raised eyebrows, round mouth. "It's almost midnight. Mom's been through a lot; I need to get her home."

"Ruby, I mean it."

"We need to find Cameron. He's the only one who knows the truth." I rose to my feet. "But I will let the pros do that. I want to get some sleep."

Cupping his hands on my shoulders, he pushed me toward Mom. "Good night, Ruby?"

"Right. Home to beddy-bye."

The night was pitch black and cold as Mom, her cat, and I trudged to her Caddy. Our breath was visible against the dark night.

"I'll drive, Mom. You look more tired than me."

I heard a faint "thank you" behind me.

It took three tries to start the Caddy.

"I don't know what we are going to do with only one car." The cat rested inside Mom's coat with just its calico head sticking out.

"I wonder if the police will find my Valiant." After Mom was out of earshot, I'd told the police about checking the animal lab for Jimmy. I was pretty sure they'd find my Valiant there too. Mom didn't need to know that Jimmy had stolen my car.

"Ruby?"

I pulled out onto the street. "Yes."

"I don't want you to move out."

"Thanks, I can't afford it anyway." I smiled at her. Her face looked a little brighter. If Jimmy got out of town with my Valiant, I'd be saving pennies for another clunker. "Thank goodness we got all that casserole to eat through the winter."

Mom laughed faintly. She tugged on a button on her ratty brown coat. "God takes cares of us, doesn't he?"

I knew she was saying that to reaffirm the truth to herself. I pressed the brake as I came to a stop sign. "That he does. That he does. He doesn't give us what we want, but he gives us what we need."

Mom turned sideways so she could look right at me. The cat stuck its head out of her coat. Its yellow eyes glowed in the dimness of the car. Warm emotion coursed through me as I stared at the two-headed lady who was my mother. *Yeah, God gives us what we need.*

I turned onto the street that ran between the university and the museum. Up ahead was the field where Dale's body had been found after he had been killed somewhere else.

A light flashed in a high window of NED. I slowed down. The museum went dark again. "Mom, did they give you a key to the museum when you signed up as a volunteer?"

"It's in my purse." She rooted through her purse and held up a single key on a key ring. "What are you thinking?"

"I think I know where Cameron Bancroft is hiding." I had a vague memory of Cameron talking at the dedication, saying he'd done an internship at NED—that he liked to hang out in the loft. I didn't know the layout of the whole museum, but the flashing light had been in a high window.

After hitting the blinker, I turned into the museum's parking lot. I brought the car to a stop close to the entrance.

"Stay here where it's safe," I instructed Mom sternly.

A quick scan of the parking lot revealed only one other car, and it was parked in the far corner of the lot. With only a single streetlamp illuminating the area, it was hard to tell the make and color of the car, but it was definitely not the lurker's Volkswagen I had chased. At this distance, it looked like one of those fashionable and pricey trucks that converted to an SUV. Cameron probably owned more than one car.

"Aren't you going to call Wesley?"

"Of course." Even if I was having trouble with that interdependence thing that has to happen in a relationship, I wasn't a total moron. If Cameron was inside, I would need some help. I didn't care to be choked with my own clothes again—death by fashion is not my idea of a good time.

The cat had crawled out of Mom's coat and now rested on her shoulder. "Maybe you should wait until he gets here."

I snatched the key out of her hand. "You know I'm no good at that waiting stuff." The door of the Caddy clicked open smoothly. I winked at her, which did nothing to diminish the worried-mom look on her face: furled forehead and black eyebrows drawn so close together that she had a unibrow. I patted her cool hand. "Pray for me. I'll be okay."

"Be careful. Please, be careful."

I pulled the cell out of my purse. "I'll call before I go inside."

I slipped out of the car and walked up the sloped sidewalk to the museum entrance with only one backward glance at Mom as she sat in the Caddy.

Chapter Twenty-one

Despite my heavy winter coat, the wind chilled the exposed skin on my neck and face. The cold cut through my blue jeans. I crossed my arms and bent forward. My cowboy boots echoed on the concrete. *What I'd give for some birds twittering in the trees or even an owl's cut-to-the-marrow hooting. A little noise to accompany me marching to my doom would be nice.*

I stopped outside the museum entrance. *Maybe I should just wait.* When I'd called the station, Officer Cree had answered. Wesley had stepped out, but Cree said he would get the message to him and send another unit to the museum if he had to.

I stepped back and stared up at the window where I had seen the flash of light. No, I couldn't wait. If Cameron was in there, I didn't want him getting away again.

I shoved the key in the hole. The door was already unlocked. Mom's key hit the walls of my purse with a thunderous jingle. My hands trembled as I clicked the door and pulled it open.

I planted my feet on the tile by the welcome desk and scanned the area around me, tilted my head and surveyed the ceiling, listened for footfalls. *Come on, Cameron, where are you?*

Light spilled out from the reception hall where I had attended the dedication in October.

I walked past the theater entrance. Taking evenly paced strides, I made my way toward the light, making sure to salute Sacajawea, her baby, and the canoe on my way by. She had been a better woman than I would ever be. The sound of instrumental music grew more distinct as I made my way past the displays on west-ward expansion and barbed wire. Was a string quartet doing some midnight practice?

As I walked through the westward expansion exhibit, I glanced up at the dark windows of the loft. I turned the corner into the reception hall. The scene was very end of the world—like people had just vaporized and left their stuff. Music spilled out of a CD player on the floor. Tables draped with white linen were arranged around the room. A ski jacket rested on one of them. Each table held a flowering potted plant as a centerpiece. Against the walls, large photographs of bears and bobcats snarling at the camera, claws visible, were mounted on easels.

"What are you doing here?"

I jumped. My heart contracted. All the air expelled from my lungs. I turned around to face . . . Lorelei Philips? "What . . . what are *you* doing here?" *Brilliant comeback. Not.* I took in a deep breath to slow my heart rate. I'd been expecting Cameron to come bar-reling around the corner, wielding a knife.

"The film festival. It's tomorrow night." She lifted the film can-isters she was holding. "I wanted to run the footage one more time." She'd pulled her wavy auburn hair up into a soft bun. Some of the hair was held back with jeweled bobby pins. She wore kha-kis and a white, button-down shirt. Lorelei Philips had a gift for looking totally casual and totally glamorous at the same time.

Considering I have trouble getting my socks to match, I found her appearance very intimidating. "Yeah right, the film festival."

After glancing over my shoulder at the reception area, she let out a small feminine breath of air. "I put students in charge of setting this up, but I'm such a perfectionist, I had to make sure it looked okay. Do you like the centerpieces? I brought them from home. They're oleander. I started growing them when I was teaching down south."

My mouth went dry. "Oleander?" I croaked.

She smiled at me and did a sweep of the tables with her hand. "So what do you think?"

I glanced back at a coyote with its face stuck in something bloody and unidentifiable. Then I looked at a wolf bearing its teeth to the camera. "Looks good." My heart rate increased tenfold. Boy, did I want to run back to my mommy.

Lorelei set the canisters on a corner of the table. "So why are you here?" She crossed her arms and narrowed her round eyes at me.

"I'm a—were you up on the third floor in the loft?"

Lorelei tilted her swan neck. "There's a loft in here?" She leaned over, clicked off the CD player and took a step toward me. "You still haven't told me why you're here."

If Lorelei ever wanted to give up professordom, she'd do well as a prosecutor. Her stare had a penetrating Superman quality, like she could see underneath my clothes.

"I saw a light and thought Cameron might be hiding in here. He tried to hurt me earlier tonight. The police think he might have killed Dr. Aldridge and then Dale Cutler." I now knew that wasn't true. Cameron didn't have a strong-enough motive to kill two men, but Lorelei did. Aldridge wasn't killed because of greed or because of the potential loss of someone's reputation; he was killed because of love.

Lorelei gazed at me for a long moment. I watched her nostrils move in and out as she took in a deep breath. "Oh." She turned her back to me and proceeded to straighten the tablecloth. "I've been here since nine. I don't think there's anyone else in the building. Hope you find him." She tugged on a corner of the tablecloth. "It's a terrible thing to kill someone."

The hair on the back of my neck stood up. My skin felt itchy. What had I seen in her airbrushed expression? She'd drawn her mouth tight for only a second, but I didn't think she was on to me.

A photograph of two eagles against white fluffy clouds and blue sky caught my attention. The eagles were joined together, twirling through the sky. "Are they fighting in the air?"

Lorelei looked up at the photo but not at me. "Actually, they're mating."

"Funny how love can look like violence." Even as I took a step toward her, cold water seeped through my veins and arteries, threatening to freeze. My stupid need-to-know compulsion made me ignore the little voice that screamed in my head, *Run, Ruby, run.*

"I don't think eagles feel love, just instinct." She tugged on a corner of a tablecloth too hard, causing her film canisters to spill to the floor. She cursed and kneeled on the floor.

"Let me help you with those." I kept hearing her voice from a week ago, "Strong arms," she had said. "Strong hands." As I picked up a canister and placed it in her hand, I had a flash of visual memory watching her open and close her fists. *Strong hands.*

"Thank you," she said sweetly.

I gripped the canisters until she made eye contact with me. My heart pounded a mile a minute. "I bet you really miss Theodore," I croaked. *Come on, Ruby, don't push it.*

"I do. I really do."

"Theodore was afraid of Cameron. He was getting ready to turn him in. He had a loaded gun in his house."

Lorelei strode across the room and snatched up her ski jacket. "Really." She slipped into the coat and zipped it up. "I'd love to chat with you about this, but I'm tired. It must be past midnight."

She moved toward the hallway that led to the exit. I stepped in front of her. Then I took two steps back, remembering her strong hands. "What exactly did Dale say to you that night he came to see you?" I saw a flash of anger—or was it fear?—in her eyes. "I'm just trying to figure out why Cameron killed him," I added.

"I told you. He was paranoid and scared. He wanted to know if I had any copies of his freshman film project. He wanted to stay at my place. I told him no and sent him away."

"Didn't you say you gave him a cup of tea?" *Oleander tea. Hardly a future market in that. Drink it one time and die.*

Lorelei took a step back. "Yes, to calm his nerves."

Dale must have figured out that Lorelei had killed Aldridge. He'd come to her house to confront her and to get a copy of the video to finish up that business. My mind began to work like a visual card catalogue. It had to have been Dale who had placed the article on top of my research at the library all those weeks ago. The article had had a picture of Aldridge at his desk with Lorelei standing behind him. Even then, he had wanted me to make a connection between Aldridge and Lorelei.

Lorelei backed into a table. "I loved Theodore. Dale was a good kid. I miss them both." She turned sideways. Her fingertips touched one of the oleander flowers.

The line between love and hate is thin, Dr. Philips. Aldridge said

*he wanted God more than he wanted you. Your ego couldn't deal
with the rejection.* "Hope the film festival goes okay." I sounded
downright cutesy and friendly. If I didn't reveal that I was on to
her, she would drive home, and the police would go and get her. I
didn't have to be anywhere near her strong hands.

Two black tears streamed down Lorelei's cheeks. Because of the
amount of mascara she wore, she already had a major case of rac-
coon eyes. "You'll have to forgive me. Thinking about Theodore stirred
up feelings." She wiped her eyes. "You should come to the film festival. I'm really proud of the work the students and I have done."

"I'll think about it."

"Good night, then. I'll probably see you around campus." She
strutted confidently out of the reception hall. I pulled my cell out
of my purse and dialed the station-house number. I wandered
past the displays—the chair made with longhorn cattle horns, the
stuffed buffalo, displays about Native Americans. The phone rang
and rang.

A door slammed above me. I clicked off the phone. Had Lorelei
gone up to the loft?

I studied the dark windows of the loft that looked out on most
of the museum. I saw no movement or flicker of light.

Maybe she had lied about knowing about the loft just like she'd
lied about killing Aldridge and Dale. What would she go up there
for? I hadn't heard the outside doors open and close.

I stared at my phone. Cree had said there was a cop on the way.
I should just wait.

That geriatric Nancy Drew inside my head kept egging me on.
Come on, Ruby. You want to know if she is really in there, don't you?
I bolted up the stairs.

My hand touched the doorknob and I twisted it. *What is it with me?* I am a dedicated couch potato—a total egghead. My idea of a big adventure is to lie on the couch and read Rex Stout, not live it.

The door swung open silently, and I felt along the wall for a light switch. Careful to make sure the door stayed ajar so I had some light coming in, I patted the wall. There had to be a switch here somewhere.

Fueled by my wild imaginings, my heart rate accelerated. I ran into something with wheels. A baby carriage maybe. It rolled several feet on squeaky wheels.

Mental note: *Next time I'm up here trying to be quiet, bring WD-40.*

The door closed behind me as the carriage crashed into something and stopped.

I held my breath. In the near total darkness, my other senses clicked up a notch. I stood very still.

The old-stuff aroma was almost overwhelming: old books, old clothes, and a scent I couldn't distinguish that was somewhere between wet leather and vinegar on the smell continuum. I could just make out the raspy inhale and exhale of another human being.

I dared not take a step—dared not give away my location. Sooner or later, I would be in need of inflated lungs. I held my breath long enough that my stomach twisted tight in an effort not to exhale.

Slowly, I let out the air and waited for Lorelei to make some sort of move. Blood drummed in my ears. All the moisture left my mouth. I counted. *One Mississippi. Two Mississippi.* My leg and arms muscles contracted—ready to bolt if I had to.

Something or someone made a sound like a baby crying from a long ways away. I turned my head in the direction of the noise.

A light flashed on the other side of the room and then was gone. In the momentary illumination, I'd seen an Indian head-dress and a broken china doll not far from me. The doll had a black chasm where her left cheek should be.

Feet pounded across the floor. Where had Lorelei gotten a flashlight?

The darkness disoriented me. I eased my way toward where I thought the wall was. The flash of light caused murky dots to float across my eyeballs.

Again, I heard the cry, muffled, like a baby far away or covered up with something.

Lorelei had clicked the flashlight on and off to figure out where to hide, but she didn't want to give me time to find her. Best if I just got out of here and guarded the front door.

Stepping softly, I felt along the wall and moved toward where my kinesthetic memory told me the door was. My toe hit something solid. Pain shot through my foot and up my leg. I yowled quietly. I tried not to dance around and knock things over. I tried not to make noise. But I was pretty sure I had given away my location.

Behind me, a flashlight clicked on.

I drew my fingers protectively to my neck, expecting to have to fend off Lorelei's strong hands at any moment.

"Ruby, it's me."

You could have knocked me over with a microbe. *Of all the people . . .*

Chapter Twenty-two

I turned slowly. The flashlight lit up half the loft, creating broken and fading circles on the low ceiling. He looked different somehow from when I had last seen him. Part of his face was in shadow. The slouched posture suggested weariness.

He had propped the flashlight up on the floor beside the trunk where he sat. A big gray cat crawled into his lap. Two more cats meandered toward the trunk. The presence of the felines explained the muffled baby cries. "How did you find me?"

"It was an accident. I came looking for your partner." I glanced toward the big windows that looked out on the museum. The westward expansion history display was completely still. I could see the antique wagon, the jail, and a set of antique revolvers and other weapons under glass.

"He's not my partner. He's just one of the guys I fenced stuff for."

"So there's others?" Jimmy's answer surprised me. He hadn't dodged the question with his usual verbal zigzags.

He stood up and shoved his hands into his jeans pockets. The cats circled around him.

I shook my head. "Why, Jimmy? Why? Mom would have let you stay at her place for as long as you needed."

He wandered over to three headless dress dummies lining the wall. "I tried to do what she wanted. I did." He punched one of the dummies in the stomach. The jab was halfhearted and weak, as if his arm were made of clay. "Cameron's supposed to bring me some cash—and a car that will get me out of town."

"Didn't you take my car?"

"It's parked out back. No offense, Ruby, but I don't think it would make it out of town."

"Hey, it's paid for, and I didn't steal it." Pity and anger mixed together inside of me. I paced the loft. I picked up the doll with half her face broken away.

"Cameron said this was a good place to hide."

"I wouldn't count on Cameron." I smoothed over the hair of the doll. "He's probably halfway to Jamaica by now."

"You found the video. Cameron was worried you would." Jimmy spoke in a monotone. "In a way, I'm glad you found it." He sat back down on the trunk. Cats flocked over to him. "You'll take care of those cats I left at the house, won't ya?"

"You know, Jimmy, you could have gotten out of town if you hadn't come back for those cats."

"I . . . I think part of me wanted to get caught." Gently, he placed a cat on the floor and stood to his feet. "I don't want to live like this anymore. I don't want to be me. Sorry I took your Valiant. I didn't mean to hurt you."

For the first time since Jimmy had come back, he was being straight with me. I appreciated that. It suggested that he was changing—that there was hope for him. But honestly, I was too angry to have a mushy family reunion moment. My throbbing headache served as a reminder of how low he could sink. He'd steal from his own family.

After placing the doll in the baby carriage, I made my way to the door. "Cops will be here in a minute." I stared out the window of the loft. The place was completely still, dim and lifeless. What was taking them so long? "You can turn yourself in if you want."

Jimmy swept his foot back and forth across the floor. The gray cat rubbed against his still leg. "I was going to take these cats with me."

"Mom and I will take care of them, providing we don't have to return them to the animal lab. One thing I've just got to know, Jimmy."

"Yeah."

"That first night you came to the house. You were trying to break in to get whatever you thought was in the attic. You didn't want to see me and Mom, right?"

"I'd been watching the house for a while. I thought no one was home. I just got it into my head that Dad had money stashed in some secret account. He was always so uptight about keeping records. I thought there would be a paper trail—a ledger or something."

That was my brother, always looking for the big windfall. I opened the door. Light washed through the room, revealing the relics of Montana history: dummies in antique dresses; fur pelts and traps; broken papier-mâché dinosaur parts.

"Do me a favor, Jimmy. I don't want Mom to see you . . . not yet. It would be too hard on her. I'll send the cops up after Mom and I are gone."

"I didn't want to hurt her."

"Be honest. Yes, you did." I couldn't look at him again. "See ya."

Wesley, or whoever was coming, was taking forever. I stared out at the quiet floor below me, then tromped down the stairs and past the display of the history of barbed wire. The door above me slipped shut. I walked past the covered wagon.

I heard footsteps on carpet. Jimmy needed to stay up in the loft until I could get Mom out of here. I thought I had made that clear. I turned slightly.

A cool hand cupped over my mouth, traveled down my neck, and pressed against my vocal cords, hard and tight. The scent of lilac perfume assaulted my nose.

Believe it or not, while Lorelei was suffocating the life out of me, I actually had time for two coherent thoughts. The first went something like this: *Of course Lorelei wouldn't have run out. Her modus operandi was to kill whoever figured out what she had done to Aldridge.* The second thought went something like this: *Jimmy, where are you? Get down here right now and help me! Jimmy!!!*

I tried to twist free of Lorelei's strong hand, which she had shoved under my chin. She clamped her other hand around my arm just above the elbow and dragged me backward. To say she had strong hands was an understatement. She was giving me a major ouchie. The pressure on my chin was such that my head arched back at a painful angle. Each inhalation was a struggle. My eyes watered.

Once she got both hands around my neck, I knew it would be curtains for me. I turned my head sideways, and she exerted pressure on the back of my neck. My twisting resulted in my getting my face planted against the display of antique guns under glass.

My scream of protest came out in an incomplete gurgle.

I reached behind me, touched Lorelei's leg, and pinched it. I know, pinching is lowdown and dirty fighting, but I was running out of both air and options.

The pinch was enough to make Lorelei groan in indignation and let go of my arm.

I angled my torso and twisted out of the grip she had on my

neck. The force of this little maneuver cost me my balance and I stumbled to the ground. But I was free. I knew I couldn't hope to win a fight with her, so instead I scrambled to my feet and raced toward the exit.

Stupid idea. Not only was she stronger than me, she could run faster too. Before I'd gone ten paces, she dragged me back, twisted me around, clamped both her hands on my neck, and backed me up against the stuffed buffalo. I dug my fingers into her wrists—trying to pull her off. I couldn't breathe, couldn't move.

I stared into her brown eyes, saw her murderous intent. Air. Air. I needed air.

I formed the word *please* with my lips. My vision dimmed. I felt dizzy.

She was crushing my breathing tubes. The soft fur of the buffalo rubbed against my cheek and neck.

I gasped. I knew this feeling. I had been underwater before and run out of air—knew that awful suffocating feeling that made me flail my arms to the water's surface while panic set in. Meshy darkness slipped over my eyes. All I saw were white bits of light floating by.

I thought about my mother and my brother—and Wesley. My hand reached out for something solid. *At least I get to see Jesus,* I thought.

The pressure on my neck vaporized. I sucked in a raspy, gasping breath of air. I coughed. I blinked hard, preparing to see what heaven looked like. The web of mesh that had spread across my eyes dissipated. Heaven looked like—my mother holding a rolling pin?

Apparently, the way station on the way to heaven was a Salvador Dalí painting.

I bent forward, wheezing and gasping for air. Lorelei lay unconscious on the floor.

Mom patted my back. "You had quite a scare there, dear."

Resting my hands on my thighs, I angled my head toward my mother, the saver of my life. She had that big obnoxious purse slung over her shoulder. "Really, Mother, a rolling pin?"

"Honestly, Ruby, don't give me a hard time. It was for a craft at the center. I forgot to take it out." She pointed at the unconscious Lorelei on the floor. "This lady is not nice."

"I love you, Mom."

Wesley, dressed in full uniform, rushed around the corner. He had this gift for showing up when all the hard work was done. Just once, I would like him to actually rescue me and have me conscious for the event.

I placed one hand on my hip and waved the other. "It's okay, Officer, the senior citizen took care of it."

My mother squared her shoulders and smiled. "We have it under control, Wesley."

Wesley's glance traveled from the two of us to the unconscious woman on the floor.

I put my other hand on my hip as Wesley ambled toward us. "What took you so long?"

"Cameron came into the station and gave himself up. He said he was putting all the money from selling the books back in the university coffers." He touched my shoulder. "I didn't think you would find anything here."

"I'm glad you got here . . . finally."

Lorelei stirred on the floor. She moaned. Mom lifted her rolling pin. My mother—a one-woman SWAT team.

Wesley ran his hand up and down my arm. "I'm glad you're okay, because I would like to just hang out with you—not dating—and I couldn't do that if you were dead."

"So true," I gushed.

Somewhere between ushering my mother out and meeting the police coming in to do all their official stuff, including arresting a very disoriented Lorelei Philips, I glanced up at the windows to the loft.

Jimmy was there with his hand pressed against the glass, fingers spread open. Mom walked about twenty paces ahead of me. I slowed down so I could tell one of the officers to go up and get Jimmy after Mom and I left.

My brother stood ghostlike at the window. All I could see was his hand and the pale white skin of part of his face.

There would come a time when, girded up by prayer, Mom would be strong enough to visit him in prison, strong enough to face that reality. But that time wasn't now.

And maybe I could lay my prayers down like bread crumbs for my brother to follow. Maybe, just maybe, his heart would change like Theodore Aldridge's had—like mine had—and he would find his way back home . . . for good. My brother was not beyond God's love. I had to believe that. After all, thieves hung next to Jesus.

I kissed my hand, turned it toward Jimmy, and whispered goodbye to my brother.

Chapter Twenty-three

I hefted a bag of alfalfa cubes onto Josiah Carmichael's flatbed. My thirty-one-year-old arm muscles burned from the strain. I had missed that feeling.

I brushed my buckskin gloves against each other. "You know, Josiah, we're giving away a free cat with every twenty-pound bag of feed." Hands on hips, I stepped back to catch my breath, which came out in puffs in the crisp December air.

From his flatbed, Josiah chuckled as he adjusted the bag of feed he'd stacked on top of two bags of gleaned grain. "I'm not falling for it, Ruby." He stood up straight and winked at me, his eyes two beads in a sea of wrinkles. "Besides, I took one last week. The little tabby's having a ball killing mice in my barn."

Josiah jumped off the flatbed with the energy of a man half his age. He tilted his tattered baseball cap to me and climbed into the cab of his rig.

As his truck rumbled away, I closed my eyes and enjoyed that tingling chill on my skin—the cold that tells me I'm alive. I was back at work full-time at Benson's Pet and Feed, not because it was the only job I could hold down, but because I was choosing to be there.

The week before, I had turned in final grades for my classes and said good-bye to the university—probably forever. The only tie I kept was with Celeste. Right before the semester break, I'd gone up with her to walk the halls and pray. I spent a little extra time outside the department head's office, which now belonged to Donita. I put a large amount of chocolate in a pretty dish outside her office. I wrote one word in large letters on the card: *Congrats.* In smaller letters, I wrote: *P.S. I need the dish back. I borrowed it from my mother.* I thought about getting her a card with cute Christian sayings all over it, but she would have seen right through that.

A light went on in the outer office. The door swung open.

"Donita, I didn't know you were in." I rose to my feet.

"I fell asleep at my desk." She rubbed her temples and readjusted the chunky book she held in her hand.

I touched the book. "Still hanging out with Ivan, I see."

Her face looked pale without makeup. She kneeled down and picked up the card and candy. "Thanks." She read the card. "Does this mean you'll cut the Jesus talk?"

"I can't help myself. It bubbles up out of me."

She stared at me, and I smiled back. A hot pink scarf with a bow on the top served as a headband for her wild hair. Donita, the Russian scholar who dressed like she'd fallen out of an eighties music video.

"I don't have anything to put these in. I'll get the dish back to you." She picked up one of the chocolates. "Listen, I got a little more pull now that I'm head of the department. I could look into something permanent for you." Leaning against the doorframe, she popped the chocolate in her mouth.

"No, thanks. I was here for the wrong reasons. I have a job I really love."

"Okay." Donita brushed her hand over the bowl of chocolate. "Thanks, this was nice." She slipped back inside the main office and then into her own smaller office.

"You're welcome," I said to the closed door.

"Quit lollygagging." A voice that was music to my ears chimed from the back door of the feed store. "Git yer hiney in here and give me a hand. We're in the middle of a rush."

Georgia Benson, owner of Benson's Pet and Feed, stood with a fist on her ample hip and a smile on her round face. She was dressed in her usual business attire: a ratty denim jacket, Levi's, and new white tennis shoes. The only non-regulation part of her uniform was the Santa hat—complete with jingle bells—that was propped on her head.

"Coming, Georgia." Georgia's idea of a rush was two people, so I wasn't too worried. My moon boots crunched through the snow. Georgia's a rancher widow, so she has kind of made the shop a hangout for retired, failing, and just-gettin'-by farmers. Some customers come to drink the cheap coffee and never buy anything. Georgia's got a new espresso machine, but trying to talk a cowboy into having a latté or mocha is the diplomatic endeavor of the decade. We have few converts.

As Georgia put her arm around my shoulder and ushered me in to deal with "the rush," I caught a glimpse of the mountains that surround Eagleton. The Lord was being quite extravagant with his paintbrush today. Clouds rested low on the horizon with clear azure blue above them. Sun slanted through the sky, creating a warm band of crystalline gold across the snow-capped mountains—like a blanket of jewels or a robe of diamonds.

Everywhere, God reminds me that he is not through with me yet; what he began in me, he will finish. I hear his voice in my ear: "Do you see what I see? So beautiful." Even if I can't see it myself, I trust that he knows what he is doing—after all, he is the omniscient Ruler of the universe.

Inside the feed store, Wesley sat at the counter with his father, who sipped from a mug of coffee—or as he calls it, "a cup of joe." The elder Mr. Burgess had both hands wrapped around the coffee mug. He was about a foot shorter than Wesley with fluffy, Einstein-like hair.

Wesley tilted his head to me in greeting.

With no verbal exchange, Georgia yanked the coffee mug out of Nathan Burgess's hand and refilled it. Her version of hospitality. Don't ask me why, but I had really missed her abrupt, rough-around-the-edges demeanor.

I'd missed this place. I'd missed the bags of feed, the fertilizers, the baseball hats and coveralls, and the calf vaccine in the fridge right next to the muffins. I'd missed our resident cat, Her Majesty, a Siamese with mood issues.

I'd missed the people who start sentences with phrases like "you folks." People who say they paid "two bits" for something when they mean a quarter. People who get up before the sun to check heifers about to give birth. People who grow the food that feeds the world.

Georgia squeezed my shoulder and pointed to a woman on the far side of the store with her back to me. "She's been waiting for you, and another woman came in with this for you." She pushed a piece of paper toward me.

"Another woman? What did she look like?"

"Like a paint factory exploded on her." Two other people milled through the store. "I'll take care of them," Georgia said.

The woman at the far side of the store turned and met my gaze. Greta Aldridge. I waved her over to the counter after setting the folded piece of paper aside.

Greta had dyed over the blond streak in her hair. Her bangs were curled and combed back so the harsh line across her forehead was gone. "Hello, Ruby. Eliot said you called and had something for me." Her almond-shaped eyes looked clearer, despite the dark circles underneath. A tint of natural color on her cheeks softened her face.

From below the counter, I pulled out the stuff we had found under the floorboard in Aldridge's and my old office. "Dr. Aldridge left these behind. Everything is here except a tape that is evidence in a crime." I spread out the journal, the Bible, Benjamin's drawings, the ratty baseball, the picture of Aldridge with Xavier Konrad and Cameron Bancroft, and the flat pink rock. "I thought you and your sons should have them."

Without a word, she picked up Benjamin's drawings, examining each one carefully. The faintest of smiles crossed her face. She rolled the baseball around in her gloved hand. "Eliot's." Then she picked up the photograph.

"I think he kept it because it reminded him of his friend," I said. Or maybe he had kept it because he felt guilty about taking the money that Konrad had willed for the books. Turns out Konrad died of natural causes. I was wrong on that one. My speculating without evidence had almost cost me my life at the strong hands of Lorelei Philips. *Maybe Wesley is right. Maybe I should leave the detecting to the professionals. Nah.*

Greta nodded. "He was close to Xavier." Her hand touched the notebook.

"That's his journal. Greta, I know you didn't want to believe that he had changed, but—"

Greta sank down onto a stool at the counter. "I'd gotten so comfortable relating to him as the selfish alcoholic who only cared about his work. When he started being so nice right before he died, I couldn't trust it." She pulled off her leather gloves with a jerky motion. "I had trusted before and been hurt."

I pushed the rock toward her. "I'm not sure why this was in there."

Greta's lips quivered. She reached across the counter for the stone and placed it in the palm of her hand. "I can't believe he kept this." Greta brushed the rock with her fingertips. "One of our first dates we went on a picnic by a river. I found this rock and gave it to him. He kept it—all those years." Her eyes glazed. "He was working on his Ph.D. at the time. He was worried and stressed. I told him to rub the rock when he felt anxious. A worry stone." She shook her head. "He kept it."

"He was trying to make things right," I said. "I'm sorry he didn't have more time." I reached out to touch her hand. She jerked away from my touch, and then in an odd gesture, she put her hand close to mine so our fingertips touched.

With her free hand, she flipped through the journal and read. "I love Jesus. That's all I know, all I truly know, but it is enough." Her fingertips slipped over the top of mine. "Thank you for giving me these things. It will help Eliot and Ben."

It will help you too, Greta, if you let it.

Greta pulled her hand away, slipped on her leather gloves, and gathered up the contents of her ex-husband's telltale heart, holding them close to her chest. "I'm glad you found out who killed him. My picture of him just fit better if I believed he had killed himself—I didn't want to believe anything else." She looked at me. I thought I saw a thank-you in her expression, even if she didn't say it. She turned and headed toward the door, high-heeled boots clicking on the linoleum.

Having dealt with the rush, Georgia continued to hang up decorations, wreaths, and ornaments for the miniature Christmas tree on the counter. As she drove a nail into the wall, each miss with the hammer was punctuated by a curse word. She's a tough old bird, but I love her. Besides my Mom, I think she's the person I care about most.

I opened the folded piece of paper and read the typed, unsigned letter: "If you want to see your mother's dish alive, bring two stuffed weasels and a bag of chocolate to Leota's Grill at two tomorrow. P.S. Ivan will be there." I folded the letter and put it in my back pocket. That was a ransom drop I'd have to make.

Several of the cats Jimmy had rescued milled around the store. One of them hopped up on the stool by Wesley's dad. Nathan Burgess reached out a gnarled hand and stroked the cat's head. Two other cats lounged on the shelves. No one around here seemed to mind that they bought new overalls with cat hair on them.

While Georgia strung yet another strand of lights, I leaned across the counter and smiled at Wesley as his father went into a spiel about how the Mafia controlled the cheese industry.

Wesley raised his eyebrows in an I-told-you-so sort of way.

Georgia slipped past me as she stapled the multicolored lights to the wood of the counter. The place had more Christmas stuff than the seasonal aisle at Wal-Mart the day after Halloween. Next to St. Patrick's Day, Christmas was Georgia's favorite holiday.

Nathan Burgess continued: "'Course everyone knows that pony express riders were transferring secret government documents from D.C. to San Francisco. There has been a whole shadow government in existence since the 1860s." Nathan paused for dramatic effect, sucking his lips in.

I pulled a muffin out of the refrigerator and set it in front of him. "Here's a gimungous snack for you, Mr. Burgess."

Wesley rose to his feet. "You are coming out to help us feed the cattle later?" I detected a quiver of insecurity in his voice. Did he actually think I wouldn't want to hang out with him after I met his father?

Nathan picked up the Take-a-Penny, Leave-a-Penny box Georgia had sitting by her cash register. He opened his mouth as if to say something, and Wesley's shoulders tensed.

"I'll drive out as soon as I'm off my shift, Wesley."

Wesley swung his arm around his father, and they walked toward the door. I listened to the chimes.

Ten minutes later, the door chimed again. I looked up from the receipts I was sorting. A man in a cowboy hat and sporting a belt buckle the size of a saucer ambled in.

"Hey, Larry. Got a fresh pot of coffee."

"Actually, I think I would like to try one of them newfangled espressos Georgia's been bragging about."

I wiped muffin crumbs off the counter. "Pull up a chair, Larry. I'll make you the best espresso you ever had."